Totally Bound Publishing books by Liz Crowe:

Brewing Passion
Tapped
Lightstruck
Adjunct Lovers
Conditioned
Gravity

I0658956

Brewing Passion

GRAVITY

LIZ CROWE

Gravity
ISBN # 978-1-78686-329-4
©Copyright Liz Crowe 2017
Cover Art by Posh Gosh ©Copyright September 2017
Interior text design by Claire Siemaszkiewicz
Totally Bound Publishing

Published in 2017 by Totally Bound Publishing, Think Tank, Ruston Way, Lincoln, LN6 7FL, United Kingdom.

Totally Bound Publishing is an imprint of Totally Entwined Group Limited.

GRAVITY

Dedication

I humbly dedicate this novel to anyone who continues
to fight addiction in any form.
Be strong.

Chapter One

Brock stared around at the bustling atmosphere of his brother's successful brewery, trying like hell to stifle the urge to bolt.

He knew he was only here thanks to Evelyn, his brother Austin's wife. If it had been up to Austin, he, Brock, the man's long-lost twin, would have been tossed out on his ear. Working here wasn't that bad. They kept him busy—which was something he'd demanded of them.

He had to be kept busy. Anything less would be a disaster.

"Hey, Brock," one of the office chicks hollered for him.

He blinked and slapped a smile on his face. "Yeah, sorry. Here. I found this new reporting system for your inventory management. It's mobile-based so anyone back in the warehouse can pull it up on their phone and make entries." He handed over the computer tablet, forcing himself not to stare at the woman's tits. She took it, patting his arm, brushing it with those self-same very large, very nice tits.

He gritted his teeth and palmed the anti-anxiety pill he kept in his pocket. He wasn't due to take it until noon but he knew this was going to be a 'one of those days' day

Sweat beaded his forehead as he turned from her and almost ran over Amy, Evelyn's too-cute-for-her-own-good assistant. She batted her long lashes at him. Her full, red lips moved. He blinked at her too, not hearing a word, aware only of the smell of her perfume, or shampoo, which almost covered the distinct, sexy odor of her skin.

"Sorry, I gotta…go…" He stumbled out of the main office, breathing heavily and cursing the genetic lottery that had gifted him with this weakness. Okay, *all* these weaknesses.

He ducked into the men's room and threw the lock, then leaned against the door, willing his stupid body to behave like a grown man's and not that of an out-of-control teenager's. He knew his problem of course — he'd been living with his curse long enough to realize his own triggers.

He'd not been sleeping well — again, his fault as he'd slid off the wagon with exercise. But he was so sick of the routine — he was fucking bored with it, with all of this. But that was not the original problem.

"Stop," he said, turning so he could slide down to the floor with his back to the locked door. "Just stop."

He rested his face on his arms and waited, knowing it would pass. It always did.

Flashes of memory hit his brain — the smells and tastes of all the women he'd fucked paraded around, poking and prodding and teasing him. The sweet but ghostly memory of a heroin high made him shiver. The edgy, brittle perfection of a night out on nothing but X plus a hit of coke made his face burn.

He wanted it. He wanted all of it. He *needed* it. Why didn't anybody understand how much he needed it?

"Fuck," he muttered, banging his head back against the door. "Fuck. Fuck. Fuck. Fuck." He hit his head harder and still harder, until the pain broke through his nervous system and his rigid dick went limp.

Trembling all over, he got to his feet and stuck the pill into his mouth, wincing at the metallic taste. He tossed it back with a handful of tap water, then splashed some on his face. The ants were marching again — up and down his spine, back and forth across his scalp — which meant he'd muscled past stage one and was now on to stage two.

Great.

"Fucking great," he said to his reflection.

The man gazing back at him surprised him a little — he'd gotten used to the gaunt, haunted, yellow-eyed image of a junkie. This guy looked, dare he say, normal?

The eighteen months he'd spent in brutal, cold turkey rehab, alone in Minnesota at an expensive, parent-funded facility, had been the worst. But he'd woken one morning to face the therapies, the kitchen work, the gardening, and the endless group discussions with one thing on his mind — finding his brother.

He had checked himself out, declared himself healed, free of all the demons that had chased him since his adolescence and had hitchhiked his way to Michigan. After a week spent in a roach motel, shivering his way through the long nights, realizing that he now was the proud owner of a two-million-dollar trust fund thanks to the accident of his latest birthday, he'd bundled himself into the public library, set up an email account and reached out to his brother's fiancée — the lovely Evelyn.

It had worked out, thank God. And all had been fine — until he'd seen Caroline.

A trigger, as his many therapists warned in his rattled brain. Something well avoided for his own mental and emotional health. But it was a free country and his oldest, longest-running, most loyal in the face of his bullshit girlfriend had no reason to know he was back in Michigan. She'd wandered into the FitzPub with some friends after work, looking mouth-watering in a short black skirt, high heels and plain white blouse. She'd had a few beers and left, not even knowing he'd seen her.

But now, thanks to that single view of her, here he was again, battling like a son of a bitch for control of his body, his mind and his sanity.

A loud knock on the door made him jump and curse under his breath.

"Hey, you okay in there?"

It was Austin. Fucking guy had a twin brother radar that was eerily sharp. Brock dragged his fingers through his thick hair, attempting to calm his racing pulse and clear his mind of the many things that were tempting him.

"Yeah. I'm fine," he croaked out.

"You sure?"

Brock waited a beat, unlocked and opened the door, his happy-go-lucky, everybody-loves-Brock grin plastered on his face. "Never better, brother. Never fucking better."

He slapped Austin on the shoulder, pushed past him and whistled his way down the hall. His hands were shoved deep in the pockets of his nerdy workplace khakis, curled into tight, painful fists. His brain was still reeling through it all—settling firmly in one place. A place where he was fucking some random woman, while another random woman waited for her turn.

When he turned the corner, he leaned against the wall, his heart racing, his face covered in a sheen of sweat. He needed to get laid. Maybe that would help.

No, Brock. It won't. You don't know how to have normal, healthy sexual relationships, remember? It's one of your many failings.

"Fuck that," he muttered, glancing around, his vision suddenly sharper. He saw Amy, she of the pretty smile, the sweet ass, and the flirty glances. He lifted his chin and grinned at her. She gave him a little wave.

He took a breath and wandered over to her. "Hey, uh, I was wondering…could I buy you a drink sometime?"

She smiled, fluttered those lashes at him and cocked one hip, most likely without realizing she was doing it. He knew about these things now, having spent ten years off and on in various therapies and detox clinics.

Compulsive sexual behavior had been the diagnosis—coupled with addictions to, in varying orders, alcohol, pot, cocaine and opiates—ever since he'd been caught screwing the substitute high school AP English teacher in the back of her car. He'd been sixteen then. He was now thirty-eight. He had a job, thanks to his brother and his brother's wife. He had a place to live, thanks to his trust fund.

He'd been clean for a year. But the demons were roaring back thanks to her—Caroline, his one most-powerful trigger—and he had no idea how to fight them.

"Sure," Amy said, startling him. He'd almost forgotten they were standing and looking at each other. "How about tomorrow night?"

"Uh...yeah..." He backed away from her, knowing he shouldn't, that he couldn't. Amy was a sweet young woman and had a big-time crush on him, the twin brother of the brewery owner. He was the quintessential bad boy—catnip, for some reason, to nice girls like her. He swiped at his lips, already feeling her curves under his hands, the no-doubt lovely tight squeeze of her pussy around his dick. "I'll...uh...call ya."

He ran, needing space, and air, and another pill. Anything to set him straight. As he fumbled with his car keys, a hand landed on his shoulder. He threw it off, spoiling for a fight and yet unwilling to have another one with his brother.

"Brock," a voice, not his brother's, said. He turned and came face to face with her...Caroline Reilly. "I thought that was you."

He sagged back against the car and closed his eyes, praying for strength even as he sensed it ebbing out of his exhausted, compromised system. He felt her hand on his arm. Her familiarity soothed him. Thanking his timing on the medication, he opened his eyes, smiled and gave her a quick hug. "Hey, Caro, good to see you." He used their old shorthand, making her name sound like the corn syrup brand.

She sighed into his chest and put her arms around him, which forced him to shift away from her, unwilling to go there—to go anywhere—with her again. He gripped her upper arms and stared at her. "I'm glad to see you looking so great, and, you know, happy."

A tear slipped down her face. He bit back his knee-jerk, illness-based reaction to this, and simply let her go. She swiped at her eyes.

"Sorry," she muttered. "It's good to see you, too." Her smile lit up all the dark recesses of his mind, as it always did. As it had done for so many years. She touched his bearded jaw. "Looking all burly and shit."

"Yeah, it's the atmosphere. Brewers grow beards. I mean, I'm not a brewer but…you get me." He put his hand over hers, holding her in place for a few seconds before letting her go again—as usual, the hardest thing ever. Taking a long breath, he forced himself to be distant from her. It was his only hope, if he wanted to remain above the chattering, clamoring noise in his head that was rising again, urging him forward.

"Yeah, so, please tell me you have a boyfriend."

She rolled her eyes. "No, not really. Not now, anyway."

"Ah, okay."

Shit.

"Well, I just wanted to catch up with you…you know, see how you're doing." She crossed her arms. Her eyes went flat. Relief flooded his system. He was back on familiar ground.

"I'm pretty good." Lame, he knew, but it was all he had. He needed her to go away, far away, before he did something stupid. "As good as I can be, I suppose."

"Working for Austin?"

"Yeah, well, you know what they say about beggars and choosiness."

One corner of her lips lifted. He gulped and shoved his hands into his pockets, willing her to leave him alone. They stood, staring at each other, their respective pasts filling the silence like a dark, deadly smoke.

"So," she said.

"So," he said.

Another tear slid down her cheek. In opposition to everything logical in him, Brock reached out and touched it, then put it to his lips. The taste—salty and so familiar—made him shiver and his mind lurch forward. But he kept control over his body. He had no other choice.

"I'm glad you're back," she said, backing off from him, as if sensing his massive inner struggle. "I love you, Brock."

"Caro…"

"No, no, no need to say anything." She pulled her dark denim jacket tighter across her slim torso. "It's my curse. I get it. But I also understand why I shouldn't." She glanced behind her at the FitzPub front door. "I won't come back here, don't worry."

"No…I mean…it's okay." But it wasn't and they both knew it.

She tilted her head to one side. A gust of wind blew her red hair across her face, making Brock battle a nauseating urge to grab her, toss her in the car and run away with her. Again. "You really do look good. And that makes me happy, whether you believe me or not."

"I do believe you." The expensive hours of therapy had made him admit that. That his issues with regard to the beautiful Caroline were exactly that—his, not hers.

"I'm glad." She blew him a kiss. He made as if to catch it, and left his closed fist up, unsure where he wanted that ghost kiss to land. She smiled, turned and ran into the crowded parking lot.

Chapter Two

The smooth, white expanse of the sheet felt cool as Kayla passed her palms over it, sucking in the bleach-y scent. She'd always loved fresh, clean sheets — she'd had them so rarely in her life.

"Hey." The voice behind her made her flinch. "No sitting on the beds."

"Right, sorry." She got up and shook out the somewhat less clean duvet over the sheets, re-covered the pillows and put everything back together before grabbing the bag of garbage she'd collected from the room. "I'll swipe down the bathroom," she said, not meeting the eyes of her co-worker. As part of her probationary period in this crappy job, she'd gotten paired up with one of the hardcore, long-term cleaners and, to a person, they hated her guts.

"Yes, do that." The woman flopped into the chair by the open window and fired up one of those smokeless cigarette things. "Make it fast. You know, how I showed you yesterday."

"Right." Kayla pushed the cleaning cart into the dingy alcove between the bed space and the bathroom. As she stared at the filthy sink area, overflowing with empty beer bottles and pizza boxes, she gave herself the usual mantra-like reminder that this was her life now.

Employed. Drug-free. Poor as shit, but other than that, without any real worries.

"Don't fuck it up, K," she said under her breath as she shook out a fresh garbage bag and started scraping the detritus of what looked like a nice party into it. The bottles clinked together as wafts of old beer and pot filled her senses, triggering her synapses even as she used all her mental power not to grab the bottles and turn them up into her mouth.

Once the sink was cleaned out with near straight bleach so strong she'd gone home the last few nights with her fingertips faded, she turned her attention to the toilet and tub. With a sigh, she put on fresh gloves and picked up three used condoms, an empty tube of lube, more beer bottles. The tub was disgusting, ringed with dirt, while the fiberglass shower walls were streaked with God knew what. She sprayed, wiped, splashed hot water all over it, then set herself to the task of cleaning the toilet and the floors.

"Hurry up in there," her minder called.

She emerged, eyes streaming and nose running from the strength of the chemicals. "What's the worst thing you've ever found in a room?"

"Girl, you do not want to know that." The woman heaved herself up from the chair and checked her clipboard. "Come on. We're behind. You're taking too long on those toilets."

"It was pretty gross."

"They're all gross. People are disgusting. Ask any hotel room maid." The woman tucked the clipboard under her arm and glared at Kayla. "But we're on the clock, and the manager doesn't pay overtime. Let's go."

Kayla nodded and pushed the cart out of the room, after looking back once, recalling all the times she'd disgust-i-fied a hotel room, leaving behind way worse than what she'd found in this one. Shutting the door on the room, and the memories before she allowed them to take hold and pull her into a mire of longing for those days, she turned, resigned to another long day of sheets, bleach and berating.

"Hello, I'm looking for Kayla Hettinger." A stranger was standing on the balcony of the one-and-a-half-star no-tell motel where she now worked. The stranger was a strikingly beautiful woman with long black hair and light-brown skin, a Latina, Kayla figured, but without a trace of any accent.

Her minder turned toward the newcomer, her usual frown etched deeper into her dark skin. She took a quick look at the other woman and launched into a barrage of rapid-fire Spanish which was met with a response in kind. Kayla stood between them, waiting for the angry conversation to end, studying her ragged fingernails and jonesing for a hit, a pop, anything to get her through this day that stretched out in front of her like an endless, empty highway.

"Come with me," the strange, gorgeous woman said, grabbing her arm and tugging her away from the cleaning cart.

"Um, what?"

"You go with her, you're fired, do you hear me, girl?"

"Hang on a second," she said, yanking herself out of the other woman's grip. "What the hell is going on? I don't know who you are or what you're doing but I need this job right now, lady."

The woman sighed. "I'm sorry, Kayla. I'm Melody Rodriguez." The woman waited, as if seeking acknowledgment of this fact of her name. Kayla blinked at her, feeling her boss's gaze on the back of her neck like a pair of lasers.

"Yeah? So?" She took a step back, hand to her neck. Bleach smells filled her nose.

"I'm... I know your brother, Trent. And I think he'd love to know you're alive. Much less working here in Grand Rapids."

"My brother." Her voice remained flat as she allowed her brain to open that tiny room she'd shut off long ago. The one where she had a brother, a house, a mother. A life.

Her supervisor-slash-tormenter made a throat-clearing noise. But Kayla barely heard it. "I don't think..."

The other woman—Melody—smiled at her. "I run a bar. The FitzPub, over at Fitzgerald Brewing. Come with me and we can talk about a job, maybe?"

Kayla recoiled from the woman's outstretched hand. In her near forty years of life, no one had ever offered her a single kindness, one iota of helpfulness without an ulterior motive. She stared down at the cracked concrete balcony for a few seconds.

"You don't want this one working at your bar," her minder scoffed. "She's a junkie. She'll drink up all your profits."

Kayla glanced over at the woman. Her pulse raced. Her mouth felt packed with cotton.

Melody spat something in Spanish at her supervisor, who called her a whore. Kayla knew enough Spanish to recognize that word. "Come on, Kayla," Melody said, turning slightly to indicate Kayla should precede her away from the dirty hotel rooms and hateful fellow employees.

"Don't come back," her former minder grumbled behind her.

Kayla kept her gaze pinned to Melody's dark one. Her heartbeat hammered in her ears. She tried to swallow past the lump in her throat.

"It's all right," Melody insisted. "You're safe with me."

The woman behind them harrumphed again. Kayla peeled off her latex gloves, tossed them into the rolling trashcan and followed Melody without looking back.

"We did you a favor. Don't come back here looking for any more charity." The sound of the hotel employee's voice followed her across the balcony, down the steps and to Melody's car. She hesitated, her fingertips resting on the door handle.

Her brother. She was going to see Trent.

Tears burned her eyes but long years spent not giving away any emotion stood her well. She blinked them back, got in the strange woman's car and stared straight ahead. Luckily, she'd also had plenty of practice getting into strange cars on a whim, or in search of something better.

Melody turned to face her. "I'm…um…dating your brother," she said, her pretty face flushing at the words. "He may kill me for doing this, but after he told me about you I went off on my own to track you down."

Kayla raised an eyebrow, amused and yet anxious at the same time. "So, he doesn't know I'm here, back in town?"

"Nope, not yet anyway." She put the car in gear. "But he loves you and was so worried and I...well, I guess I wanted to do something to make him happy."

"Lucky guy." Kayla couldn't even picture him anymore, much less as a grown man with a grown woman for a girlfriend. He'd only been eleven when she'd run away — escaped — from the hell she'd been inhabiting.

"Yes, well, he's had some troubles, too. He has a daughter. She lives with him most of the time. Taylor. She's seventeen, you know, going on thirty."

"Hmm," Kayla said, her mind spinning as her skin began to crawl with a need to escape. She couldn't handle this right now. She'd moved back to Grand Rapids without a thought to even contacting Trent, even as her subconscious mind reminded her daily that she should reach out to him, to let him know she was alive, and more or less well. As she squeezed her fingers together, she started her inner counting trick.

Count to a hundred. Then two hundred. If you still want to bolt after that, do it.

Nine times out of ten, she didn't.

It was that tenth time that always got her in deep shit.

Breathless, even after a two hundred count, she defaulted to her old faithful method, pressing her short fingernails on her left hand into her right upper arm, triggering the pain. The blessed, mind-calming pain.

Chapter Three

"Here, hold Her Highness for me," Evelyn said, handing Rose to him over the top of the cluttered work table. Brock took the baby in one arm and set the computer tablet in front of his sister-in-law. "Thanks." She tugged the tablet closer to study it while he walked around the large office, jiggling the fussy kid.

He'd discovered his inner nurturer as Uncle Brock and never turned down the opportunity to hold his niece. If anything, it calmed him. His therapist had walked him through endless discussions about it but he preferred to simply appreciate the sensation of her warm, milky-smelling body in his arms, the scent of her light-blonde hair, the way she would grin at him, flail her arms and bop him on the nose with a giggle.

Now that she was mobile, she couldn't stand to be held, which kept his brother and Evelyn on their toes. They had a full-time nanny but if they were both working late, she would bring the baby to the brewery after five, like she'd done today.

The brewery was in the middle of a massive ramp-up of product as the decision to export beer overseas had been made, in light of the domestic competition in the craft beer sector. They had high hopes for a massive sales rise, but in the interim it meant running the brewery on a twenty-four-seven cycle. Something that had necessitated bringing in Ross Hoffman, the guy who was the biological father of the little girl who was attempting to climb his shoulders.

"We are fucking certifiable," Evelyn groaned before putting her head down on her arms. "We'll never meet this goal. I don't care how many people Ross runs through in there."

"Well, he's not really doing the running through, you know. Hey, cut it out." He pulled Rose off his head, wincing as she brought two handfuls of his hair with her. He tucked her under one arm like a flour sack, making her squeal and giggle as he galloped around the space a few times.

"I know. It's Elle. Between them, she and Ross are gonna make this happen, but I'm not sure at what cost, personnel-wise."

"I guess it's a good thing their, ah, chemistry worked out so well."

She shot him an arch look as he flopped onto the couch, exhausted from a four a.m. run, and a full day of work as the official brewery gopher. Rose clambered up his torso again, then settled herself on the back of the couch, kicking at his shoulder, sucking her thumb and studying her mother from across the room.

"Yes. I suppose that it is."

His phone buzzed with a text. As he dug it from his pocket, he felt the regular evening ritual creep up on him. The ant army was mustering along his spine, readying themselves for the march up to his scalp. He sighed and stared down at the message, blinking when he realized who it was from.

Hey, Brock. Wondering if you'd like to come over tonight for dinner. It would be safe. Other friends are coming, too. XO. Caro.

His little niece chose that moment to straddle his neck and yank his hair, which was a perfect distraction. He tossed the phone down and stood, delighting the girl, who kicked and flailed and made word-like noises that sounded like "Bock! Bock!"

Evelyn glanced up at her daughter, who was currently astride Brock's shoulders. "Great. She says that before she says Ma or even Da?"

"I have that sort of effect on ladies, you know."

"Or she could be doing her chicken imitation. She's somewhat fascinated by them, or at least videos of them." She returned her focus to the tablet screen, scrolling through the production and sales projections for the coming weeks.

"Nice. Way to crush my tender ego, evil bitch," he said as he headed for the door. Sitting was no longer an option. Caroline's invitation remained on his phone, burning a hole in his brain. He needed to move around. "Want anything?"

"What?" She glanced up. "Oh, sure. If you don't mind."

"The usual?"

"Yeah, yeah. Don't drop my kid in the mash tun on the way."

"I'll do my best." He held on to the girl's legs as he made his way down the metal steps from Evelyn's office to the original brewery floor. Elle, their new lady brewer, a petite German chick with wild-ass dreadlocks, tatts and piercings as far as his eye could see and an attitude just shy of a four-star general, had demanded that they run production not only in the main, modern brewery one building over, but also in this smaller, original version. Brewer-types scurried around, ramping up for the second shift as he wandered among them, allowing Madam Rose to soak up her fair share of attention.

He heard a door slam, a loud curse and a string of German. He walked over to let Elle see whose tender ears she was abusing before heading into the pub to fetch a beer for Evelyn and a ginger ale for himself.

Ginger ale. So lame.

But it was his only option, now.

Elle smiled up at the little girl as he took a few seconds to admire her in her labeled T-shirt, cargo shorts and rubber boots — the de rigueur brewer's uniform. But on her it was especially nice since she always cut the neck of the T down to the black sports bra and sliced off the sleeves, leaving her lean, inked arms in full view.

"Looking good, as always, m'lady," he said, tipping an invisible hat to her when he heard the answering growl of German behind him. Ross, the just-as-bossy prima donna German brewer Austin had met in school in Munich and who had, somehow, inserted himself in the middle of Austin and Evelyn's relationship a few years prior. Resulting in the precocious girl now yanking on his hair again like a horse jockey.

He knew everyone was stressed beyond belief and making small talk at this point was useless. Besides, he'd spent a fair bit of energy flirting with the exotic, sexy Elle only to receive her firm rebuff — before she turned her attentions to Ross.

"God damn it, Hoffman, I knew you were a complete idiot, but I…" she was saying in accented English.

He wandered away, leaving them to their German-English tangle of argument. As he walked through the empty hallway behind the brewery that connected to the FitzPub, he hummed and chatted with Rose. Which allowed him to keep the evening ant-march at bay.

He rounded the corner and headed into the kitchen, pulling Rose down off his shoulders. There was too much hot grease and other crap flying around in there to be safe, much to Her Highness' chagrin of course.

"Chill, sister. You'll have plenty of other reasons to be pissy at me. Save it for a future moment." He held on to the girl, waved at the cooks and other staff, then emerged behind the bar. The smell of beer hit him hard as it always did. He choked down the urge to fill a pitcher of Fitzgerald's finest anything and drink it all at once.

Melody, the hot little Hispanic number who ran the place, was laughing with some patrons at the far end. The three bartenders were pouring, taking food orders, the usual. Once he set Rose on the bar near Melody, she proceeded to try to crawl down the expanse of sealed concrete.

"Whoa there, Miss Thing," he said, snatching her back up and installing her on his shoulders once more. It seemed to be the safest place. "Jesus, she wears me out."

Melody bumped his shoulder. "Everyone's worn out these days, eh?"

"You can say that again." He smiled when a woman he'd never seen before approached him and put down a coaster. "Hel-lo there," he said with a grin, at the precise moment Rose sneezed. He felt the splatter against his cheeks and the top of the hand he had out to greet the lovely, strange new FitzPub employee.

"Gross," the woman said, handing him a napkin. She didn't even acknowledge the girl sitting on his shoulders. Odd, since that was the first thing most women noticed. As he swiped at the Rose snot, he watched her pour two beers for someone else, then turn back to face him.

She was tall, very thin, with huge, greenish-brown eyes, full lips and sharp cheekbones. Despite the heat, she wore a long-sleeved version of the FitzPub T-shirt, which engulfed her as if she were playing dress-up with someone else's clothing. She smiled at him — if he could call it that since it was more a soft lifting of the corners of her lips for a few seconds, before she busied herself, pulling empty glassware out of the bar-level dishwasher and stacking them on their appropriate shelves.

"Who is that," he whispered to Melody.

"Huh?" She looked up from her phone. "Oh, that's Kayla. She's Trent's sister."

"Trent? Your main man? Captain Business?"

She rolled her dark eyes at him. "Yes. Him."

"Ah, I see." He eyed the new chick's rear view as she stretched to reach the highest shelves with the clean glasses. "I also see the resemblance."

Melody shot him a look. "Hands off, lover boy," she warned. "That girl is a hot mess."

"Yeah? And I'm not?"

"Whatever. Listen, Trent and I are having people out to the lake house in a few weeks, once this craziness is done here. You're invited. Bring a date." She blew him a kiss and headed around the bar and into the kitchen, talking six miles a minute *en Español.*

"We're a regular United Nations around here, aren't we, Princess?" He kissed Rose's chubby knee and sat for a few minutes, watching Kayla work. She was graceful, like a dancer, but never met anyone's eyes for very long. She had a habit of tugging the already overstretched sleeves of the shirt even farther, as if hiding something.

And like that, he realized he was gazing at a fellow junkie. "Takes one to know one, kid," he said, raising a finger to get her attention.

"Hi, I'm Brock Fitzgerald." He held out the hand that hadn't gotten befouled earlier. She did that weird almost-smile thing again and touched her fingertips to his before giving her sleeve another tug.

"Kayla," she said, her voice soft and sing-songy. "Nice to meet you. This is your place?" She gestured around the bar.

"Ha! Hardly. Or better yet, I wish. It's my brother Austin's place. Well, his and Evelyn's, I guess." He pulled Rose down, mainly because his neck was getting a little too warm all of a sudden. "This beautiful creature is Rose Fitzgerald. My niece."

"I see," Kayla said as she observed the girl from a safe distance. "So what can I get you Mr. Fitz—?"

"Oh, Jesus, please do not call me that. It's Brock. And I need a double IPA and a ginger ale. I'm running the beer up to Evelyn." He smiled by way of covering his embarrassment at drinking ginger ale.

But her smile went a hair past ghostly as she pulled a to-go cup with a straw from under the bar and sipped. "I love the ginger ale myself," she said, turning to pour his drinks.

Yep, he thought, as he held Rose on his lap and she giggled, grabbed the coaster and tried to cram the entire thing into her mouth. "Too many carbs, doll face." He snatched the thing away from her and held it over his head while she worked her way into a snit. "Somebody needs a nap." He tossed the half-masticated round of cardboard toward the garbage behind the bar, missing by half a mile.

Kayla picked it up and threw it away then put the two drinks on the bar, well out of Rose's reach. "So, how exactly are you going to get two drinks and that," she pointed her elbow at Rose, "up to Evelyn's office anyway?"

"Easy peasy," he said, slipping the girl back up to his shoulders. But she had other ideas and went stiff as a board, as her snit worked its way into a full-throated howl.

Kayla raised a dark eyebrow at him. He shrugged and pulled Rose back down, tucking her under his arm once again. "One at a time, I guess, unless I can convince your boss to let you take a few minutes away and give a guy a hand."

She glanced over her shoulder. Her eyes had gone from light and amused to clouded and anxious during the time it had taken for him to speak. He frowned at the sight of what could be a bruise under her jawline. But then convinced himself it was a shadow. And either way, none of his business.

"I don't know. I'd better not." She ran a hand around her neck. Her nails were short, the edges red and inflamed looking.

A hot mess, he mused, as he imagined himself running his lips along her collarbones. His face flushed hot when she met his gaze again as if sensing his dirty thoughts. He cleared his throat and busied himself trying to calm the pissed-off baby.

"Go on," Melody said, having emerged from somewhere. She patted Kayla's arm. "He's safe."

Before he could mount a decent argument against that, Rose let out a screech that made the whole bar turn and stare. "Exit, stage left." He hurried around the bar, holding the girl out in front of him like a hood ornament while she kicked and squawked, not even checking to see if anyone had bothered to grab his drinks and follow him.

But Kayla had indeed done that, and once he made it to the foot of the metal flight of steps up to Evelyn's crow's-nest-style office, Rose was calmly sucking her thumb, her sweaty head pressed into his neck.

"You're a natural at that," she said, waiting for him to ascend the stairs before her.

"Yeah. I'm as surprised as anybody about it, too." Aggravation hit him then, right between the eyes. He was an almost thirty-nine-year-old man, reduced to running around at his brother's beck and call, up to and including playing after-hour nanny to this kid. Forced to drink ginger ale and avoid women since he had no big-boy control over himself.

This kid you love, don't forget that.

He smiled when his inner nice guy emerged, calming the devil that had attempted to escape. His usual evening battle. *Nothing new to see here, folks. Move along.*

He sighed and leaned against the wall, so exhausted that the thought of climbing the steps made him dizzy. Kayla waited him out, silent and observant, not offering to switch with him, he noticed. Another oddity for a female as the sight of the droopy, sleeping, blonde-haired little angel almost always brought out their inner mama hen.

But something about her presence calmed him in ways that no woman ever had. He felt himself relax, even as he got a closer look at her and realized that, but for her extreme thinness, she was an absolute stunner. "Okay, up we go," he said to himself as he headed upstairs.

Evelyn glanced up from the spot where he'd left her, glaring down at electronic spreadsheets and futures reporting, her blue eyes bloodshot, her shoulders slumped. "Oh my God, can I ever use that." She got up and stretched, then took the beer from Kayla, downing half of it in one gulp.

"Damn, now I'm really jealous of my stupid brother," Brock said before laying Rose down on the couch and covering her with a small blanket. She shifted around and opened her clear blue eyes, smiling up at him.

"Bock," she said, making little gimmie-gimmie motions with her fingers. Undone by this, he sat, brushing her hair back off her forehead until she dropped to sleep.

"Dude, you are a goner," Evelyn said. He blinked as if emerging from a trance, mad at himself for not saying more to Kayla. But of course, she'd faded, vanished into the ether.

And a damn good thing, too, he reminded himself. *The last thing you need is to fall for a fellow junkie.* Besides, he had a date tonight.

He picked up his abandoned phone and typed out a reply to Caroline, not allowing himself to think about it, or for his logical mind to talk the rest of him out of it.

I'll be there. But I need your address, and a time.

He hesitated, then sent it.

"You do realize that she'll grow up and go out on dates someday, right?"

"Like hell she will," he said. He rested a hand on the tiny girl's chest, as dead serious as he'd ever been. "Her father and I will make sure that never happens."

Evelyn chuckled and shook her head, finished the beer and sat back down while Brock stared at the messages emerging on his phone, telling him where to be, what time to be there and realizing that he might just have made a horrible mistake.

Chapter Four

"Are you sure about this?"

"Yes, I'm fine. Lay off me, will ya?"

Brock glared at his brother, who'd shown up right on time, as he was emerging from a long, scalding shower which had done exactly nothing to clear his rattled brain. "I never should've given you a fucking key," he muttered as he toweled off his hair, baring his backside to Austin, who'd been draped across his bed, half asleep. "You really don't have to babysit me."

"Tell that to our mother, please," Austin said around a jaw-cracking yawn.

"I will," he said, rubbing some random white pasty product into his dark hair, something the hot chick who cut it every four weeks insisted he buy. "At our next intolerable family dinner, how about that?"

Austin groaned and dropped his arm over his eyes. Brock watched him a few minutes, his sympathy muscle flexing in a fairly healthy fashion, which was a good sign about his general state of mind.

"You're gonna work yourself into a stroke, my brother," he said before pulling on a pair of black boxer shorts and rooting through his closet for a pair of jeans.

"Uh," Austin grunted from underneath his arm.

"Then I shall be forced to do the brotherly thing, I suppose." Austin raised his arm. "And marry your smoking-hot wife for you."

"Fuck you, loser," Austin said, the arm back in place again.

"No thanks. That's just weird."

"You're weird," Austin mumbled.

"Dude, if you want to have a weirdo contest, why don't we tell dear Virginia about the actual paternity of her precious grandchild, eh? Maybe at the next family dinner?"

"Go to hell," Austin said.

"Lame. You really *are* tired." He smacked his brother's leg so he could sit and pull socks from the drawer next to his bed. He sat, elbows on his knees, hands dangling for a few seconds. The ants had been stupefied by the hot water, but they were gathering momentum again, ready to begin the Brock full-body march. The only thing that he'd found would stop them was sex. But the problem was, once he started down that road, he couldn't stop, no matter what sort of pharmaceutical cocktail he'd ingest.

Exhaustion stole over him again and he flopped back next to his brother, staring up at the circulating ceiling fan, willing the skin-crawling sensation to cease, desist, leave him in peace for one damn night. By the time he realized what was happening, his teeth were chattering and someone was covering him with a blanket. On reflex, he rolled onto his side, curled into himself as tight as he could and began mentally reciting the Serenity Prayer.

It didn't help, but it kept his mind occupied for a while, so the moment could pass. When he emerged from the warm cocoon, groggy and head-achy, Austin was there, holding a glass of water and a fistful of pills. He sighed and threw off the cover, taking the water and swallowing the pills, wincing at the slimy taste they left in his throat. "Thanks," he said, looking down at his lap.

"No problem," Austin said, slapping him on the back. "But I'm on the record as against this little dinner party idea. You know I like Caro, Brock. That's not the issue. You put that girl through so much…"

"Spare me the memory lane journey, please." The ants were also groggy, but mustering again. He rose and stretched, relishing the soreness in his chest and arms. He'd hired a new trainer and demanded that the guy push him ever harder. The guy had done so, right to the brink of making him almost pass out a few days ago. He loved it and its mind-blanking numbness.

Fucking or other forms of exercise, he thought as he shuffled into the bathroom to brush his teeth. *That'll be the name of my sought-after memoir someday.*

When he emerged into the main room of his condo, Austin was in the kitchen, drinking water and eyeballing his phone. "Go on, already. Beat it. Go home and service your wife or something."

"I'm going. Hey, did Melody ask you about the lake house weekend coming up?"

"Yeah," he said, splashing water from the kitchen sink up onto his still sleepy face. He'd forgotten about until now. "Whatever."

"If you want, you could bring Caro. As a friend."

He tossed the kitchen towel down on the empty countertop. It was a prop, just like every other damn thing in this room. He couldn't cook to save his life but he made a mean PB&J and knew his way around a soup can when he didn't have the energy for any other options. "Sure. I'll do that." Anger took over again. Fury roiled in chest, shoved its way up his gullet into his throat, filling his sinuses and skull. Choking him, as it always did. "Go home, Austin," he said, glaring at his brother.

Austin met his gaze, his cool, steady, normal-guy expression striking a match to Brock's smoldering nest of rage. "Stop fucking staring at me like I'm a god damned freak, will you? Jesus." He stomped out into the living room and flopped down in one of the leather chairs his mother had delivered to this random, sterile, cookie-cutter condo. He buried his face in his hand, willing Austin to go so he could be mad in peace. It was another stage and he had to get past it before he left for Caroline's little dinner party. He felt a hand on the top of his head. He ignored it and ignored it some more until the door clicking shut made him take a loud inhale.

The air filled his lungs, making his blood pump faster, so fast he believed he could feel it swooshing through his pulmonary system. *Tha-thump. Tha-thump. Tha-thump.*

He could picture her — not Caroline with her full, perfect curves and her thick auburn hair. But the other her. The new her. The odd bird, junkie her he'd met today.

Kayla. Dark hair, mysterious, haunted eyes, thin frame, nervous tics and all.

He groaned as his body responded in its usual fashion, hardening all over. He limped to the bedroom and took care of things, willing his mind blank and not full of Kayla the junkie, a.k.a. the last person on Earth he should be jacking off to right now. But he lost that battle and cried out into the darkening room, phantom tasting her skin, her full lips, her sweet pussy, coating his hand and the clean shirt he'd wanted to wear tonight.

With a grunt of disgust at himself he rolled off the bed and tossed the now sticky shirt into the hamper. As he yanked another one off a hanger without looking at it, he left his jeans unzipped, his still-hard cock exposed to the cool air in hopes it would soften.

It didn't. But that was his life, wasn't it? His fucking curse to be the twin who got the triple dose of pervy, the double dose of addiction, the quadruple dose of loser.

He stared down at his dick, thinking boring, unsexy thoughts, the way his therapist had urged him. But it took almost an hour before he felt equipped to go out in public, to his ex-girlfriend—hell, his ex-fiancée's condo—for some kind of a lame ass dinner party with 'friends'.

Chapter Five

Kayla lay awake, hearing the thuds and wails, the screams and groans, the gunshots and whatever the hell else all around her. It was almost soothing in its regularity, its familiarity, after a night spent slinging expensive beer and overpriced bar food to a bunch of rich assholes and their insufferable dates.

She pressed the heels of her hands into her eye sockets, willing the vision of him out of her mind. Willing him gone from her memory banks. He was just another Richie Rich anyway. Just another asshole, eye-fucking her when he thought she didn't know it.

But she always knew it. She'd spent her entire life knowing it.

The heat in the upper room where she was squatting pressed down on her body, forcing her to remain as still as possible as if by her stillness she might escape it. She took tiny sips of the wet, damp air. Reminding herself that she was lucky to have this illegal space at all. That she was lucky to be alive.

Lucky. That wasn't a word she usually associated with her life. But it seemed to be shining a weak light on her the past few weeks, at least in relation to the shit she'd slogged through from the time she'd been thirteen. Lucky to get caught up in a drug bust, where she lay, dying from an overdose of pain pills and booze. Lucky to be so poor and nameless that the hospital had had to take her in, revive her, feed her a few days. Lucky that a nice lady doctor had taken pity on her and found her a coveted spot in a government-paid detox camp. Lucky that the camp had made her work so hard she'd almost forgotten her daily need for a hit, for a pill, for a drink.

Almost.

Not so lucky that one of the guards had caught her outside smoking an illicit cigarette one night and demanded that she blow him in exchange for her silence.

She sighed and let the sweat drip down her face, knowing that it would cool her skin and so resisting the compulsion to wipe it away. She rolled onto her side and let her legs dangle off the edge of the mattress. Her feet hurt, but in a good way, a hard-day-at-a-job-she-actually-liked way. It had only taken her a few weeks to get into the groove and flow of the place. And Melody, her rescuer, seemed to be pleased with her performance so far.

She had the day off tomorrow, which was not something she looked forward to like a normal person would. Hours to sit and stare at walls did nothing for her, so she planned to take a long walk, drop in at the library and read, anything to keep from having to be alone with her thoughts.

She'd put her foot down and insisted that she wasn't ready to see Trent so Melody had agreed to keep her presence a secret as far as was possible. She'd enlisted Evelyn in this, too. And Trent was super busy working on some new massive real estate development deal anyway so he was hardly ever at the bar.

Her baby bro — the real estate mogul. She smiled into the stifling room while thinking about him, letting herself visit some of her oldest memories after a lot of years stuffing them under a pillow and smothering them out of mental self-preservation. She'd seen a picture of him on Melody's phone and had been shocked at how tall and handsome he was. But the sight of his face had set her back a few days. Because he looked an awful lot like his father. The man not her father, but who'd stuck around long enough to drink away what money they'd had, slap her around a little, then take all of that a step further when she'd turned fourteen.

She squeezed her eyes shut, unwilling to go there right now.

With a groan, she sat up, letting her bare legs stick out on the floor in front of her. The pain in her feet focused her for a few minutes, but the urge was back. The need to do something to release the intolerable pressure building in her chest, her neck, her head.

When her stepfather had made his first forays into her childhood bedroom, she'd been afraid, of course, but something in her, some innate positive creature, had reminded her that he must love her.

She'd been so stupid and weak, she'd sought him out during the days he'd been home without work. She'd bring him beers or sandwiches and he'd smile at her, pat her on the arm, kiss her cheek, tell her what a nice girl she was. So much nicer than her mother.

He'd come to her at night, make her cry, and leave her room with kisses on her forehead and cheeks and promises that if she never told anyone, he would love her forever.

She forced herself to her feet and stumbled into the adjacent room with the moldy shower, cracked toilet seat and leaky sink. Tears burned her eyes but she stopped them, calling on her training. *Nobody likes a crier*, he'd said to her. A lot.

She dropped to her hands and knees and pressed her hot face against the toilet seat, waiting for the inevitable. But she'd only eaten a few bites of soup and her body seemed determined to hang on to it for now. As she leaned back the room spun a few times, then righted itself. Which served to increase the pressure. Pressure under her skin so powerful she wondered how she didn't just explode into a million pieces.

Gasping in pain, she stood, lifted the lid of the toilet tank, and found what she was looking for—a tiny ziplock bag with a few crucial items.

Not pills. Not anymore. She'd never go back to that.

As her fingers closed around the sharp, German-made blade, she sighed in anticipated relief. Just holding the cold metal between her finger and thumb calmed her racing pulse. The pain in her feet and hips faded in anticipation.

She pressed the blade to an old cut, ready to slice through the thick scar tissue, eager to release the horrific pressure under her skin, she recalled the man she'd met today. Brock. His handsome yet sad face. His deft touch with the little kid. His sweet smile.

"No," she said, startling herself as she opened an old wound with a grunt of pain. "No. No. No. No. No."

The blood beaded up, then began to flow down her arm — a warm, familiar, soothing sensation. Kayla sighed and dropped her head back. The voices building in her head — mostly her stepfather's but a few others' along the way — receded in the face of the pain. But another voice, and a different face, filled her mind as she sobbed, keeping as quiet as possible. Because nobody liked a crier.

The sound of a buzzing phone made her gasp and sit up, slipping around in the coagulating blood on the bathroom floor. Her neck ached from being jammed up for God knew how long after she'd passed out on the floor and dropped over onto her side in the small space. Her arm throbbed. But her head was clear. The pressure was gone. And that was all that mattered.

Pressing a thin towel over the fresh cut, she stumbled out into the other room, still shocked that anyone would have a reason to be calling her. It took her a few seconds to register that it was Melody, her boss.

"Hello?" She tried to keep the tremor out of her voice. She was dizzy, weak, hungry. But she needed to sound normal. She wanted to keep the job at the FitzPub.

"Hi, Kayla. It's Melody. Listen, I'm wondering if you're available to open tomorrow?"

"Yes, I am." She pressed the towel against the oozing wound and made herself focus on this conversation. "No problem."

"I gave you a key, right?"

"Yes. I have one."

"Great. Okay. Thanks!"

"No problem. Thank you."

There was a beat of silence. "Kayla, I really think we need to tell Trent."

"I know you do. But I… I need a little more time." She closed her eyes, seeing his face in the photo and unable to not superimpose the voice of her stepfather in her ear, the smell of old booze and sour sweat out of her nose, the pain… "I'll do it soon, I swear. I need to go, though. I'll open tomorrow. Talk to you soon." She ended the call and fell back on the mattress, panting and praying that the pressure wouldn't build and forcing the invasion of Brock Fitzgerald's face, eyes, smile out of her head.

Chapter Six

Brock sat clutching his water bottle, watching Caroline and her friends get drunk and wondering how long he could wait before they left and he could do what he wanted—what he needed—with his pretty ex-fiancée. She hadn't changed much. The bubbly laugh, the toss of hair, the twinkle in her eyes when she'd look at him.

He did his usual funny, charming, self-deprecating, water-drinking thing for her. A show, he now knew. A preamble for later.

He sipped and observed her doing her mating dance, in front of an audience of her work friends—including a guy who was staring just as intently as he was. His body hummed in anticipation. Even as his brain yammered at him not to do it. Not to stick around for the inevitable end of this night of torture.

Because it would not be an end—not for him.

He sighed and emptied his third bottle of water, getting up to help clear the wine bottles and dessert plates from the room, figuring he might as well be busy while the evening trundled along its pre-determined path. He smiled as Caroline's drunk friends hip bumped him, giggling at their daring. As he loaded the dishwasher, he allowed his mind to go blank. The pills were working their way through him now and he was less fraught, less tense, more willing to go slow with her. To enjoy the night in her bed.

But he shouldn't.

He couldn't.

Caroline Reilly represented his lost years—years spent fucking, drinking, smoking, shooting up. Years he was embarrassed at this particular moment to long for, to wish himself back to, for no other reason than that he had no worries, no responsibilities, and could do whatever the hell felt good.

He wiped his hands on a towel and turned around to watch the show a little longer, half-convinced that he should leave while she wasn't paying attention to him. He was her catnip, her pop, her hit, her deepest, darkest urge, in living, breathing form. They'd been perfect and yet awful together for so long. What in the world she was doing inviting him over, getting drunk and doing all the things she knew damn well would encourage him—showing off, flirting with the other guy so hard that poor dude was near pop-eyed?

The music pounded through the Bluetooth speaker. The girls danced around, sliding against each other while his male compatriot-slash-audience member sat, gaga at the potential. Brock sighed and pulled his phone out of his pocket and sent a quick text to his brother.

Yo. You were right. I should never have come here.

He stared at the words after he'd sent them, smiling when he got a message back within seconds, even at this hour.

I'm always right. Do you want me to come get you?

He sighed and looked back into the living room. Caroline was staring at him now, her deep-green eyes flashing, her hips undulating to the music. He smiled and tucked the phone away, crooked his finger at her and put a pillow over the voice in his head that kept reminding him that this…kiss…this…touch…this…all this…was all a very bad idea.

His phone buzzed in his pocket. A call this time, from Austin, no doubt. But he was busy now and he let Caroline take the hand he'd had up her skirt and lead him down the short hallway, past the giggling friends and into her bedroom. He hesitated for a count of three after she shut the door and turned to face him. Then he lost himself in her for hours.

The sex wasn't perfect. He was out of practice. But her familiar smell and taste and feel under his lips and fingers brought it all back. Afterward, they slept, arms and legs tangled together, sweat drying on their skin, his face buried in her hair.

He woke with a start when the darkness was only beginning to fade into dawn, and disentangled himself, needing water, a shower, space. But obviously wanting something else if his traitorous hard dick was any indication. The ants were crawling all over him now, tickling his ears and making his fingertips tingle. He leaned on the vanity, staring into his flushed face. He felt good but wanted more. Needed more.

"Fuck," he muttered, splashing water on his face before ducking into an ice-cold shower for a few seconds, emerging with his teeth chattering and his cock at half-mast. After wrapping a towel around his waist, he wandered out into the living room. The girls were still there, as was the guy. All passed out on the couch in various stages of undress. He stood and observed the women with a clinical eye. One was curvy, with full hips and breasts like Caroline. She had a fully waxed pussy, he noted with a sort of clinical detachment, something he'd never cared for.

The other one was a dark-skinned near-goddess. Her nipples were hard, tempting, like drops of chocolate. He licked his lips, took one step toward the scrum, hand on his revived erection tenting the towel. He'd bet money that her pussy was a light shade of brown too but she had on a skirt. Their mouths were hanging open. The dude was snoring. Brock backed away, citing some mantra or another as he went into the kitchen.

He downed two glasses of water and stood, berating himself, until he felt her hands on his shoulders, his arms, around his waist, her lips against his back. He turned and held on to her for dear life, sucking in deep breaths of all that was Caroline.

He grabbed her arms and pushed her away. "I can't do this, Caro. You know that."

She nodded, her eyes bright.

"I'm gonna go now. Before I do something really stupid, okay?"

She nodded again. "I was drunk. It was a mistake." Her voice was low and soft, but serious, as she always was. His serious, sweet, amenable-to-try-anything Caroline. His first love. His first fuck. The girl he'd screwed over so many times and in so many ways he'd lost count.

He poured her a glass of water. She drank it, thanked him and put the empty glass on counter, pulling her robe tighter around her body. "But it was good, right?"

He nodded, tucking her hair behind her ears, cradling her face in his hands and kissing her long and deep. "It was," he whispered. "And that's why I have to leave."

"I know." She leaned her forehead against his. "I'm sorry. I was being selfish. But I've missed you...so much."

"I love you, you know," he said, surprising himself. "But I'm the worst thing in the world for you."

She sighed and swiped her eyes. "Go on, then. Beat it." She smiled at him and slapped his ass.

And for the first time in a long while, he had nothing—no witty rejoinder, no snarky response. He stared at her a few minutes, memorizing her. "Could we be friends, maybe? I could use a few of those."

She sniffled and poured more water. "Maybe," she parroted him before drinking and staring at him over the rim of the glass. "Yes, I think I'd like that. I mean...if I can't have you any other way." She stared pointedly at his bare chest.

He took a breath. "Okay, so come with me up to the lake. It's in a few weekends. Some get-together, Melody and Trent's place."

"Who?"

"Melody's the manager of the pub. She's hooked up with Trent Hettinger. He's—"

"I know who he is. You know him?"

"Only via Austin and the brewery crew. So, will you? I'll make sure we have separate rooms. I understand his lake house is less cabin and more mansion."

"Wouldn't surprise me," she said. "He's rich as God. Hot too." Her eyes twinkled at him when he frowned. "Okay, fine. I'll go. But as your friend." She flicked his nipple, making him yelp. "Can you help me with them?" She pointed to the truncated-looking orgy in the other room.

"Yeah. Let me get dressed." He headed to the bedroom for his clothes, his mind at peace but his body fighting him every step. His curse, he figured. But he felt as if he'd won a major battle just now as he and Caroline got dressed in silence around her tousled bed. He sent two quick texts before assisting her in rousing the partiers and shoving them out the door before helping with a quick clean-up. One to his brother, who was livid, as usual. And one to his therapist, requesting a Sunday, emergency appointment.

Later, he patted his belly, which was full of scrambled eggs and toast. "Gotta go, babe. Thanks for the laughs." Trying to keep it light, while every nerve and molecule in him was screaming for him to reach for her, hold her, kiss her, fuck her until neither of them could walk. He put his dishes in the washer and downed the last of the coffee. "Don't," he said, flinching away from her touch. "This is hard enough, as you well know."

She sighed and stepped away from him. "I don't know about this, Brock."

"Well, you don't have to come with me." But he had to chew the inside of his cheek to keep from begging her to promise that she would.

"I know." She pulled her hair back into a thick ponytail. He tried not to stare at her nipples that were poking through the thin fabric of her T-shirt. "*Can* we do it? Just be friends, I mean?"

He slumped against her counter, keeping his distance as the ants resumed their circuit across his scalp, down his neck, spine, arms and legs. Shivering, he closed his eyes. She slid into his arms and held on to him, whispering something that he couldn't hear over the roaring in his ears. The roaring of need, of sick, uncontrollable desire.

Gently, he tugged her off him. "Thanks. I'll check in with you later." He touched her nose. "I have to go now and pay my therapist time and a half to talk through this giant mistake I made with you."

She seemed to deflate. He touched her cheek.

"You're not a mistake, Caro. You're not the problem. It's me. We both know it. And I want to be your friend, but that's it, okay?"

"Okay." Her voice was rough with emotion. "I love you, Brock."

"I know," he said, heading for her door, his head pounding and his entire body yearning to turn around and go back to her.

Chapter Seven

Kayla spent an hour setting the chairs down and wiping all the tables and the expansive concrete bar. The silence was odd but soothing. Since she'd never worked a Sunday open, and typically took the later weekday shifts, she'd never been in the place when it wasn't already noisy and teeming with patrons.

She chose the music theme — a non-committal jazz-like station — and sat a few minutes, taking in the calm silence of her new workplace. As she wandered behind the bar, letting her fingers trail along the cool, clean surface, she realized what she wanted to do, right now.

She grabbed her backpack from underneath the cash register and pulled out the cheap sketch pad and charcoal pencils she'd treated herself to after an especially good night of tips. The 'art thing' as she'd come to think of it had begun during her last days at the detox camp. Her therapist had been aggravated at her when she'd kept insisting that she had no real hobbies — she didn't like reading, didn't play any instruments, hated to cook, didn't sew or make anything else with her hands and had no real desire to do any of it. But she'd needed something, the woman had kept saying to her, while Kayla had kept shaking her head, telling her that was part of her damn problem—nothing to distract her. No job. No real prospects. No hobbies. No significant skills, unless you counted blow jobs and faking orgasms. Oh, and rolling joints and mixing cheap martinis.

"Stop it," she muttered as she sat and stared at one of the tables, with its flower stuck in an old beer bottle, the condiments, the rolled utensils and stack of self-serve coasters. Something about it struck her. It was representative of her new world, up to and including the flaws in the wood, the stains on the chairs, the sad dip of the two-day-old flower in its faux-chic bud vase.

The therapist had presented her with her first sketch pad and charcoal pencils. She'd scoffed but after a day of glaring at them from across her small cell-like room, she'd opened the book and drawn the first thing she'd seen—the contents of her bedside table. A box of generic tissues, a half-empty glass of water, five different pill bottles, most of them tipped over, a cracked lamp.

She'd shown it to her therapist the next day, encouraged when the woman had seemed surprised by it. The final weeks of her time in the camp had been spent scribbling and scraping away on the pad until she'd filled it up and worked the pencils down to nubs.

When she'd been set free from that place, with nothing in her possession but a backpack full of shitty drawings, a bus pass, an address for a halfway house and twenty bucks for food, something about her hours spent being creative had given her hope. She'd used the ticket to get home to Grand Rapids, after almost twenty-five years away, realizing that she wanted to reconnect with her brother, now that she was clean. The stack of sketch books was tall enough to serve as her bedside table in the warehouse, alongside the mattress. She'd gone back into them and filled every possible corner of both sides of the paper. Then she'd made herself wait until she had three hundred bucks put away before allowing a thirty-five dollar purchase of fresh pads — the sheets grainy and cheap but blank — and some new pencils.

It freed her for a few minutes — the act of drawing. She had zero delusions about her talent, regardless of what the therapist had said about her early forays. But she had all kinds of faith in its power to distract her from her worst urges, her most violent memories. As she let her hand move, she kept her eyes on the subject as the soft jazzy music filled the air around her.

When the door slammed open, the sun shone in, blinding her for a moment. "We aren't open yet," she called, flipping the sketch book closed and tucking everything away in her bag. It was only ten-thirty but she'd forgotten to lock the door behind her so she figured she might as well earn a few bucks early.

"It's me," Melody called out.

Kayla blinked, confused. Her boss' voice sounded strangled, as if she had a cold. Or she'd been crying. The woman walked around behind the bar so fast Kayla couldn't get a good look at her. She ran through the kitchen that was occupied with cooks doing prep work. Following her, worried in a way that she chalked up to female intuition, she waited outside the staff restroom door that had just slammed behind Melody.

"*No es bueno*," one of the cooks said. The other one made a clucking sound with his teeth but shrugged at her.

Kayla waited a few minutes, then heard the bar door open again, so she headed out, a smile on her face, ready to earn more sketch book money.

It was freeing, the art. But it was also freeing to only be worried about that — not about where to get her next hit, or how to pay for it. Not that she wouldn't love to have one. The sweet rush to the brain, the odd sensation of swelling in all her nerve endings, ready to receive all the good the world had to offer. How colors were brighter, sounds more compelling, her sense of touch intensified. Until she lost the high and her body staggered into needy mode.

She shook her head at herself as she approached the couple settling themselves at the end of the bar. After about an hour, she heard a new voice in the kitchen behind her. A somewhat strident, bossy-sounding female speaking rapid Spanish. When she had a spare second, she ducked her head into the busy kitchen and saw a woman who was a shorter, older version of her boss, helping Melody out of the bathroom.

"Hi, Kayla, sorry," Melody said. "This is my mother. She's…here to help out this afternoon. A couple of the guys are down with the flu."

The older woman smiled and shook Kayla's hand then cluck-clucked at her daughter, who looked as if she had the same problem as the missing kitchen staff, toward her small office at the back of the kitchen. She shot a worried glance over her shoulder then shut the door behind them.

The bar was getting busy, so Kayla headed back out, eager to lose herself in the work for a few hours. She'd almost forgotten about Melody and her mother's presence but after a while realized the older woman was, indeed, working away in the kitchen, chopping, stirring, prepping, bossing the rest of the staff around like a pro.

Once things had calmed down a bit, she started putting away cleaned glassware. She greeted the second shift of bartenders and servers then filled a couple of beer orders, loving the way she felt in control of this, of herself, for the first time in years. She'd even managed to flirt back with some of the older guys who were semi-regulars, and with the cute young guy sitting alone and watching a Tigers game on one of the televisions.

She grabbed a towel to wipe a few spills, humming under her breath before she saw a man perched on the edge of a chair, fiddling with his phone. All the blood drained from her face. Her ears went buzzy. Her knees weak. He frowned at her.

She swallowed hard, opened her mouth, but nothing would come out. Her vision began to dim from the outside edges, going gray and fuzzy and strange. It was Trent, of course. She'd seen the picture of him—the broad shoulders, olive-skinned face, strong jaw and nose. She'd know him anywhere.

But he looked so *much* like his father—her stepfather and abuser—it burned her throat like acid. The hand she put to her throat was ice cold. The man's— Trent's—eyes narrowed further. He rose, something in his expression making her realize he recognized her but didn't want to believe it. She took a step back and decided to jump right into this thing.

"Trent, it's me. Kayla," she managed.

He got up and ran around the bar, then was standing in front of her, towering over her. She attempted not to cower. Something about him was so powerful. Something not at all unlike his father, until that man had let the drink get to him, weaken him enough that she could whack him in the head and run away one cold fall night.

She put a hand on Trent's chest and felt his heart pounding against it. As she sensed herself sliding to the floor, he gripped her arms, firm but not too tight. "Kayla," he said, his voice low and gravelly. "It is you."

She nodded and before she could disentangle herself, he had her crushed to his chest. She sighed and let him hold her a few minutes, then pulled away, anxious from the close contact. "Sorry," she said, tugging at the sleeves of her long T-shirt. "I'm sort of not great with…hugging."

He nodded. His eyes — the exact color of hers, an odd mix of green and brown — were shining. His smile so wide it was cartoonish. He opened his mouth to say something, but someone called his name from the kitchen. He stood, blinking fast. "Wait, so, you work here? For Melody?"

She nodded. "Don't be mad at her. I wouldn't let her tell you. I needed to…see you first."

He ran a hand around the back of his neck. Someone called his name again, louder this time. He held up a finger. "Don't leave. I'll be back and we can talk."

She smiled. "I'm working, remember? I'm not going anywhere."

"Jesus… Okay, I'm coming, Josefa, *uno momento*." He stared at her a few more seconds, shook his head then headed into the kitchen.

By the time he made it back out to the bar, it was busy again, demanding all her attention. He sat, watching her as she worked. She felt that strange thrill of familiarity again combined with a distinct fear, given his sharp resemblance to her tormentor. The man who had yanked her innocence away from her, leaving her a shell, ready to accept anything and anyone who'd fill it up.

At one point, she glanced over at him and saw he'd been joined by a pretty teenaged girl. She hesitated before heading over to them, not sure she could stand being around someone so lucky to have Trent as a father, money to pad her life, real paternal love to cushion her landings. But when the girl smiled at her, she unstuck her feet and fixed a smile on her face.

"Oh my God, Dad, it *is* her. She looks *just like* you!" The girl jumped up in her seat, leaned over the bar and gave her a tight hug around the neck. Kayla suffered it as long as she could then pulled away. "I have an aunt! I *love* it!"

"Hi, you must be Taylor," she said, fiddling with the girl's coaster, unable to meet her eyes. She felt dirty, filthy, slimed with the disgusting detritus of her past. She knew a sign was flashing over her head, neon and complete with arrows pointing down and saying, "Slut. Whore. Junkie."

She gulped and took a few steps back from her brother and his perfect daughter, as a sick surge of jealousy filled her gut. She blinked fast, gave them a little wave and turned away, hoping someone at the other end of the bar needed a refill. They did, and she was able to ignore Trent and Taylor for a while longer. But they stayed put, waiting for her. Finally, she gave up and faced them, bringing her lidded ginger ale cup with her.

"Where have you been all this time?" Taylor beamed at her. Trust the teenager to jump right into the morass and stomp around. "I mean, are you a journalist or something? Some kind of world traveler?"

Trent put a hand on his daughter's arm, keeping his soft gaze on Kayla. "Honey, lighten up. Give her some space."

"Sorry. I'm sorry. It's just so *weird*, you know?" She raised her smart phone and held it up, then typed away on it. "I just Insta'd you. That okay?"

"Since I have no idea what you're talking about, I guess so." Kayla smiled, unable to keep from getting caught up in the girl's enthusiasm.

"Me neither. It's like Greek or Latin," Trent said, pushing his empty glass toward her. "Do you mind?"

"Of course not," she said, happy to have something to do with her hands. "Taylor? Another root beer?"

"No, thank you." The girl patted her flat belly. "I will take some of the crack fries, please. Extra spice."

"Okay, I'll put that in for you. Trent? Hungry?"

He shook his head, still staring at her in wonder. She smiled at him then looked away, her face burning hot, her heartbeat pounding in her ears.

She put the basket of fries in front of Taylor, who smiled up from her phone. "You're so thin," she said, giving Kayla a frank once-over. "How do you do it?"

"I don't have much appetite. It was the drugs."

When Taylor choked on her fries, Trent pounded her back then trained his gaze on Kayla. "We have a lot of catching up to do," he said.

"Yes, we do," she agreed, giving the bar a perfunctory swipe with a towel. "But I'm not one to mince words, fair warning."

Taylor glanced at her father then stared at Kayla. "So fuckin' cool," she said, tucking into the fries like a little kid.

"Language," Trent warned.

"Something like that," Kayla said as she refilled the girl's water glass. "It is really good to see you," she said to Trent.

His grin widened. "I never thought I would see you again. I just figured you were dead."

"I was, kinda, for a while." He reached out and grabbed her hand, folding it between his two giant ones. She pulled away on reflex, fiddling with her shirtsleeves and strands of dangling hair. "Sorry. I'm not…into touching."

"No, I'm sorry. Will you come to our house tonight maybe? Have dinner? Stay?"

"I can't do that. Not yet." She studied them — her family, her blood relatives. "I will though, soon. I promise."

Taylor finished her fries and glanced at the ever-present phone. "Brad's here, Dad." Trent's face fell, his gaze darkened. "It's fine. We're just studying." She rolled her eyes. The rush of emotion that filled Kayla's chest was an odd mix of jealousy and protectiveness.

"Studying, eh," she said, putting the dirty basket in the tub under the bar.

Trent raised an eyebrow at her. "Be safe, Tay."

"I always am, jeez." She reached out and grabbed Kayla's hand, gave it a squeeze then let go before Kayla could wriggle free. "I'm so glad to see you, to meet you. I can't wait for you to come over. I could use some help with this guy." She punched her father's shoulder then got up and kissed the top of his bald head. "Love you, Daddy."

"Yeah, yeah," he said, watching her as she flounced through the bar, drawing plenty of eyes in her yoga pants and T-shirt. "God, I hate being a parent some days."

"I admire you for giving it the old college try," Kayla said, taking his empty. "More?"

"Better not. Just some water. I actually should go." He glanced around Kayla as if hoping Melody might appear. "She was pretty sick."

"Yes," Kayla said. They stared at each other. "I wish I were better at this."

"At what? Coming back from the dead? Making my day? I'd consider you pretty damn good at it." He leaned forward then righted himself when she moved the corresponding space apart from him. He frowned at her. "Kayla, you...you ran away. I know why."

Her heart seemed to skip a few beats then caught up with itself. "Oh. Well...okay." She looked down at the rubber mats under her feet. She shut her eyes against the urge to scream. "I'm sorry."

"For what?" His voice was sharp, with an angry edge to it. She glanced up at him, her pulse racing.

Don't hate me. Please. Don't hate me.

"I killed him. Did you know that? I killed my own father."

"He's...dead?"

"Yeah, the sick fucker. He killed our mother on his way to Hell. But I beat the living shit out of him and he never woke up from it." He said this with a level of matter-of-factness that made Kayla hate the sick son of a bitch all over again.

"How old were you?" She took a step toward him, permitting herself the few pleasant memories she still retained of him, of them, as sister and brother, playing, reading, eating, hiding from his temper-prone father and making a game out of it.

"Too young," he said. "But I was acquitted once it was determined what he'd done to our mother. Self-defense. Which it was, of course. Asshole beat on me pretty heartily most days, too."

"I am so, so sorry, Trent." She put her hand on his then withdrew it as if he'd shocked her.

"Stop saying that, God damn it." He scowled at her, making her heart pound and her throat close up with raw, primal anxiety.

Don't hate me.

She'd said that a lot, at the end. She'd also said it to her last pseudo-boyfriend, who'd been her dealer for a while until he'd sniffed out her inner needy little girl and turned it to his advantage.

"Don't hate me," she said, meaning it.

Trent stood to his full height, towering and powerful again, soothing her with his presence. "We're going to work on this. I'll find you a therapist and pay for it. Anything you need."

"No, no you don't have to—"

"You may not want me to touch you yet, but I will by God help you get through this. We're family, Kayla. You and Taylor are all I've got left in that arena."

"Taylor's mother?"

"Not in the picture anymore. And thank your lucky stars for that." He slumped against the bar chair, checking his phone for the hundredth time.

"And Melody?" She crossed her arms, feeling brave all of a sudden. "She's not family?"

"Not yet, but she will be." His lips were set in a firm line. "But I really do have to go. I need to check on her, okay? I'll… We'll talk. You call me." He flipped a business card onto the bar. "Whenever you're ready. I won't push you but please know I need to help you, and I will. Whatever you need me to do."

He had an expression on his face then that shot her straight back to their childhood. He'd always been a worrier, even as a little kid. And since she'd practically raised him, even though she was only five years older than he, she recalled that worried Trent face. She reached over the bar and touched the line between his eyes. He smiled and let her. Her hand dropped.

"I'll call. I promise. Probably sometime this week."

The bar door opened, sending a shaft of late afternoon sunshine into the dark space. For some reason, she glanced around Trent, wanting to see who'd walked in. Her face flushed and she put her cold palm to her throat when she spotted Brock, re-shouldering a backpack and blinking as his eyesight adjusted to the gloom. Trent seemed surprised by her reaction then turned to see who'd caused it.

He raised a hand at the man, then treated her to the sort of protective glare that surprised her. "Brock Fitzgerald is a fucking hot mess, Kayla," he muttered under his breath.

"Yeah, Trent. I guessed that, thanks." She swallowed past the lump forming in her throat and grabbed up his beer glass and Taylor's water. "Takes one to know one."

He glared while Brock settled himself at the opposite end of the bar and opened up a laptop without glancing at either of them. Then he sighed. "I have to go check on Melody."

"Go, already." She flapped the bar towel at him. "And don't worry about me. I don't like to be touched, remember? Mr. Hot Mess isn't getting in a country mile of me. But he does seem like he could use a friend. So, I may give that a shot. Relax."

"Fine," he said, jamming a ratty Tigers ball cap on his head. "Talk to you soon."

"Yes. Soon." She smiled.

He shook his head again and mumbled, "I still can't believe it."

She sighed, arranged her face in a neutral expression, then poured and served Brock his ginger ale. He grunted at her when she put it on a coaster next to his computer. "Don't spill it," she warned before heading down the bar to assist some other newcomers.

When she checked back on him, he'd drained the drink and was still pecking away at his keyboard. "Hungry?" she asked as she passed by him.

"Maybe," he said, not looking up. Without asking him, she put in an order for a mushroom burger, something she'd developed a hankering for in the last few weeks. Her taste buds were shot and she found eating to be a waste of her time, most days. Going for days high as a kite had a funny way of training your body not to require food at regular intervals. Something told her Mr. Brock Fitzgerald had familiarity with that. But the way the earthy, rich portabella 'shroom was grilled, then served hot with a slice of locally sourced white Cheddar and a side of borderline kimchi level fermented slaw hit her long-dormant taste buds like a sledgehammer.

She ordered it up for him then served it with a small jar of grainy, horseradish mustard. He blinked at it then up at her. "Damn. You're a mind reader. Cool."

"No. I'm not. But whenever I'm hungry that always tastes good so..." She shrugged and plucked a strand of the fermented cabbage out of the small bowl and ate it.

He grinned at her. And it almost made her faint. He was so fucking cute. So guileless, innocent and kind. But he wasn't, of course. She knew that. Short of a secret handshake, a junkie knew another one as if he or she were staring into a mirror. She offered him a small smile, refilled his soda then ignored him, alarmed at her reaction to a guy who was very possibly the worst thing that might ever happen to her.

You are such a sucker, she thought as she kept a peripheral eye on him, eating and staring at his screen as if it contained something crucial to his existence. Every now and then, he'd catch her looking and smile at her, making her flutter like a teenager. As if she knew what a real teenager got to experience.

"Stop it," she said, staring at the beer tap she was pouring from. "You are almost forty-two years old. That guy is thirty if he's a day. And you're both the hottest of hot messes. Let it go."

"What's that?" One of the closing bartenders moved past her with a full tub of dirty dishes.

"Nothing. Sorry." She served the beers and kept ignoring Brock, letting her colleague serve him, until she realized that he'd left.

Chapter Eight

"I hope you're fucking happy."

Brock squinted up at Caroline, woozy from the sun and water and sleepless nights.

"I'm not, I don't think." He shaded his eyes and studied her, standing over him, her hands on her hips.

"I'm leaving," she said, flopping onto the oversized lounge chair next to his.

"Fine," he said. He trained his gaze out over the expanse of lawn between Trent's giant house and the boat dock, where most of the others of their long weekend party were gathered, drinking beer and splashing each other in the waning afternoon. "Probably for the best."

She grabbed his chin and jerked his face around so he was forced to look at her. "Brock, I can't be your friend."

"I gathered." He turned away from her, his heart breaking into a million pieces even as he knew this was for the best. They couldn't be anything but lovers —

emotional, passionate, and destructive intimates. There was too much between them. Too much shit in their mutual past. It was insurmountable. And this weekend away had proven it.

He wanted it to be her fault. He was dying to blame someone other than himself. He was fucking sick of being the one to blame all the time. But it was his fate, it would seem. "I'm sorry, Caro." He reached for her but she rose, holding her giant sunhat in place as she gazed down at the happier couples, doing happy normal couple things. His hand hovered in mid-air for a few seconds until he let it drop to the deck, mere centimeters from her tan, bare feet. He touched her instep, his baser self wondering if he could finagle a break-up screw.

"You're a sick asshole," he said muttered as his fingers trailed up her firm leg to her knee. He loved to kiss her there, right behind her knee. If he closed his eyes right now, he could taste her skin—warm and earthy with a hint of spice.

She stepped out of his reach. "I'm moving away," she said. "I took a job. It's in D.C. I'm leaving next week."

The brightest slash of panic, powered with a spike of anger, hit Brock in his solar plexus, leaving him breathless and, somehow, standing up staring at her.

"D.C.? Really? And you were going to tell me about this when?"

Her green eyes were impenetrable, creating a thick, jungle-like wall between them that he'd never seen before. She stood stock still, not even blinking.

"Well?" He drew back, crossing his arms, sensing control slip out of his grasping fingers. "Jesus, Caroline. Why did you even come up here with me, then?"

"Last time I checked, Brock, we're just friends. At your request, after you fucked me when I was barely sober enough to remember it?"

"I didn't...do..." But he had. God help him, he had. As sure as he was standing here, feeling as if his guts were emptying out through his pores. She lifted her beautiful, sunburned chin. The anger took over then, and he opened his mouth before his brain could slap a hand over it. "Fine. Go. I don't fuckin' care. God damned manipulative bitch."

She stood a few minutes, hand on the top of her hat, her sunglasses back in place so he couldn't see her eyes. She'd driven up here with him a few days ago in silence, hung around the other couples, speaking when spoken to but not much beyond that. The night before, their next-to-last night here in this idyllic paradise built by Trent Hettinger's hard work—something he admired and hated at the same time—she'd slipped into his room, into his bed, into his arms, her skin smooth, smelling of sunscreen and lake water. He'd struggled to drag his brain awake, as he'd been double dosing himself to get through the nights without sliding back into the familiar with the only woman he believed understood him.

They'd had sex in silence, almost on autopilot. It had not been nice or romantic or lovely, anything other than a physical release. And when he'd finished, she'd slipped out from under him and stood, backlit by the massive shaft of moonlight hitting the wall of windows behind her. Brock recalled his breathless, sweaty need for her to come back to him. To curl into him. To hold him and protect him against the demons now railing at the ramparts of his psyche.

But she'd just stood there, naked, staring down at him as he'd caught his breath. "Caro," he'd whispered.

"Shh." She'd put her fingers to his lips, shook her head and snuck out of the room. This morning she wouldn't even look at him, not that anyone noticed but him. And now, after another day of sun, swimming, not drinking anything but water, and staring at Caroline's patrician profile, her bare shoulders and legs, his mouth watering in anticipation of what he'd do with her tonight.

"I hate you, Brock," she whispered. A tear slid down her face. "And I think I finally figured that out. So, I'm leaving. Don't call me. Please. Lose my number and forget about me, for both our sakes."

He stared straight ahead, ignoring his now raging hard-on, as she touched his forehead as if in some kind of fucked-up blessing.

"Yeah? Well, it's mutual. Get the hell out of here."

This was their oldest argument. The one they always circled back around to, no matter how great the sex, or the parties, the booze, the drugs. This time, though, after years apart that he'd spent fighting physical, mental, emotional battles she would never understand only to find himself right back in the same old space, have the same damn argument, this felt final.

As it should. He didn't deserve her. He didn't deserve anything good. He was a useless, addicted, weak human being. And that was all he ever would be — toxic to anyone who cared about him.

He jumped up, yanked off his shirt and ran away from her, down the long flight of steps to the grass without a backward look or comment. Austin called his name but he ignored them all — them and their perfect lives, with their more perfect lovers and wives. Shit, even Elle and Ross had worked their shit out and were more lovey-dovey than any normal, grown couple had a right to be.

His feet hit the sand along this stretch of Lake Michigan and he ran, letting his legs and arms pump fast and still faster until his super-in-shape heart was pounding and he couldn't catch a breath. He slowed, jogging some then walking, his head down, sucking in huge, hot breaths, until he stumbled and fell to his hands and knees.

He stood up so fast he got dizzy from the heat and exertion. Trent's obnoxious mansion was far behind him. But he knew she was still standing there on that damn deck, watching him go, waiting for him to come back.

It was their usual old argument. She'd never leave him. Never go all the way to God damned D.C. She loved him. He needed her. They should get married. Yes, that was it. Get married. He could afford a whopper of an engagement ring. Girls loved whopper engagement rings, right?

He craved normalcy for himself. The sort of stability Caroline would provide was something he'd always yearned for. She'd prop him up and he'd support her in her dream to be a big shot book editor. He could afford it. Hell, he could afford for them to not work another day in their lives. But he'd do whatever she wanted. Anything. If she'd not leave.

Panic suffused his brain, slipping a cold hand down his spine. He sucked in a few breaths and took off toward the house, even faster this time, desperate to get to her, to drop to his knees and hold on to her legs and beg her in front of his brother and everybody to never leave him. His ears were ringing by the time he made it back to Trent's boat dock. It was deserted. The sun was making its too-perfect way toward the horizon, promising yet another photo-worthy sunset.

"You're too late," he said, staring up at the open wall of doors along the deck. A sudden wind blew the diaphanous curtains in and out. He heard someone laugh, then someone else. A snippet of conversation hit his ears. His chest still heaving, his legs screaming in agony, he made his slow way across the grass and up the steps to the deck.

She'll be sitting there. She always waited for me before. D.C., my ass. That was just her trying to force my hand or some shit.

But the deck was as empty as the boat dock and the yard.

"Caro?" His voice cracked. His throat was a desert wasteland, cracked and aching for water. The ants…the fucking ever-present insects, awoke at their usual time and began muttering around the base of his spine. He took a step toward the chairs where they'd fought, his heart skipping the odd beat, scaring him, until he realized that this was entirely of his own doing. He'd pushed her away, him with his bullshit about being friends, and only friends.

He could never only be her friend. He knew that now.

"Caro?" His voice broke as he shouted her name. He felt his legs buckle beneath him. Saw the deck rise to meet his knees first, then his hands. His face hurt. His throat ached. His skin crawled. "Fuck!" His voice echoed around, hitting his ears and reminding him that he was not alone here. That he had an audience.

"Fuck," he said, this time to himself before jumping up and marching past the women gathered at the door, trying not to stare at him. There was no sign of Austin,

Ross, or Trent. Trent's teenaged daughter and her minions had decamped to some other lakefront mansion for the evening, thank Christ for small favors.

He lurched to the fridge and yanked it open, grabbing the first beer he saw. It was cool and innocuous in his palm. *"Drink me,"* it urged him. *"Just one. You can do it. Don't listen to all those doctors, therapists and other experts. You can drink me. And then another me. Fuck everybody else. This is* your *motherfucking life. Go on. Drink me, you God damned pussy!"*

He shoved the neck of the bottle into the retro steel opener next to the fridge. The smell hit his lizard brain like the smell of a woman. He sucked in a breath and put the bottle to his lips.

"I don't think so," Austin said, prying the thing out of his hands and pouring it into the sink. Brock shivered in the hyper-cooled interior. His teeth chattered and his skin broke out in goosebumps.

"Fuck you, Mr. Perfect." He grabbed another bottle, opened it and right when he was about to take his first, glorious gulp of alcohol in years, Austin took it and dumped it down the drain.

They played this game through four perfectly good beers, Austin pouring them out as if they were nothing more than water. The fifth time he reached for one, Austin grabbed his arm and dragged him from the fridge. Without even thinking, he swung, connecting in a satisfactory way with his twin brother's jaw.

To his surprise, Austin just held on tighter, gripping his arms tight to his body, their faces level, their eyes locked. "I won't let you do it, do you hear me? I will *not* lose you again." Austin's voice was calm. Drops of his spit sprayed Brock's face. He tensed, struggled, knowing he was stronger, after all his workouts at the hands of his trainer-slash-torturer. But Austin didn't budge. Brock felt his brother's legs against his. The soft fabric of his polo shirt against his bare stomach. He reared back and bunched his arm muscles, determined to spring free, grab some beers and hightail it down the beach.

Just a little party. I can handle it.

"Fuck. You," he spat at Austin's face.

"I'm not letting you go. I don't care if we stand here all night."

"Christ, fine." He made himself relax. But Austin only tightened his grip.

"I love you, Brock. Stop trying so hard to prove how great you are, okay? Just be you."

"Be me? Seriously? I suck. We all know that."

"No, brother, we don't." Austin let him go so fast he stumbled forward, whamming his knees into the kitchen island cabinets. He caught himself, propping his hands on the huge expanse of dark granite countertop. Everything drained from him then — anger, frustration, energy, remorse. The urge to drink until he passed out. Everything…but resignation.

"I'll never be normal," he whispered down at the counter as if it could answer him.

"Normal is overrated." Austin patted his back, rubbing between his shoulder blades, calming him. He didn't fight it for a change, as his mind settled. "Here," Austin said, handing him his evening pill cocktail and a glass of water. He looked at them both, knowing that they would both help and hurt. They would quell the marching ant army but would also leave him depleted, limp and with a shitty taste in his mouth.

"She left, didn't she?" He took the pills and downed them, sucking back the water so fast it dripped out the sides of his mouth.

"Yeah, man. She did."

"Good. She should go. She's moving to D.C."

"Oh, well, then. Good for her."

"Yeah. Fucking great for her. Oh, Christ… Oh dear God…" He groaned and dropped to his heels, realizing what he'd done. That he'd kicked his last remaining anchor to Earth free, leaving him floating and utterly alone. Austin crouched beside him then pulled him all the way down so that they sat together, backs to the kitchen island, legs sprawled out toward the fridge. He draped an arm over Brock's shaking shoulders and held him tight.

Brock realized at that moment that he'd been wrong. His one remaining anchor was here, in the form of a man he'd despised for his normalcy, his perfection, for so many years. He still had a hard time making small talk with him.

He closed his eyes as the pills entered his system, whooshing through his bloodstream, softening connections, dampening others, coating his brain with the usual evening blanket of pharma-induced peace. He sighed and leaned into Austin's torso, letting a single tear escape before the drugs sent the ants scurrying to their hiding places. Tomorrow was another day to march, after all.

"Hey, Uncle Brock," Evelyn's voice broke through the kitchen silence. "Where are you? Somebody woke up from her nap super cranky and I can't even…"

He opened his eyes and saw his brother's wife crouched down, holding a teary-eyed, sweaty-looking toddler. As soon as she spotted him, she leaped into his arms. "Bock!" she yelped, wrapping her arms around his neck and clinging to him like a limpet. "Bock." Her voice was muffled against his skin. He patted her back and let himself relax further.

"You okay down here for now?" Austin peered at him.

Brock nodded. "Yeah. And...thanks. Although that was a very serious beer foul earlier. You'll have to pay a penalty."

Austin chuckled, leaned in and kissed Rose's cheek. When he pressed his lips to Brock's forehead for a second before climbing out from under the overhanging granite counter, Brock flinched. Evelyn patted his leg and let Austin pull her to her feet. They wandered out, hand in hand, leaving him with the baby, who kept muttering "Bock" into his neck until she broke away, her smile lighting up her face, and his soul, at least for a few minutes. "Swim!"

He grinned and got up, tossing her over his shoulder, making her squeal in delight. The group was gathered, sipping water, reading books or tablets. "I'm sorry," he declared to them as a whole. "Slipped. Caroline left. She...uh...had someplace better to be."

"Bock!" the little girl demanded, tugging his chin around with her fingers. "'Ose want swims!"

"Does she always speak in exclamatory sentences?" he asked Evelyn as she brought out the funny-looking swimsuit, floaty combo thing.

"Yep," she confirmed, pulling Rose out of Brock's arms long enough to wiggle her into the contraption. "You okay with her for a while?"

"You okay with me with her for a while?"

She patted his cheek and put the happy toddler in his arms again. "I'm more than okay with it, Brock."

"Thanks," he said as he tossed Rose up onto his shoulder before heading out of the wide-open wall of doors, down the steps and toward the sand, his mind calm, his heart at peace, the ants at full parade rest.

Chapter Nine

"Hey. This seat taken?"

Kayla startled from her semi-trance, took her fingers from her hair and set the charcoal pencil down. "Um. No, I guess not."

Brock smiled at her and slid his ever-present laptop onto the bar in front of the seat next to her. He made a show of leaning over her shoulder but she slapped the sketch book shut and glared at him. He backed away, hands up in mock surrender. "Sorry."

She sipped her ginger ale, unwilling to acknowledge the strange little tingles running along her skin at his proximity. As he settled himself and spent an inordinate amount of time flirting with the cute and much-younger-than-her bartender who'd materialized in front of him, she stared straight ahead, focusing on the gleaming line of glasses on the shelves.

"I need a meeting," she blurted out, her hands clutched together in her lap. "I'm guessing you might know where I could find one."

He turned to her, his smile that odd combination of sweet and amused. "Where have you been going?"

"A place I don't want to go anymore."

"Okay. Well, mine's at St. Francis, downtown."

She unclenched her fingers and fiddled with her straw, swallowing the panic that was sneaking into her consciousness. When she felt a hand on her arm, she flinched, sending the half-empty glass of pale amber soda and ice flying down the bar before it rolled off and landed on the rubber mats without shattering.

"Shit," she muttered, getting up and heading around to grab it. But Brock touched her arm again, firmer this time, his face neutral. "Please don't," she said, pulling away from him.

"Do you need a meeting now? I can find one for us. God knows there's hardly an hour of any day I couldn't use one."

She shut her eyes then opened them. "Yes, actually. I could."

When he turned back to his laptop, she took a few minutes to study his profile—strong jawline covered in a light-brown, close-trimmed beard, well-proportioned eyes and nose. It was a handsome face—but not too much so. She put her hands on the bar's edge, gripping it tight, to keep from touching his jawline.

"*I think he needs a friend,*" she'd insisted to Trent several weeks ago.

"Got one," he cried, startling her again. "Right here." He pointed to the screen.

She squinted at the map, noting that it was in a community center, not far from her halfway house. She shook her head. "No, that's where I was going. I can't…go back there."

"Why not?" He leaned forward, trying to catch her gaze. "What happened?"

She sighed and looked up at the ceiling. "There's this woman there and she brings her kid. And it gets on my nerves."

"Meetings aren't supposed to include kids. I know of some that offer a sort of daycare, though." He turned back to his screen. "You're not so much into kids, are you?"

"No." She didn't move, but inside, she felt as if she could leap out of her skin, crawl down the bar, lie under the taps and drink until her stomach exploded. She scratched her nose with shaking fingers. "Shit."

"Tell you what, I'll drive us over there. You've been skipping them. I know the signs. I see them in my own mirror sometimes." His smile was so kind, so genuine. She hardened herself to it. "I'll see this illicit kid for myself." He pretended to look serious which made her smile.

"Fine." She shoved her sketches and pencils into her backpack and shouldered it. "Let's go then."

He waved down the bar to the hovering cutie-pie who hadn't taken her eyes off him the whole time he'd been sitting there, then tucked his laptop into a case and held out a hand, indicating she should walk ahead of him. She shook her head, nervous, panicky, and in need of something…anything…to soothe her nerves.

He shrugged and started toward the door, holding it open for her, same for the car door. She frowned at him as he meandered around the front of the car and got in. "You don't have to try to impress me, you know."

Without responding, he touched the ignition button and the powerful, expensive, German-made motor roared to life. "Nice car," she said.

"Thanks." He pulled out of the FitzPub parking lot and into the midday traffic, whistling under his breath.

"We're gonna be late," she said, hearing the petulance in her own voice as they waited out a long red light.

"You know as well as I do that it doesn't matter." He gunned the car through the intersection, wove through the three lanes of traffic and got them to the rundown community center with four minutes to spare.

"Again, trying to impress me..." She was desperate to sound normal, or at least something approaching it.

He grabbed his phone from its holder. "Nah. I'd try something else if I wanted to make an impression." He winked at her. She blinked fast and fumbled with the door handle, spilling herself out onto the asphalt— right onto her hands and knees. Within a few seconds, she saw his shoes beneath her. A hand was on her elbow. She pulled away from him.

"I'm fine, Jesus. Spare me the hero moves already." She drew herself up, trying to act more indignant than she felt.

He grinned at her and crooked his elbow. "Shall we? I need to evaluate their breach of kid etiquette and you need some support. I can tell."

"You can't either." She sniffed and hesitated, her palms sweaty at the thought of touching him—not to mention the fact that she was flirting with him like some flighty girl.

"Oh, yes I can. You forget, fair lady, I see my own face when I'm in need of an extra meeting. I know it well."

She sighed and slid her hand inside his proffered arm, swallowing against the dryness in her throat when he patted her hand then pressed it to his side. He was warm. She could feel it emanating from his torso. It scared her for a split second. She hadn't touched anyone, much less a man, in almost five years.

He waited along with her, as if sensing her discomfort. All the while keeping her hand prisoner, pinned to his oh-so-warm side. She swallowed again. "Okay. Let's go." Her voice sounded croaky and old.

He nodded and they headed across the packed parking lot toward the doors which were propped open, welcoming the huddled, smoking stragglers. When they stepped into the hallway, with its cluttered billboards and stacks of free newspapers, she expected him to release her hand. But he didn't. He kept walking until they were in the main, chair-lined, coffee-scented room.

"Caffeine?" he asked, letting her hand go.

She nodded, incapable of speech, her vocal cords frozen from the tiny intimacy. She wrung her hands, watching him fetch them a couple of Styrofoam cups of black liquid. He smiled at her again, setting her nerves twitching. She took the cup and sat in the nearest chair before she fell over and embarrassed herself even further.

He sat next to her, sipping while the rest of the group filed into their seats. She gripped the hot cup of coffee, letting the smell of it fill her nasal passages. It was an odor she'd always associate with these big rooms, crowded with people so desperate they'd show up in the middle of a workday afternoon just to be around each other, to gather strength from their collective desperation.

She sighed and closed her eyes, putting herself in a different place in her head. A place she'd been unable to locate since she'd skipped her usual three meetings a week. Then she heard it. The distinct bleat of an unhappy toddler.

The murmurings around her quieted. She tried the Serenity Prayer but the wailing kept creeping in around the edges. She heaved a sigh and opened her eyes, catching sight of the harried-looking woman with the hunched shoulders trying to shush the kid.

"I see what you mean," Brock whispered to her as he watched the woman set the unhappy child in the chair next to her.

"I have permission," she hissed at the people glaring at her. "It's this, or I'm gonna go back to using."

Kayla stared at her and decided that she'd used that morning. Her pupils were too small and her nose was running. She had a horrific rash on her neck and up one cheek.

"Shush, please honey," she begged the kid, who was trying to climb down.

"Jesus," Brock muttered.

Kayla glanced at him. He was staring at the child who was of indeterminate gender and coated in a layer of dirt. Brock got up and threw away his empty cup then stood near the percolator, his eyes never straying from the hapless woman.

The moderator called the room to order, made some announcements, and reminded everyone to remain open-minded to the situations of their fellow persons in the room. A not-too-indirect rebuke of the glaring going on, all pointed in one direction. Kayla averted her gaze from the woman, who was swiping at her nose and trying to entice the kid back to the chair with a candy bar.

They stood and recited the Prayer. The call went out for speakers. Kayla waited, letting the simple regularity soothe her. She was in a room full of people who understood her pain, for the most part. At least they got the addiction part. Her face flushed hot as her mind turned to what therapists had always called her 'inciting incident'. The abuse by her stepfather, which had morphed from 'just' fondling to a whole lot worse over the years

She sighed and banished him from her thoughts. She was here to heal, not to dwell.

Let go, let God and all that shit.

Brock remained standing, as if unable to stop watching the child as he or she climbed up and down out of the chair, his or her mouth smeared with chocolate and other unnamable goo. Kayle took a breath and got a whiff of piss, which made her want to gag.

The speakers commenced, each giving their version of the same old story. For the millionth time, Kayla wondered how or why this even helped. It was depressing as shit, listening to all these losers.

It was the scheduled regularity of them. The sameness. The knowing what to expect and that there were others out there worse off than you.

She'd heard all the reasons. And yet, every time she came to one of these, she'd find her mind wandering, her ire rising and her frustration growing.

And now there was that damn kid…

As if on cue, he or she let out a loud howl of protest when the mother tried to pin the kid into the chair with one thin arm. The current sad sack at the podium hesitated, with a glance over to the moderator who nodded and indicated he should keep going. As if anyone could be heard over the racket. Several people got up and walked out. The mother was crying now, tears mixing with the snot that had been running from her nose since she'd walked in — high as a fucking kite.

With a final loud cry, the kid slid from underneath his mother's arm and started hightailing it to the back door. Kayla watched as if from a long way away while the woman leaned over her knees and puked.

"She's been using," a large woman in front of her said. "That's even more against the dang rules."

The moderator stood and made her slow, calm way back to the now shivering, blubbering mother. She sat and put her arm around the woman's shaking shoulders and spoke in a low voice. Kayla was frozen in place, knowing she should help, do something productive. That was the point of these stupid gatherings. To show support for each other. But many times, they were as judgmental as she imagined a group of soccer moms would be.

Mad at herself for joining in with the judgey-ness, she got up and turned toward the somewhat less fraught-sounding kid noises at the back of the room. The dirty child was in a corner, trapped by Brock, who sat on the floor cross-legged in front of him, dangling a set of keys just out of the child's reach. Kayla crouched down next to him, amazed at his patience, much less his interest.

"He looks awful," she said, listening while the moderator calmed the near-hysterical junkie mother behind her.

"Yeah," Brock said. "I think it's a she."

Up close, the kid was even worse and stank to high heaven. She drew back when she realized that the dark stain was pee, or worse. "God, that is gross."

Brock glanced at her, his eyes flat, his lips turned downward. "Like she can help it? Look at her mother."

He jerked his chin toward the crowd that had gathered around the pitiful woman. "Have some sympathy."

She sighed, sticking out her arm when the little stinker tried to scuttle away, getting her shirtsleeve coated in chocolate that he – or she – still had all over his, or her, hands.

"What kind of life must she have," Brock said, running his fingers across the matted, tangled mop of dark-brown hair. "Huh, little one? You seem pretty hungry to me." Like some kind of a magician, he pulled a package of peanut butter crackers out of his pocket.

Kayla watched as the kid eyed him, wariness in her blue eyes, already trained not to trust men.

That realization forced her down from where she'd been crouching all high and mighty, to her butt on the floor next to Brock. She smiled at the child, who smiled back at her around a mouthful of her thumb, while ignoring Brock. He handed her the crackers and Kayla opened them, holding one out. The kid snagged it and jammed it into her mouth like a feral animal, while taking furtive glances at the man next to her. She took a second one but almost choked on it she ate it so fast.

Brock picked her up and slapped her between her shoulder blades before she asphyxiated. Once she realized who had hold of her, she let out a heart-rending shriek of terror and flailed her arms and legs until Brock had to set her down. Kayla observed from her vantage point on the floor and was as shocked as anyone when the child flung herself into her lap, sobbing, but tearless, another clue as to how serious her dehydration must be.

She patted the kid's back, unsure what else to do, while the mother kept puking and sobbing and the moderator called for an ambulance. When the professionals showed up, they loaded the woman into their rig then returned for her kid.

"I'll take him," the ambulance guy said, holding out his arms.

"She's a she. And I don't think she'll go with you." By this time, the kid had herself wrapped around Kayla's neck and torso. An unpleasant warm wetness was spreading across her shirt. She tried peeling the child off but she held tight with a surprising strength.

"Are you a relative?" the man asked.

"No." Brock helped her to her feet. The kid hardly weighed anything but Kayla was starting to feel claustrophobic.

The man sighed. "Do you mind riding with us? We can turn him…her, whatever…over to the proper authorities if her…his mother ends up…you know."

Kayla glared at the guy, putting a protective arm around the kid who was sliming her neck with snot and crumbs. Her pulse was racing and somehow the thought of letting the kid go made her nauseated. She glanced at Brock. He smiled and put a hand on the kid's sweaty head.

"We'll come with you," he said, alleviating her of the responsibility. Which was a good thing as her throat had closed up and sweat dripped down her back under her shirt as if she were absorbing every ounce of the child's abject terror.

Chapter Ten

"Sir?"

Brock opened his eyes and grunted as his brain caught up with what his eyes saw. The hospital waiting room was the most obnoxious shade of aqua he'd ever seen. But hospitals were not strange places to him. He'd been in and out of plenty of emergency rooms like this one, since turning fourteen and fracturing his ankle, breaking two ribs, and flirting with a concussion after jumping from the top of a quarry wall on a dare.

He'd been as high as a kite of course. Couldn't even recall doing it after he'd regained consciousness. But he sure as hell recalled the aftermath.

He rubbed his eyes and focused on the scrub-clad person hovering over him. "Yep. What... I mean..." For a split second, he couldn't remember why he was here, since waking up in hospitals had become so much a part of his normal life. He wrinkled his nose at the smell — rubbery and medicinal.

He saw Kayla then, standing just behind the nurse, still hanging on to that damn kid from the ill-fated meeting. "I just wanted to let you know that Child Protective Services are here. They'll take the little one off your hands. You and your…friend are free to go."

He blinked fast, trying to parse this. Kayla sat down next to him. The child, now somewhat cleaner and wearing dry clothes that were too large for her, sat with one arm around Kayla's neck, thumb jammed into her mouth. She eyeballed Brock from that position, her blue eyes still wary.

"Are you sure? I mean, we can… My friend and I… We can stay…" Kayla's voice sounded pinched and stressed. Her eyes were red as if she'd been crying. He put a hand on her arm. She flinched so hard the little girl flinched and started fussing. "Sorry," she whispered into the girl's matted hair. "Seriously. You don't have to—"

The nurse looked sympathetic but firm. "I'm sorry. Neither of you are relatives. You told me yourself you just happened to be at that AA meeting today."

"Yes, but…but…Brock?" Kayla turned to him, her eyes wide, wild with dismay. She was clinging to the little girl almost as hard as the girl was to her.

He sucked in a breath. He wanted to make this right. His need to make this right was so urgent it was like a giant hand was squeezing his chest, making him breathless. He got slowly to his feet, attempting to appear authoritarian.

"Listen, what's the harm in us hanging around, keeping the kid calm? We were at a meeting with her mother—actually NA, Narcotics Anonymous—so we know what she's going through. And the kid is…" He turned and gestured to them. "She's so torn up and seems calm now, with Kayla and me."

"Sir, I understand and I'm sorry but—" A clanging alarm made her back away. "I have to go. But the CPS will be here in fifteen minutes."

"Okay," he said, his hands shoved into his pockets, watching as staff scrambled around, heading for a room with a flashing blue light over the door. "Um...isn't that...?"

The door of the room flew open, revealing a scrum of people around what he assumed was a bed, working, yelling, while various alarms and other noises blared. The door swung shut again. He swallowed and sat back down.

"Oh my God," Kayla whispered. "That's her room, isn't it?"

"Yeah, I think so."

They waited and watched. At one point, Kayla held out her hand and Brock took it, holding it tight while medical personnel poured in and out of the room. They'd followed the ambulance in his car, Kayla holding the child in her lap against the law, and had ended up at County General, what was more often known as the Medicaid Hotel. It was where you went when you didn't have a sweet safety net of insurance like he'd always had, no matter how dumb his shenanigans might have been.

The place was about as dire as you'd expect. Grimy and hot, as if they couldn't even afford to run the air conditioning full blast. The random human detritus surrounding them were dark-skinned, many bleeding, some crying, most glaring down at the cracked linoleum floor under their feet.

"Oh shit, Brock." She let go of his hand and pointed. The movement woke the girl on her lap. She let out a howl as if having a nightmare even as she woke. A couple of men and one woman had emerged, looking grim, leaving the door half open.

"Time of death, five-o-eight," someone said from inside the room.

Kayla started moaning and rocking the girl back and forth. Brock got up. His reaction to the stress was to lurch into management mode. He needed to find the proper authorities and get this kid turned over to them. The noise, heat and overwhelming stench of unwashed bodies and blood and general hospital-ness was making his gut churn. To his shock, Kayla stood up next to him and whispered in his ear. "Let's go."

"What?"

"Let's go. I'm not leaving her to…foster care or worse. She's already traumatized by God knows what. I can't let her be—"

"That's not our decision to—"

"Fuck you and your decisions. I'm leaving." She whirled away from him, clinging to the girl who had her hands locked together behind Kayla's neck.

"But…wait…"

She got as far as the elevator before a couple of nurses intercepted her and marched her straight back to where they'd been sitting. For some reason, at that moment, the beautiful determination on Kayla's face slammed into him. He was almost always the first in any room to notice the hot women and leap right in, always flirting these days. In his bad old days, he'd have his hand up one skirt and would be eyeballing the next target within hours of spying someone as drop-dead appealing as Kayla Hettinger.

But for some reason, his reaction to her had been muted. Most likely thanks to this latest cocktail of dope they had him on. That was the point of it after all — dulling his sharpest, least appealing edges. Now, however, now… He studied her face as she held on to the little girl. Her features were not perfect, taken separately, but together, she resembled an exotic model — a woman just this side of gorgeous, falling somewhere between interesting-looking and beautiful.

Five-o-eight, his mind chimed, recalling that for the time of death, as well as the fact that as of four-thirty he had missed a dose of meds — his crucial daily hit of lithium — a relatively new addition to the mix and the one thing that dulled him the most.

"I'm sorry," one of the nurses was saying as the other one began talking to the little girl, trying to coax her to let go of Kayla's neck. "But this child has to be evaluated and then turned over to Protective Services."

"Protective Services," Kayla spat out as she backed away. "Protective, my ass. It's nothing but a holding pen. And a dangerous one at that. I won't let you take her."

"Ma'am," the nurse said, exasperated, and over this whole scene.

"Don't touch me," Kayla yelped when an orderly appeared, the muscle, ready to wrestle the baby out of Kayla's arms. "Brock, don't let them."

"I'm… I…" He ran fingers through his hair. The ants were on the move, and had been for a while now. They were making their collective presence well known right now, with their typical crap timing.

She glared at him, keeping one hand on the back of the girl's head. Her face was red. Strands of dark hair that had come loose from her ponytail framed her forehead and cheeks. Her lips were full and ever so slightly ragged. He felt his body flush with blood, including the last place he needed it to, as he watched her. He turned away.

"Restroom," he choked out.

A nurse pointed down the hall. He ran, leaving her yelling for him, which made the kid start screaming again.

Even as he shoved the door open, hellbent on getting some water on his face, he realized his error. He looked at her, saw her surrounded, cornered by the medical staff, clutching that child to her like a talisman, or a shield. He sucked in a breath and headed back down the hall, determined to do something right for a change, and not just something that was all about him and his weaknesses.

"Excuse me," he said, shouldering his way none too gently through the crowd and standing next to Kayla. Tears streamed down her face, mingling with the little girl's own. "Listen. Can you give us a minute? And back off a little. We haven't done anything wrong. We're the ones who sat here with this little girl while her mother died of an overdose, all right?" He glared at each of them until they gave him some space.

Kayla leaned into him. He put an arm around her, feeling her tense the second he touched her. "Thanks. Now, if we sneak out, I think we can..."

He dropped his arm and turned her so they were facing each other. She was so hopeful, so damn beautiful it was painful to disappoint her. "Kayla. We can't just take her. They'd find us and we'd be in a shit load of trouble. You know that. I know that. Let's hand her over and then we'll—"

"No!" She pulled away, glaring at him. "You don't know shit, Brock Fitzgerald. I don't care if you are an addict. You were a fucking rich boy junkie. Your mommy and daddy took care of you all the way through. You have no fucking idea what it's like to be in the God damned system. And she's already been through so much…"

"Kayla…I'm…"

"You'll never understand. She'll get shuttled around, probably abused…"

Brock realized that a couple of new people had joined the group down the hall. Two women in cheap suits, holding file folders and wearing fake-sympathetic expressions. For a moment, he pitied them and their horrific job. He held up a hand, keeping them all at bay for a few more minutes.

"We can't just take her. You know that. Kayla, look at me."

She shook her head, keeping her face pressed into the child's shoulder as she backed up until she hit the wall between a pair of elevator doors. He walked up to her, as if approaching a rabid animal trapped under a porch. She clutched the child closer, shaking her head, tears streaming down her face. But when he tugged the girl, she let her go. As if resigned to her fate, the girl remained silent, even as she reached for Kayla before giving up and shoving her thumb back in her mouth.

"It will be all right," he assured everyone, including himself. "I'll talk to them. See if they'll consider us…uh…me or you…for temporary placement."

"Don't be stupid," she spat out, swiping at her eyes. "That'll never fucking happen."

He opened his mouth but nothing came out. Because she was right.

"It's fine. I don't care. Take her."

He handed the child off to the suited ladies, who scurried away, avoiding any further scenes. All the residual adrenaline he'd been floating on for the last few minutes flew out of him, leaving him depleted and weak, wanting a drink and a hit. He sighed and turned to Kayla, hoping they might salvage something, a friendship maybe, based on this shared fucked up experience.

She'd slid to the floor and now sat, elbows on her knees, staring into the air in front of her. He dropped down next to her, unsure what to do or say. "You're right, you know," he managed, leaning forward, parroting her stance. "About me being the rich asshole-type of junkie."

"I know that," she said, her voice devoid of any affect whatsoever. "That kid doesn't have a fucking chance. You know that, right? She's doomed. Just like I was."

"Well, maybe not."

She scoffed and rose, leaving him down on the filthy floor, staring up at her. "Thanks for the ride," she said, keeping her voice light.

"Wait, hang on. Let's go…eat something."

"Not hungry." She was already striding toward the exit door.

He sat for a solid five minutes after she'd stomped out, watching the hospital's ER staff close in around the space she'd just vacated. Making it seem as if she'd never existed.

Chapter Eleven

The darkness had been closing in ever since she realized she had to be the one to take the damn kid to the hospital. She'd fought it as long and as hard as she could. Using the child as a barrier against it, of course. Praying that it would see how good she was, how responsible she was being.

But once the tiny, smelly, human shield had been ripped from her arms, the darkness had descended, chuckling under its breath, whispering her name. She couldn't even remember what she'd said to Brock before walking away from him. As she stumbled out into the warm evening air, mumbling apologies to all the people she kept running into in her near-blind clumsiness, the sensation of wanting to leap out of her skin and hide under the nearest rock had never been sharper.

By the time she realized that she had no car here, that they'd gone to that stupid fucking meeting in Brock's car, then to this god-forsaken hospital, she also realized that plenty of alarmed civilians were eyeballing her. And no wonder. She must've looked like she was coming down off a bad trip — wild hair, sweaty, pale, mumbling about a nonexistent car.

With a hard wrench to her psyche, she forced herself to stand up straight, pull her damp hair into a half-normal ponytail and to take deep breaths. After a few seconds, she believed all the gawkers had moved on, headed toward the hospital intent on their own individual traumas. Leaning on the nearest car hood, she watched for a few minutes, reminding herself that nothing had changed. She had a job. A place to live. A start on a real life — one that included an actual family in the form of her brother and his daughter.

Nothing had changed.

But for that poor kid. That hungry, dehydrated, stinky little kid, made an orphan in front of her damn eyes, thanks to the junk her mother had shoved into her arm, or up her nose. The same junk that she, Kayla, craved right now so hard it created physical pain between her temples, tightness in her chest, shivers all through her body.

"Oh fuck," she muttered as she squatted in front of the car, trying to catch her breath. "Fuck...fuck..." She pressed her hands into her eye sockets and dropped to her butt. Her ears were ringing so loud she couldn't hear the traffic from the nearby interstate.

She didn't even like kids. What was her flipping problem, anyway? Jesus. The stupid mother had killed herself in front of her own child, sure. And the little girl was already malnourished and filthy. God only knew what conditions she'd been living in, and for how long. And she was also skittish around men — even one as kid-friendly as Brock Fitzgerald.

The tiny pebbles and other crap on the asphalt parking lot cut into her knees and palms but she couldn't feel it. Because that was what she needed — to feel something. Anything. She had to do something to release the pressure building under her skin, stretching it so tight she felt like an over-inflated balloon.

With a loud gasp that startled an older couple on their way into the emergency room entrance, she lurched to her feet and started walking. This was the shit-hole hospital in the shit-hole end of town not very far at all from her shit-hole dump of a flop house. Why not walk there?

Why not indeed?

She pulled out her phone and plugged in the address, noting that she would do well to consider her brother's offer to replace the thing — the long-cracked screen was beginning to flicker almost non-stop. But she hated the concept of taking anything from him, no matter he could afford to buy her six phones, two cars, and a house, if she'd let him.

It was almost dark by the time she shoved open the sticky front door of what was an abandoned warehouse partitioned into tiny, non-conforming living spaces. A giant firetrap was what it was, but they had strict rules about open flames — candles or anything else. Most people adhered to it — although she'd smelled her fair share of weed and cigarettes.

Her living space was on the fourth floor, in the corner, with an actual window and as she made her slow way there, all she could envision was the pain. And how she'd inflict it.

"Try this," one man had advised, when he'd finished with her and she'd been curled into a ball in the corner of the hotel room. "It'll help."

She'd looked up at him through her stringy hair, confused by the pill bottle with the blank label.

"Go on," he'd said, swiping his sweaty face with one hand and shaking the bottle with the other. "Jesus." She hadn't moved so he'd tossed at her head.

The first round, pearl-like pill she'd swallowed had made her throw up within the hour. But before that, the pain had indeed subsided. So she'd taken another one, with a few bites of stale cereal, and it had stayed down. She'd kept the bottle hidden from her stepfather for a month, but when she'd run out, her body had gone into a terrifying free-fall, which had scared him so he'd left her alone for a while as she'd sweated and shivered and puked her way through her first unwelcome detox at the tender age of sixteen.

By the time he'd decided she was well enough to resume making money for him, her intense need for more magic pills had forced her out of her shocked stupor and she'd formulated her escape plan.

She shoved the door to her space open and fell onto her mattress, sweaty and shivery, as if she were coming down from a bad high. But she wasn't. She hadn't used in almost six years. But God help her, it was as if she'd only just had her last hit. As if the past five-plus years being clean hadn't even happened. It was so damned unfair.

Her gut cramped. She groaned and curled into a ball. The skin-tightening sensation got worse, making her afraid that if she moved too much, her epidermis would crack and split, exposing everything in her to the outside air.

She felt along the space between her mattress and the prefab wall while keeping her eyes tight shut, willing away the onrushing, various unhealthy urges. When her fingertips touched the tiny plastic baggie, she counted to ten, then twenty, before tugging it free. Hot tears rolled down the sides of her face as she lay back and studied the contents of the bag.

A small box of blades, some not-too-clean bandages, a half-empty tube of antibiotic ointment—expired, she noted. She was still trembling but no longer crying as she dumped everything onto the threadbare sheet. The thin slice of cold metal felt good between her thumb and finger. So good, she held on to it a while—how long she had no concept but for the loud entry of her fellow halfway-house inmates.

The urge to cut had come upon her during the last part of her stay at the rehab camp. Once she had been assured that her body was not her own. It never would be. She'd come to view it from a distance—a coping mechanism, one of the chattering group leaders had called it once. She didn't even like to touch her own skin after a while, which had led to brutal episodes wrestling her into a shower as she'd kicked and screamed and flailed so hard she'd managed to blacken her stepfather's eye once.

Once.

As an adult in the stupid detox camp, trading blow jobs and quickies behind the garden shed to get the short relief of a cheap cig or spliff, that sensation had come roaring back, leading to an adjustment to her meds, leaving her loopy and woozy twenty-four-seven. Once she'd started holding the new drugs under her tongue and spitting them out, she was ready for all the assholes who'd come at her, thinking they could take yet more advantage of her.

She sighed, shoving all the memories of all the men and all the times she'd been used without her permission out of her head. She had control now. The razor blade flashed in the moonlight from her window as she rolled it between her knuckles, pondering its potential, how much she wanted it, how the pain of cuts on her arms must be how some people felt about sex. How normal people felt about sex—as a release, a pleasure, even enjoyable.

"Fuck that," she spat out, sitting up and yanking off her shirt and dingy bra. Her skin pebbled and her nipples hardened but she didn't look at them. They weren't hers after all. Not them. Not her mouth or her hands. Most especially not what she had between her legs. None of it belonged to her. It never had.

But the razor—it was hers and hers alone. The odd sensation running down her spine was just the precursor to the pleasure. The only pleasure she had ever found in her own body and she had one of the assholes at the camp to thank.

"Here," he'd said, handing her the first tiny plastic box full of relief. "Go on. Try it. You might like it."

She had liked it. A lot. So much that she'd ended up in the infirmary with nasty infections in both her arms and put into solitary for a month. A month she'd spent throwing her thin frame against the four walls, seeking something resembling sensation, even if it came in the form of pain and bruises.

She'd figured out that she'd never get out of there unless she stopped acting like a total whack job. And after two weeks of eating, drinking water, and not saying much, she'd been released back into the general population of losers. And she'd learned to treat each cut with antibiotic ointment and cover them with the bandages she'd snag from the infirmary.

She hadn't cut herself in months, however. She'd even admit to forgetting the need, what with exhausting herself working the bar almost every day or night. And with the effort to show a normal face to Trent and Taylor. They'd never love her the way they claimed to if they knew all her awful, disgusting truths.

With a cry of pleasure a few people inhabiting the cubicles around her took for sexual, she pressed the blade into the scar tissue on her left biceps. The blood bubbled then flowed and her cry turned to a low, satisfied moan as she sat watching it, using the razor again, and again, too much, she knew, but she was simply unable to stop herself.

The pressure under her skin diminished by the blood-letting. And it felt so good, like the sweetest release. Too late, she realized there was too much blood. She was slipping around in it on the cheap linoleum. But when she tried to get up to find a towel, her vision went wonky, making her curse and fall sideways, face down on her mattress.

Her last thought was of Brock, of his face when she'd walked away from him in the crappy hospital. Of how handsome he was, and how stupid she was to think she might be normal, for him.

Chapter Twelve

Brock sat in his new office chewing the end of a pencil and pondering the computer screen in front of him. He'd only managed an hour or so of sleep the night before and his mind felt as if it were covered by a heavy blanket. Austin had given him the new space, with a nameplate on the door and everything as CEO of the Fitzgerald Charitable Fund. More make-work, he realized, but at least he had a bit of autonomy.

He'd already lined up a couple of interns, eager poli-sci and sociology majors with mad internet skills from the local university. They were tapping away in the adjacent room, setting up their website and establishing a social media presence. The chair he'd liberated from the office furniture cemetery squeaked as he rotated, unable to settle or focus and not just for lack of sleep.

"Hey," a voice called from the half-open door, startling him out of his semi-trance. "I don't suppose you've heard from Kayla today, have you?"

He blinked and sipped his coffee gone long cold, trying to figure out who was talking to him. When Melody materialized, he put her together with the words and stood up fast, worry hitting his brain and snapping it out of its fugue. "No. I don't... I don't even know her phone number. Why?"

Melody crossed her arms and frowned. "I don't know. Thought you might."

He rolled his eyes and turned away from her, not wanting her to see how his face had flushed. "Junkies don't just know each other's info automatically, you know. I mean, we are a club unto ourselves and all but..."

"Spare me." Her voice was sharp.

"Sorry. But no, I haven't. And I'll repeat my original question. Why?" The memory of her angry, hurt expression filled his mind but he repressed it with a firm mental shove.

"She was supposed to open the bar today." Melody glanced at her watch. "But when I got here, the kitchen staff said no one had shown up at all." She sighed and slumped against the door frame. "Shit. I hope she's all right. I mean...you know."

"Yeah." He pulled his phone from his pocket and scrolled around, wondering if he'd somehow managed to capture Trent's number at some point. Which he hadn't. He tossed the device down on his desk and rubbed his face, trying to wake himself all the way up. "We had a sort of bad time, yesterday I mean."

"Oh?" Her dark eyebrows raised. He could sense her protective hackles rising.

He held up a hand. "Hold on. Stop jumping to all the shitty conclusions I see floating around behind your eyes."

Her frown deepened. "Just tell me what happened."

He sighed and shoved his hand down in his pockets, wondering where in the world he should start.

"Start at the beginning, Fitzgerald. Then I gotta call her brother and tell him. Make it fast." She snapped her fingers in his face.

He told her everything—from Kayla's rough start, needing a midday group meeting fix, all the way through to the be-suited bureaucrats wrenching the crying child out of her arms.

Melody's eyes were brimming with tears when he finished.

"I'm sorry," he said, his voice rough. "I shouldn't have... I don't know...shit."

"You did fine." She put her hand on his arm. "You did the only things you could in such a crappy situation. I have to call Trent now. We need to check on her."

"Yeah. Okay." He watched, helpless while Melody relayed the story to Kayla's brother in a condensed form and they agreed to meet at the halfway house where Kayla lived. "I want to come with you," he said, grabbing his jacket from the back of the chair.

She gave him the better part of a hairy eyeball for a few seconds then shrugged. "Fine. Whatever. But don't expect a happy greeting from her brother. He is royally pissed and is going to blame you, even though that's wrong."

"Eh. I'm used to taking the blame for random shit. I want to see for myself she's all right."

The drive through the industrial area between the brewery and where Kayla lived was made in total silence but for the computerized instructions from the SUV's navigation program. When she pulled up in front of an abandoned warehouse and stopped, they both peered up at the rattletrap building in wonder. "This can't be it," he said.

"It is, though." She pointed to the address on the navigation screen. "Let's go." She turned off the ignition at the same time as a classic Jeep screeched into the lot next to them and Trent jumped out, glowering at him before giving Melody a quick kiss and mumbling something to her in Spanish.

Brock waited, letting them lead. They all covered their noses at the rank stench as they made their way to the fourth floor. The upper hall was hot, but at least it didn't reek of piss and shit and puke like the stairwell. Trent checked his phone and motioned for them to follow him to the far end, to a cheap-looking door with a number written on a strip of duct tape.

"This is it." He hesitated, then knocked once. "Kayla, it's Trent. Are you in there?" When there was no response, he rattled the doorknob with a curse. "Kayla!" He knocked louder. "Kayla, open up."

"Maybe she's not there," Melody said, hip bumping him aside. "Kayla, honey, it's Melody. We're worried because you didn't show up for work. Open up if you're in there. Please?" She knocked and knocked until Brock couldn't stand it another second. His skin was crawling and his eyes burned. She was in there all right. He knew it—he could sense her presence.

"Excuse me." He pulled Melody back from the door gently and nodded at Trent, man to man. "Kayla, if you can hear me, move away from the door."

"Hey, hold on a second. What do you think you're—?"

He glared at the hand Trent used to grip his biceps. "I'm saving your sister's life, dude. Back off?" He made it an option, not a command.

Trent's brow furrowed but he let go of Brock's arm and stepped away, taking Melody's hand and gripping it so tight Brock could see his knuckles whiten.

"Kayla, I'm coming in. And if I hurt you I'm sorry but…" Without another word, he kicked once, breaking the cheap-ass lock and sending the hollow plastic door whamming against the wall. He took one step forward and stumbled back at the smell of blood. Trent shoved him aside, calling his sister's name.

"Kayla? Kayla…honey… Oh, Jesus. Melody, call nine-one-one, now!"

Unable to see anything, thanks to the dim light thrown by a half-window, Brock watched, helpless, as Trent crouched over Kayla's inert, bloody body splayed out on a thin mattress on the floor. Once Melody had made the call, she took up her position on Kayla's other side, patting her face and reassuring Trent that she was still breathing. Brock was frozen in place, watching this horror show tableau. "Did…someone hurt her? What happened?"

"Fuck if I know. Go downstairs so you can lead the EMTs up here," Trent demanded without looking away from his sister's pale face.

Brock swallowed the rising gorge in his throat. Her feet were bare and pale, and all he could see other than her denim-covered legs. Trent had draped her torso with a sheet and was holding her, making soft noises, while Melody patted her face. His feet wouldn't budge even when he commanded them to.

"Go, God damn it, Fitzgerald," Trent barked at him as he cradled his sister to his chest. "You deaf, or what?"

Brock nodded, turned and pounded back down the disgusting stairwell, emerging into the cool morning air with a gasp as he heard the ambulance's siren in the distance. He waited, his pulse racing, his ears ringing, and led them up the four flights and down the hall to the open door to her room. Trent and Melody moved away as the medic got to work, checking her vital signs, hooking her up to some fluid, covering her mouth and nose with an oxygen mask before lifting her onto the gurney.

"What did she take?" one of the medical guys demanded of the group.

They all looked at him.

"Nothing," Brock said.

The guy seemed skeptical, but when his partner found a blood-encrusted razor blade, they got busy trundling her down the hall, the stairs and into the ambulance. Before the doors closed, he heard her voice — weak but definitely hers.

"Which one of you is Brock?"

Trent stepped forward but Melody held out an arm. He stared at it, then at her. Brock moved closer to the ambulance. "I am."

"Get in. She's calling for you and if it'll help her blood pressure, I'm all for letting you ride."

Without a glance back at Trent, he climbed into the back of the rig and sat on a jump seat next to Kayla. Her arms were a bloody mess but he kept his eyes on her face as he took her hand and said, "I'm here. You're gonna be all right."

She nodded, trying to take off the oxygen mask with one trembling hand.

"No, no, leave that. It's the good stuff. Enjoy it while you can."

She nodded again, her face wet with tears, her eyes dark with pain. Brock held on to her hand the whole time, letting go when the back doors opened and they took her away from him. When he saw Melody's face around the ambulance doors, he flinched, realizing he hadn't moved from his perch.

"Come on, hero man. Let's go make sure she's okay." Her smile released something in him, allowing him to draw a full breath as he rose, and climbed down to join her.

The differences between his most recent emergency room experience, not twenty-four hours prior, and this one, were stark. This waiting room was half full, and had TVs on in every corner, a coffee maker running, and magazines available for perusal. It smelled like hospital of course—there was no getting around that. But it was sparkling clean relative to the shit hole where they'd sat with the kid while the mother had died down the hall. Actual medical staff were out in the waiting room, taking temperatures and talking with the walking wounded.

Brock dropped into the nearest chair—not hard molded plastic but with a faux leather cover and soft cushion. He leaned forward, elbows on his knees, and began to pray.

Chapter Thirteen

"I'm not listening to it another minute. That place is a shit hole and I refuse to let you live there."

Kayla sighed and leaned forward on the table, wrapping her fingers around the warm cup of tea. Trent had been blustering over this all morning and she was getting sick of hearing it. But she wasn't about to back down. She didn't deserve anyplace nicer, and besides, she was sort of used to the smells, noises, and general crappy ambience of the halfway house. Taylor rolled her expressive eyes and sipped sweet hot chocolate while her father stamped around, making alpha male noises.

"Is he always like this?" she asked, watching him, amused but at the same time anxious over making him unhappy.

"Yep," the girl said as she tapped away on her phone and twirled one lock of dark-brown hair around her finger.

"Tell you what, baby brother. How about a compromise?"

Trent ceased his march around the room and glared at them both. "Daddy, you look ridiculous right now. Chillax, already."

He sighed and looked down, then back up, a smile fixed to his face. "That better?"

"Not really. I gotta go. Study date with Brad." She hopped down off the high bar chair and headed toward her room.

"Study date," her father growled as she passed by him. "Right."

"Love you, Daddy," she said, patting his cheek.

"I'm sure," he said, before turning his attention to Kayla. She sipped and stayed silent, watching this tiny drama unfold. "So, what's your compromise proposal?"

"I'll let you pay for the therapist you keep harping about, but I'm staying at the halfway house. It's actually a requirement of my government-funded rehab program, you know."

He grunted and sat, before finishing off Taylor's hot chocolate. "Does the damn government know what kind of place that is?"

"Oh, it's not that bad. It's all we deserve, really."

She flinched when his palm smacked the table between them. "I am kind of over that shit, K."

She leaned on one hand, studying him. He'd been a tall little boy, lanky and gangly when she'd finally escaped. He was still tall but strong-looking and super handsome, rocking the bald-head hot guy thing better than anybody she'd ever seen. He frowned at her. "What?"

"You turned out all right, didn't you, T?"

He groused a bit more and slumped in his seat, arms crossed, looking like the recalcitrant toddler she remembered. "Yeah. I mean, I am now." He glanced over his shoulder when Taylor reappeared, face made up, hair pulled back, lugging her backpack. "Be home by dinner," he warned.

"Sure thing, Daddy-o." She rubbed his scalp and pecked his cheek, then gave Kayla a one-armed hug. "Glad you're all right, Aunt Kayla," she said.

Kayla overcame her innate queasiness at the contact and squeezed back. "Thanks, honey. Be smart, you know, on the study date." She felt her face flush. Who was she to give advice to a normal teenager?

Her phone beeped. Taylor smiled and waved at them, sliding the heavy metal door to the loft shut behind her. Kayla checked the screen of the new phone Trent had more or less shoved down her throat, with his and Melody's numbers pre-programmed in.

"Brock will be here in ten. We have a meeting."

Trent frowned deeper at her. "Why do you do it to yourself, K?"

Her pulse quickened and she collected their cups, ignoring his question as she rinsed them and put them into the dishwasher. She sensed him standing behind her, looming and protective. She turned and pushed him away, dropping her hands once he'd moved. "I need space, T, okay? I'm not going to all of a sudden be normal — I'll probably never be normal. You'll have to deal with me as I am, or not at all." Her heart slammed against her ribs at her impertinence. She lowered her face and flinched so hard when he touched her cheek that her elbow hit the tea kettle and sent it into the sink with a loud rattle and crash.

"I'm not going to hurt you, K," he said, his voice rough, his face a mask of agony. "You're safe now."

She shook her head, refusing to look at him. She'd been told that so many times — you're safe. I won't hurt you — as long as you do what I want you to do. Her logical mind knew Trent wouldn't hurt her. That he'd jump in front of a moving train to save her. But the deeper, darker part of her, the part that had taken years of training to produce, wouldn't allow her to take him at face value — not yet.

She watched as the hand he'd tried to touch her face with curled into a fist and slammed down on the stainless-steel counter next to the sink. "So help me *God* I wish I could revive that son of a bitch so I could kill him all the hell over again."

She sidestepped him, dry-mouthed at his anger. Another reflex reaction, she knew, but one she'd never shake.

"You can't fix me, Trent," she whispered, backing away from him. "I know you want to but you can't."

He turned to face her, his eyes dark with worry. "I could, if you'd let me try." He reached for her, but she recoiled, rubbing her arms and hating herself for making him so miserable. "Sorry."

"It's fine. I'll be fine. It takes time, though. And all your money plus a lot more isn't going to make it happen any faster." She pulled on her jacket, wincing when the fabric scraped against her still sore left upper arm. She'd been lucky, the doctor had insisted, as a nasty infection had settled into her wounds once they'd had her stabilized from the blood loss.

Lucky.

She smiled to herself.

No. She'd never be lucky. She just had to move forward, not worry about the past and focus on the future. Or some such similar happy horseshit.

Her phone beeped again, indicating that Brock had arrived and was waiting to take her to their thrice-weekly meeting. They'd changed venues, since the thought of being in that space where the woman had more or less died in front of her kid gave her the creeps. It meant a longer ride, but it was worth it.

"Don't worry about me. You have enough to occupy your mind, I think." She raised an eyebrow and pointed at the stack of invitations she and Taylor had just that morning finished addressing. "Papa…"

He groaned and fell onto the couch, his arm over his eyes. "Yeah. That."

"You're lucky, Trent. Melody is an incredible woman and will be an amazing mother."

"I didn't even want *one* kid…" He sighed. "But look at me now."

"Yes, just look at you." She shouldered her bag. "Get those into the mail today, please. Melody's orders."

"Yes, ma'am," he said, giving her a weak salute. "I hope…well, I hope that I can live up to what she expects of me. Sometimes I wonder about that."

"You already have. Now go and make some more money or something and leave the rest to karma, or the universe."

"Will do. But…"

"Nope. No buts. We're good here. I have someplace to be."

"I'm just worried about Brock," he blurted out, surprising her. She turned from the industrial sliding door to his loft. "Sorry, it's the brother in me, worrying about your…friend."

She set her shoulders. "That's all he is, Trent, and all he'll ever be, okay? We're good for each other that way."

"Brock Fitzgerald is a—"

She held up a hand. "Don't go there, please. No labels. He's no more fucked than I am. Lay off him."

Trent shook his head and waved her gone. But his words echoed in her mind as she rode the elevator down to the lobby of the much nicer converted warehouse. She smiled at Brock when she climbed into the passenger's side of the expensive sedan, and studied his profile as he drove them all the way across town to a Presbyterian church in a wealthy neighborhood where they were joined for an hour and a half with people as desperate to be normal as they were.

He reached for her hand during the final prayer. She let him take it, recalling how he'd held on to her in the ambulance. He was the one person she didn't mind touching her, at least that much, and she felt comfort knowing she was providing him with the same.

Chapter Fourteen

"I don't know how you do it," Brock said as he polished off the last of his burger and fries.

"Do what?" She licked the sriracha off her fingers, relishing his wince of pain.

"You know what," he said. "Put that horrific crap in your mouth."

"I've put worse in there," she quipped, not realizing her mistake until the words had flown from her lips. He grinned at her then leaned back, his long, strong arms draping the top of the booth and drawing the attention of a table full of lovelies nearby. But his eyes stayed on hers, throwing off her hard-won equilibrium in a hot second. She looked down at her hands. "You know what I mean."

"I'm sure I don't," he said, his voice soft. "But I could guess, if you want me to."

She glared up at him through the fringe of her bangs that Taylor had insisted she try at their last too-expensive salon day with Trent's credit card. "None of your beeswax, nosy," she insisted. But her voice was shaking. The new therapist was dragging all sorts of shit up from her well-buried past which had led to her need for more meetings to cope with the urges to pop a pill and forget it all, or to cut and cut and cut until there was nothing left of her but ribbons of flesh and bone. She swallowed hard.

"I know," he said, raising a finger to get the waitress to bring the check. "Just establishing how much I know, relative to how little you're willing to tell me."

He leaned forward, mesmerizing her the way he'd done a lot lately. He was so damn good-looking, she hated him for it sometimes. Ridiculous. But it wasn't fair, having this handsome, compassionate, equally fucked-up male dangled in front of her like so much catnip when she'd sworn off the stuff years before, out of sheer self-preservation.

"Stop it." She blew a puff of air upwards so the fringe flew out of her eyes.

"Stop what?" He tilted his head, increasing his adorable quotient ten-fold.

What was the matter with her? She had no business flirting or interacting with a member of the opposite sex in any way that resembled a normal relationship. She had no idea what to do with her hands, or her restless feet, or her careening thoughts as he stared at her, silent, and unthreatening.

"We—you and me—we're just friends, okay, Fitzgerald? Nothing more or less. I'm grateful to have you as my friend. So you can stop…doing whatever it is you're doing right now to make me feel like a freak at the damn circus."

"Did you hear? The last big circus closed. Hurray for the animals."

"The…what?" She shook her head. "Don't change the subject."

"You said circus first, my dear."

"Are you always this annoying?"

Stop flirting, Kayla. You don't even know how to do it right.

His grin widened, showing off the dimple revealed since he'd shaved off his beard. Kayla's heart did the oddest sort of stuttering thing, making her gasp and grip her chest. He frowned and reached for her arm, soothing her with the simple contact, his palm to her sleeve-covered skin. "You all right there, hot stuff?"

She took a long breath, wondering if she might be having a heart attack. What did that even feel like, anyway?

"Seriously, Kayla, you're really pale all of a sudden. Do you need me to—?"

She pulled her arm out from under his hand and shook her head, staring at the check the waitress had just deposited on their table. She reached for her purse, knowing how much she owed since she ordered the same thing every time—black bean burger with hot pepper cheese and sweet potato fries, all doused with super-hot sauce—and since Brock had given up weeks ago trying to convince her to let him cover their post-meeting lunches.

"Gotta pee," she mumbled as she headed for the bathroom, her mind awash with images, none of them she had any frame of reference for. All of them involving her, and Brock, and kissing.

She was shaking so hard when she made it to the bathroom, her teeth chattered, echoing and rattling. What would the man think if he knew she'd never once been kissed?

Regardless of all the terrible, degrading actions she'd done or had done to her, she'd never once allowed anyone to kiss her. Her stepfather had been strict about this. It was business, he'd insisted, as he'd taken the men's money. "No one kisses my little girl," he used to say.

She sat as long as she could without making him worry about her, rocking back and forth. She was filth. She was dirty. She was nothing but a hole — three holes, to be exact. No one wanted her for anything but her holes.

She'd been told this in no uncertain terms for so long, the mere concept of someone — of Brock Fitzgerald — looking at her in any way but clinical was so crazy as to be unthinkable.

But yet he had done. He did it a lot. The more time they spent going to meetings, eating lunches or dinners, getting comfortable in their ongoing razzing of each other, the more she would catch him outright staring at her.

"What? I got a booger?" she'd ask.

"No," he'd reply. "I like admiring beautiful things."

"Oh, shut up and leave me alone," she'd always respond.

He'd smile, look away, and they'd resume whatever discussion they'd been having about a book they were reading, or a movie they'd like to see.

She groaned and leaned forward, willing her food not to make an ill-timed reappearance.

Brock — he was the star of most of her dreams lately, she'd admit to that. Dreams that would start one way — fun, and funny. Gentle, and kind. Sweet, and nice. Then he'd kiss her and she'd wake up screaming.

She was beyond redemption. She ought to set him straight and end this useless flirtation that would go nowhere. It wasn't fair to him, after all. He ought to feel free to find a normal woman. Someone he could kiss who wouldn't scream. Someone he could… Could make love to, without worrying that she'd flip out and start cutting herself.

With a sigh, she got to her feet, splashed some water on her face and opened the bathroom door, only to come face to face with Brock himself. He had his hand raised, as if about to knock. His eyes were full of concern. She stepped back, hand to her throat.

The very air between them seemed to crackle with energy. But she had no frame of reference for it. Even though she'd had sex with more men than she would ever admit. She'd done awful things, things foisted on her as a child, encouraged by her as an adult in exchange for her next pop. She had never once had a real orgasm — other than the ecstasy she achieved from cutting her own flesh.

"I've never been kissed," she whispered, wonderment at her own outspoken craziness whirling around in her brain. "Did you know that? I'm forty-two years old and…" Her throat seized up, precluding any more words.

When he touched her face, his palm was warm and comforting. She leaned into it, wondering how long this would last, how long before he demanded something of her she couldn't provide.

This is Brock. He won't do any of those things, not if you don't want him to.

Bullshit. He's a man. All men want whatever the hell they can get or take by brute force.

"I will kiss you, Kayla." He swiped the pad of his thumb over her lips, giving her the strangest, weak-kneed sensation. "But not until you want me to." He put his lips close to her her ear. "You don't want me to. Not yet. Do you?"

She closed her eyes and leaned toward him, her body yearning for something she'd never had before. Even as her mind was screeching at her to escape. "No," she said, her voice cracking on the one word.

He kept plenty of air between them, his gaze never leaving hers. "When you're ready, you'll know. And then you just tell me, okay?"

She nodded, a single tear sliding down her hot cheek and dotting the cuff of his shirt. He let go of her, leaving her bereft and relieved at the same time. She clutched her bag to her chest, unable to stop staring at him as her mind pulled her away while her body urged her forward in ways she didn't understand.

"I'm not normal, Brock. I... I've been... I've done... It's..."

"Sh, sh," he insisted, pulling her into a nice, comfortable hug. "We've all done. We've all been. You don't even want to know some of the shit I've gotten into."

She sensed herself molding against him, putting her arms around his waist and marveling as she did it at her first, intimate embrace. She pressed her face into his shirt, sucking a deep breath of him—a bit of maltiness from the brewery that they all carried around with them made her smile, combined with what must be the natural smell of his skin. Her knees were shaking again but he held on tight, his mantra of "Sh...sh...it's all right," filling her mind and drowning out the fear.

The sound of a clearing throat forced them apart. She swiped at her eyes and reached for her bag that she'd dropped in her haste to hug him back. But he snagged it first, handed it to her with a smile and held out his elbow. "I don't know about you, but I might commit murder for a banana split right now."

She drew away from him.

"Bananas in ice cream are an utter abomination to humanity, Fitzgerald. I think you might need help." She found herself feeling strong after the close contact, not shaky and weepy like usual. As if some of his inner strength had permeated her, taken hold inside her. She tucked her hand into his arm.

"Oh, honey, I need help all right." He led her to the door and out into the lengthening shadows of a perfect West Michigan late summer afternoon. He drove them to the local Dairy Queen, and ordered a large split, "heavy on the bananas," and double chocolate fudge and whipped cream. When he brought the thing to their tiny concrete table with a triumphant flourish, she wrinkled her nose.

"That is disgusting."

He handed her a long plastic spoon and dug out a huge bite. After shoving it into his mouth, closing his eyes and making weird, ecstatic noises, he pushed the thing over to her. She scooped up a tiny helping of the hot fudge and ice cream, avoiding the banana.

"You don't know what you're missing, lovely lady," he said, taking another monster-sized bite of everything.

"Oh, I'm pretty sure that I do."

"So about this wedding..."

Startled by the quick change of subject, she set her spoon down and reached over to wipe a blob of chocolate from the corner of his mouth with her napkin. It was the most natural seeming gesture in the world and neither of them commented on it. "What about it?"

"I got my invite and am pondering my plus one."

She glanced up at him as she tried to maneuver a bite of ice cream out of the dish. "I'm in the damn thing so I'm going anyway."

"Yeah, but…" He grabbed her hand. "I see you're gonna remain as obtuse as ever and make me do it the hard way."

She lifted her chin. Her ears were starting to ring and her palm felt sweaty. She resisted the urge to tug it out of his grip and wipe it on her jeans. His gaze held hers, rapt, in that damn way he had. That way she'd been trying to resist like mad in the weeks since her cutting mishap and hospital stay.

"Kayla, would you do me the honor of being my official date for your brother's happy nuptials up in Petoskey?"

She frowned at him. Or at least she tried to. "I'm in the thing, like I just said. I'll have, you know, responsibilities and shit. I may not be very much fun."

"You will be. It's gonna be a great weekend." He kept a tight hold on her hand. "I, uh, meant that, you know. About the kiss."

Her face got so hot she worried it might catch fire. She dropped her gaze. He took her chin and lifted her face and in his eyes she saw something she'd never, ever seen. She saw respect, and trust and honest concern.

Not love. Not yet. Don't rush this…thing, whatever it is.

She smiled at him and patted his cheek. "Sure thing, handsome. I'll be your date. But don't think you can get away with that kissing thing just because the ambience is all romantic and shit. I'm not gonna be that easy."

He grabbed her hand and put her knuckles to his lips. She flinched, but the sensation crawling up her spine was pleasant. And when it hit her brain, her world seemed somehow brighter.

Don't be ridiculous. He's a man. And men only want one thing from you.

She tried to pull away but he held both her hands now, the gross, melting goop of ice cream, banana and chocolate between them. "I'm not… I…"

He shook his head. "Kayla, stop assuming you know what I want from you."

She blinked fast, shocked that he'd somehow figured out her deepest fear. He gave her hands one more squeeze then let her go and picked up his spoon. "My favorite stage…all melty." He scooped a dollop of the dessert into his mouth. She watched him, frozen by her own feelings, and terrified by the enormity of what she'd just agreed to do. To be his date. To her brother's wedding. An event that would span an entire highly choreographed set of days that would end on Saturday night with a sunset ceremony and dancing under the stars.

She shivered, but when she dug deep into the reason why, all she saw was Brock.

And all she heard was his promise to kiss her…as soon as she was ready.

Chapter Fifteen

"Yo, Earth to brother. Calling my brother...hello?"

"What? Hey, cut it out." Brock waved Austin's hand out of his face, annoyed that he'd been caught staring into the distance at his desk—the desk he occupied thanks to the ongoing goodwill of said brother trying to get his attention at that moment. "You're a pain in the ass."

"Hardly. You all right?"

"Yes, I'm fine. Clean as a whistle. Taking my pills like a good boy, all right? You know because you make me check in every day at four-thirty, remember? Now, beat it."

"I will. After you tell me more about this." Austin turned his computer tablet around so Brock could see the screen.

Local Brewery Throws Weight Behind Clean Water Efforts, the headline blared.

"Yeah, those kids," he said, hooking his thumb over his shoulder at the room where his interns were eternally tap-tapping away on behalf of the Fitzgerald Foundation. "They're pretty good at the publicity shit."

"Don't be modest, Brock. This story's gotten picked up by *USA Today* and *Huffington Post*. My inbox is stuffed full of requests for interviews. Well done, my brother."

"Over a million hits on HuffPo," a voice piped up from the interns' room.

Brock shrugged. "They speak their own language. But that's good, right?" he hollered back in the direction of the keyboard noises.

"Yeah, boss. It's great."

He rotated the squeaky office chair back around so he was facing Austin again. "The water thing was your wife's idea. I just ran with it. Turned those kids loose with the online and press release bits. *Voilá.*"

Austin chuckled and shook his head. But Brock couldn't take any pleasure in his brother's kudos. Yes, he'd done all upfront legwork—reading research about the poisoned water problem in Flint for hours, talking to local officials, the pediatrician who'd made the initial discovery—and that was the interesting part. More hours spent on budget proposals to fix the problem, and yet still more on hold, waiting for the big shots in Lansing to answer his questions about what it would really take to fix the lead pipe problem in the city.

Once he'd had all the facts at his disposal, he'd made the decision to allocate that year's funds toward it, but not via the government. The grassroots group spearheading the clean-up had been ecstatic to receive his phone call and, not long after that, his giant donation check. He'd kept his interns in the loop at every stage and they'd worked miracles, building the Fitzgerald Charitable Foundation's social media presence during his research period, and reaching out to the right press people to make their big announcement.

Hence the now-national level attention being paid to his brother's brewery's dedication to cleaning up the water in a Michigan city much poorer than theirs. His phone had been blowing up with requests for interviews too — from as high up as *The Today Show* and a few others he'd never heard of but had been assured by his pack of youngsters that they were 'awesome'.

But it was all somehow muted. And he had no one but himself to blame for that. His anxiety over the wedding weekend had grown to near epic proportions. Now that the event itself was literally around the corner — as in, he was packed and ready to drive up to Petoskey after shoving the infants out of the office for the evening — he was having a hard time swallowing his own spit.

What had possessed him to make it semi-official anyway? They were fine as junkie meeting and ice-cream-eating buddies. Why upset that particular apple cart?

"So, I hear you're Kayla Hettinger's date for the big event this weekend."

He was so startled to hear these words echoing his ongoing inner debate, his elbow slipped off the edge of the desk, which compromised the fragile equilibrium of the office chair and he found himself dumped onto the floor, staring up at the ceiling.

"Jesus, dude. Nervous much?" Austin held out his hand.

Brock rolled to his hands and knees before climbing to his feet. Ignoring his brother and the concerned stares from the peanut gallery behind him, he set the chair back on its rollers and closed his laptop.

"Nervous doesn't even begin to describe it," he said, staring down at his desk, unsure why he felt the need to chat about it. He and Austin had an understanding sort of relationship. He understood that he was only tolerated if he toed the line. While Austin understood that he could spin out of control at any moment. They didn't communicate much outside that, other than via logistics regarding Evelyn and Rose, if his presence was required to assist with either. The times Austin had saved his ass — like the last time he'd been out at the lake house where he'd find himself again soon — all went unremarked upon. He knew his own embarrassment level over them and Austin, to his credit, seemed to respect that by not bringing it up.

He sighed as his shoulders slumped against the hard reality of his circumstances. Not that he was anything but grateful for it — up to and including this latest responsibility for the foundation. But at this particular moment, he was so confused and rattled about Kayla, he felt the words bubbling up his throat and spilling from his lips before he could stop them.

"I think I love her," he said, flopping back into his chair.

"Hmm...that might get complicated," Austin said, his expression sympathetic.

"Yes, *muchas gracias*, Captain Obvious." He leaned onto the desk, forehead on his arms.

"You thought you loved Caroline Reilly, too. How is this any different?"

A flash of anger forced him to lean back and meet his brother's gaze. "What the hell is that supposed to mean?"

Austin held up a hand. "Nothing, I guess."

"So, I'm not allowed to have honest feelings about a woman? Just because I managed to fuck everything up relative to Caroline?"

"That's not what I meant." Austin was standing now, his jaw clenched in a way Brock recognized. "Never mind."

Brock was aware that the ubiquitous tapping from the room next door had stopped. The brothers glared at each other a few seconds.

"Brock," Austin said. "I'm sorry. I'm not... I don't mean to be judgmental. I swear it."

"Hard not to be. I get it. I've not been the most reliable human being on the planet most of my life." He propped his dress-shoe-covered feet up on the desk and his hands behind his head, attempting to seem like he didn't care.

But he did.

"Well, that's not what I meant either."

"So, what do you mean, Austin?" He kept his face as neutral as possible while his brother wrestled with his inner judgmental guy, amused and discouraged by the whole thing.

"Look, from what little I've been told about her, Kayla is not exactly without her own baggage." Austin hesitated. Brock waited for the second half of that statement. "Pretty heavy baggage, too."

Brock flexed one biceps by way of showing his ability to tote said heavy baggage. Austin rolled his eyes. "Far be it from me to talk you in or out of anything, relative to the fairer sex..."

"But?" Brock was baiting him now but couldn't stop himself. As if he needed to hear his own misgivings about a relationship between two people as fucked up as they were spoken out loud — by someone else.

"But shit, man, you have a hard enough time getting through some days. How could adding another person just as...challenged to that mix be anything but...a mess?"

Brock sighed and put his hands on the desk, staring down at them as if they might answer all his questions. "Honestly? I have no idea." He felt Austin's hand on his shoulder.

"I get it, though. There's no accounting for women and what they do to us."

"Yeah, that. Good thing they're soft and smell nice — to make up for the PITA factor, eh, brother?"

Austin gave his shoulder a pat then withdrew. "I'm behind you, whatever you decide. But her brother may prove a barrier, you know. He's a pretty protective guy."

"He'll be distracted this weekend, I'm willing to guess." But Brock's gut churned at the thought of pissing Kayla's brother off, regardless of his more or less virtuous intentions. "She's no more of a mess than I am. And it's not like I'm looking to...to..."

Austin chuckled and slapped his back again. "Dude, I don't think I've ever known you to be tongue-tied over a female. I'll take that as a good sign."

"I don't know," he admitted, letting his feet drop to the floor. "But whatever I know or don't know, it's almost time to get on with it." He glanced at his watch. "You guys going up tonight, or tomorrow?"

"Rose travels best at night, so we're gonna caffeine up and head out tonight, but not until after nine."

"Thanks for listening," he said, meaning it.

Austin shrugged. "I wasn't much help."

"Nope. But you always were useless."

Austin grinned at him, went for a mock-punch to his jaw, which Brock mock-blocked and did the same to Austin's gut. Man-speak for "Enough about feelings, already. Get me a beer."

"I'll see you there, then. I'm leaving from here, once I toss some candy to the kids."

"Hey!" a voice floated out over the resumed keyboarding.

"You know what I mean," he called over his shoulder. "Get ready for me in there, youngsters. Time for my daily debrief. You'll be on your own here tomorrow."

Austin turned as he was about to head out of the door. "Are you staying at the house?"

"Nope. I wasn't invited and didn't think it would be politic to show up for breakfast with the family in my PJs without Trent inviting me."

"Good call. So you're at the Inn?" He named the centuries-old set of cabins on Lake Michigan where they'd spent a fair share of summer fucking-around time as boys and teenagers. Their mother now owned half the deed, along with her Fitzgerald in-laws. The place wasn't used anymore, given how busy Austin and Evelyn were with the brewery and the fact that their closest cousins were west-coast dwellers and had been for several decades. The collection of buildings included one large, genteel but ramshackle main house and four more updated cabins that were managed by a rental company.

"Yeah. I figure it's about time someone blew the cobwebs off the furniture up there."

"Watch out for the ghost."

Brock shot him a thumbs-up. "I'm counting on him for company. I don't see this as a sleep-over sort of weekend for me and the current object of my heart's desire."

"Good plan."

"Give me some credit," he quipped as he put his work away in his worn backpack. "Go on, Judge-y McJudge Face. I gotta feed the peanut gallery then get on the road. I *am* invited to a family dinner tonight, I'll have you know."

"Good for you, Brock," Austin said. "I'll catch up with you at Trent's house tomorrow."

* * * *

The two-and-a-half-hour trip flew by too fast and before he was ready to face it, he was parked in the long driveway in front of Trent's massive lakefront mansion. Memories of his last trip here filled his head like smog. He'd been sure he and Caroline would make the friends thing work, but of course they hadn't been able to stay out of each other's pants. They were both too pre-programmed for that sort of abstinence.

And it had ended here — or rather Caroline had possessed the grownup ability to end it. That had nearly sent him spiraling downward. His typical response — and one that his brother had nipped in the bud, thank Christ.

As he wiped the sweat that had beaded on his face, he resisted the extreme impulse to succumb to the pity party building up steam in his chest. He took several deep breaths, repeating one of the mantras suggested to him by one of his many therapists through the years.

You are in control of you. You are in control of you. You are in control of...

"Fuck," he spat out, giving the steering wheel a smack and wincing at the pain in his palm. *Time to act like a God damned grownup man, Fitzgerald. She's in there.* Kayla—the equally-if-not-more-fucked-up woman who had so compelled him for reasons he couldn't justify.

The urge to kiss her outside of that stupid bathroom at the restaurant had been so strong. It had seemed perfect. The Old Brock—Mister Ladykiller Himself— would not have hesitated. He'd have gone for it, hard. And the night would have ended badly, to say the least.

The New Brock—Mister Sensitive for Now—had held back and the look of sheer relief on her face had been worth it. Of course, this weekend held all sorts of possibilities. None of which at this precise, sweaty, head-pounding moment seemed very attractive to him.

With a sigh, he climbed out of the car he'd had to park at the end of the long drive behind all the vehicles already stationed here. The afternoon was hot, and the sky was a bright, clear blue. But rain was forecast for the coming days, in a wishy-washy fifty percent way, leaving the wedding party at a loss on what to do about the huge tent they had on standby.

Kayla had texted him earlier.

Poor Mel, she's sick as a damn dog from the pregnancy, weepy over the potential shitty weather and how Taylor's behaving. I had to take Miss Thing outside and give her what for just now. I think it helped. I hope so. Trent's pacing the floors like a caged tiger. Hurry up already. I need some help!

The thought of her needing him, of anyone needing his help with anything, was comforting, so he'd pressed the pedal harder and made it from the brewery in record time. Of course, now he stood here, gawking up at the three-story, arts-and-crafts monstrosity of a lake house, heart racing, feet frozen in place.

"Hey! Fitzgerald!" He jumped at the sound of her voice, then caught sight of her, leaning out of one of the upper windows. "Get your ass in here. Please?" Her smile was so wide and natural-looking he sensed a bit of his tension release.

The realization that they were both caretakers in their souls hit him as he half-ran up the drive to the side door. Odd, considering that junkies were considered to be the worst sort of selfish — the kind that preyed on the people who loved them the most. He'd done his fair share of emotional vampirism, he'd admit that. But his parents had been unwilling to admit that he even had a problem worth addressing beyond grounding him and taking his car keys away. It was as if he had to prove to them that he was, indeed, sick enough to warrant their full attention that drove him to some of his worst deeds.

"Only you can control you," he muttered as he pulled open the door and headed into the large mud-room off the kitchen. The memories of Caroline tried to take hold again, digging into the frontal cortex of his brain with raptor's claws and forcing him to stop and grip the high granite countertop to steady himself. If he closed his eyes, he could see her, hear her, smell her as her memory ghost moved around the giant kitchen he was staring at now.

She was and always would be a part of him, a physical extension of himself in a way, but one that was toxic, like an appendix gone bad. And he was an even worse vestigial organ for her — he was her addiction as she'd said so many times. He was her crack. In some ways, even harder to beat than his own, first to booze, then to sex, then to opiates. Because no matter how shitty he'd treated her — and he'd been forced to face up to some real doozies in that department — she couldn't *not* come to him whenever he'd call or text or show up at her door in whatever state of wrecked he might be.

"Hey, it's about time." His eyes flew open at the sound of Kayla's voice. He was shaking when he ran a hand down his face, but he pulled it together and smiled at her, relieved at her interruption. "What's wrong?" She moved close to him, too close. He could smell her — something so opposite of Caroline that it turned his mild shivers into tremors. Sunscreen and lake water and sand filled his senses but with an undercurrent of something that was everything Kayla. A sort of vanilla-infused spice with the mildest hint of sweat. "Brock? Do you need some water?"

He closed his eyes against the urge to grab her, shove her up against the wall of this stupid room and fuck her so he could shove Caroline out of his damn head once and for all. Unfair. Unfair to Kayla, but also to him and to the now-absent old girlfriend.

To his surprise, when he opened his eyes and took the cool glass from her, his body didn't do its usual lurch into over-the-top horny. He downed the water. Kayla held out her hand and he gave it back to her. Her thin but striking face was tan — she'd been here for almost a week of near-perfect weather already. Her hazel eyes were shaded more green than brown in contrast to the bronzed tint of her skin. When she reached out and put her fingertips to his cheek, he blinked, expecting the usual surge of inappropriate desire. But his brain remained in charge, and his skin prickled at her touch.

"Thanks," he croaked out.

She nodded, turned back to the sink to refill the glass then returned. He took in the filmy sundress, the bikini top straps around her neck, her bare feet with their pink-painted toenails. As if to test his tenuous, new-found self-control, he shifted to one side so he could appreciate the way the sun's angle backlit her figure. After a quick twinge below his belt, he moved back to where he'd been and downed the water, berating himself for being so craven. Even as he congratulated himself for how normal he felt.

Any red-blooded, healthy man would see a beautiful woman in a bikini not very well covered by a thin dress and get that below-the-belt twinge. Any normal guy. Could it be? Had he conquered that demon? He cast his mind back to the many post-meeting lunches and dinners they'd shared, laughing and joking and eating and being…regular people. He'd never once, until that last time, given any thought to her body, or how she'd feel, smell or taste. Which was at odds with how he'd operated for so long he realized now that he should have noticed.

But he hadn't. He'd enjoyed her pleasant, snarky, intelligent company. Her beauty had not been lost on him. Any man who claimed that was a flat-out lying asshole. But he hadn't required all his willpower not to leap over whatever table lay between them, to kiss her, feel her, inside and out. Not once.

The sight of her now filled him with something else. A sort of peaceful happiness — as if now, together, they could conquer this super-stressful weekend together and have some fun doing it.

She had to peel his fingers from around the empty water glass to get it away from him. "Better now? Or do you need some more time?"

He nodded. "I'm good. Seriously. Thanks."

"This place will do that to you." She tilted her head, which made a lock of her dark hair slip from the messy bun.

Without thinking, he reached for it, tucked it behind her ear, noting the sweet flush under her tan. Again, he didn't get that sick testosterone and adrenaline-fueled compulsion to shove her to the floor and stick his dick in her just for the mental and emotional relief it might offer. All he wanted was to hold her in his arms.

She didn't move as he let his fingers trail across her shoulder, which were red and peeling, and exposed by the dress. He watched his own hand, fascinated by it, as it moved down the arm she kept clasped tight to her body, concealing what he knew to be thick scar tissue from her years of cutting. Her skin was pleasantly warm under his palm as he cupped her elbow and tugged her close. She only hesitated a moment, as if sensing his need for her proximity.

"It's all right," she whispered as she slipped her arms around his waist.

"I know," he agreed as he pressed his face into her hair, half-worried his body might betray him. He did get that twinge again but he kept a firm mental grip and allowed himself this surprising, tender moment. She felt fragile, bird-like, as if her bones contained air or smoke. And that gave him the strength he needed to keep his dick at parade rest, although the sensation of her breasts smashed against his chest made that a bit of a challenge. A normal challenge — like a healthy man might face when holding a woman in his arms.

She pulled away first, leaning back and raising one eyebrow at him. "You good now? Because I need your help with the circus out there."

He smiled and let himself have a brief brush of his lips along hers. She stiffened. But he didn't go any further. He knew she wasn't ready for anything more, yet. He was eager to explore the parameters of this new way of feeling — of being turned on but not so much so that it felt out of control. Of being happy just to be in a woman's presence, to be of use to her and her family, with the knowledge that more could — and very like would — develop later.

"Sorry," he said, pulling away from her, but noting how she swayed in his direction for a few seconds. "Come on. Let me survey the damage."

"Da-aaaaaad! I told you she…" The loud cry of an unhappy teenager filled the air before trailing off. Followed by a matching, loud masculine roar of indistinct, angry words.

Kayla sighed and rolled her eyes. "I told you. This weekend is going to end in bloody murder before it ends in a wedding, I swear to God."

Chapter Sixteen

Kayla stretched out on the couch, letting the murmurs of the others in the room soothe her. Brock's burst of laughter made her smile even as she half-dozed. He'd been so amazing over the past twenty-four hours, jumping straight into the fray and forcing Trent out of the house and down the beach for a long, punishing run within minutes of his arrival. Then that first night, cracking jokes with Ross and Elle, who'd been put in charge of the food and booze for the weekend. He'd even forced a smile and one giggle out of Taylor, which had raised his positive points quotient for Trent, she knew.

Tonight, the night before the wedding, they'd all jumped into playing cards while the staff Trent had insisted on hiring did the cleaning up after the family dinner. When she'd realized she and Brock were going to be left alone once everyone else made their way upstairs to their rooms, she'd flushed hot as that odd rush of nervousness-tinged anticipation had filled every corner of her being. She'd decamped to the couch, thinking she'd go to sleep, her typical evasion measure. But it eluded her so she'd gotten up without saying anything to him and headed into the kitchen, wishing there were something for her to do. But it was sparkling clean and ready for the big day.

She stood in the doorway, watching Brock as he sat, feet up on the large leather ottoman, sipping some kind of herbal tea Elle had made for them all "to help them sleep." The sudden realization that she wasn't at all nervous or scared made Kayla square her shoulders and march herself back out into the living room, change the tunes to something mellow and bluesy and flop into one of the big chairs opposite the couch. When she put her feet up on the ottoman, their toes touched. Neither of them flinched away.

"I'd give my left nut for a joint right now," Brock said, surprising her at first. She sighed and crossed her arms behind her head, stretching her legs out and relishing the tingling of her skin from her days in the sun. "Sorry," he muttered.

"Don't be. Me? I might commit murder for a bottle of Pinot Noir and a cigarette. I'm feeling mellow tonight."

He chuckled but kept his gaze up at the ceiling. "You weren't kidding about the trauma drama. Jesus, please-us." He ran a hand down his face and drank the last of his tea. "It sucks, thinking I'll never be past any of this."

"Junkies for life," she said, parroting one of the many phrases they were taught. One is never 'cured' of addiction. One simply 'lives with it'. Or not, as the case may be. A brief memory of the dead woman and the smelly, squalling, helpless little girl wafted across her consciousness. She shuddered and closed her eyes.

"Indeed," Brock said. The silence between them felt soft, quiet and natural.

When the music changed to something she loved— *Stand by Me*, the original version by Ben E. King—she opened her eyes and found Brock standing to her left, his hand held out. She frowned, but his grin did its usual number on her nerve endings, making her think and do things she'd never, ever believed would be a part of her life. His palm was warm and calloused against hers as she let him pull her to her feet.

"We're doing this now?" she asked as she molded herself against him as if she'd been doing it for years. The sensation of his firm body next to hers soothed her, as it had done the day before when he'd walked into the house in the middle of an anxiety attack.

"Yes, I think we are," he said. One of his hands found the small of her back. The fingers of his other hand threaded through hers. The music filled most of her soul. Brock Fitzgerald—fellow junkie and hot mess extraordinaire—consumed the rest of it. "This is nice." His breath blew the straggling hair that had sprung free from her ponytail. She was beyond exhausted, emotionally and otherwise. But she'd never felt more alive.

"Yes," she admitted. "It is." They danced together in the empty living room to the soft music until the song ended. One of her other favorite songs dropped into the playlist— *At Last*, sung by Etta James.

"Don't let go of me yet, if you don't mind," Brock said, putting a bit of pressure with his hand on her back. Kayla had always wondered what it might feel like to be in this position, held by a man who wanted nothing more from her. He sighed into her hair. "I'm not trying to go too fast here or anything. I hope you don't mind. It just feels so great, holding you like this."

She sighed into his chest, wondering if she might be inhabiting some kind of a dream state. But reality intervened and the song ended. Something lame she couldn't even identify filled the air so she disentangled herself and headed for the phone that controlled the sound track. When she turned around, tugging her hair back into its utilitarian ponytail, he was standing where she'd left him, his hands tucked into his jeans pockets. "I'm ready," she said as Bob Dylan's *Tangled Up in Blue* filled the large room. She waited, unsure what to do next, realizing the full extent of her non-knowledge, her sick, fundamental dysfunction and wishing she'd kept her stupid mouth shut.

"Nice song," he said, not moving either. "One of my favorites."

She nodded and started fussing with her hair, nervousness making her pulse race. By the time he'd made it across the room and stood in front of her, she understood that all her skin tingling had nothing to do with nervousness. He was humming under his breath as the few centimeters separating them seemed charged in a way that made the small hairs on her arms stand at attention.

She fixed her gaze on the front of his shirt—a pale blue polo-style that hugged his muscular torso and upper arms, emphasizing his strength and giving her the oddest sensation deep in her belly. A sort of liquid gooiness, not unlike the melting ice cream they'd shared so many times, arguing over anything and everything, from the legitimacy of bananas in dessert to that week's political news. Her arms rose, seemingly of their own accord and her hands explored the firm terrain of his chest.

He cupped both her elbows and let her touch him. She stroked the incredible real estate of his torso, in wonder at his physical perfection. In their bare feet, he stood tall enough that she had to rise up on her tiptoes, but as she did it, she realized that she was making the first move. At the initial touch of her lips to his, she flinched, unsure of what to do next but already loving the sensation.

The full sensory experience of the moment overwhelmed her. The smells—sunscreen and outdoors—were so healthy, and ones she'd forever associate with him. Her first kiss, she thought, closing her eyes when he slid his hands up her arms, across her shoulders and alongside her face. He kept his lips closed, letting her do the exploring and ongoing first-moving but he angled his face the right way, alleviating her momentary confusion over what to do with their noses.

His warm, rough palms felt so wonderful alongside her cheeks. Her heart pounded a drumbeat and all she could hear when she traced the closed seam of his lips with her tongue was a loud whooshing noise. It drowned out everything. That, along with the realization that her entire body was flushed, alive and flowing with the blood her eager heart was pumping faster than ever through her veins, she pressed further, breaching his lips and sensing his slight shiver when she did so.

It was odd, this kiss, but more perfect than anything she'd ever experienced. Her mind was a blessed blank, free of any ugly memories or horrible words she used to hear while men hurt her. She'd been worried that the moment she allowed herself to be physically intimate with Brock, her past would invade her consciousness and ruin it. But all she knew was him—his lips, the sound of his breathing, the way one of his hands moved down to the small of her back so their bodies were now pressed close, no light or air between them. There was nothing more or less than this, and him.

She relaxed, wrapping her arms around his neck. He inhaled through his nose, surprising her, but she felt his tongue against hers then which eclipsed everything in her entire universe. Her whole body was alive, every nerve dancing, every muscle and sinew on high alert. She opened her mouth wider, and shivered so hard at the sensation of it, of part of him being in a part of her now even if it were only his tongue. He had to grip her tighter to keep her from sliding to the floor.

Her mind continued to fuzz over as her skin got hotter, almost too hot to bear. She could tell he was holding back, not pushing her, letting her set the pace. At that moment, she acknowledged the full range of her feelings for him. When she probed farther into his mouth, feeling rather than hearing the low moan coming from somewhere deep in his chest, something seemed to burst in her, lighting her from the inside out at the thought that he wanted her. Despite her ugly history, the way she'd been used like some kind of a pre-pubescent sex doll.

No, stop, she commanded herself. *Don't think of it. Don't go there. Be here, with Brock. This man, kissing you as if his life depended on it.*

She believed that she could taste his need for more, to push harder, to go deeper. She broke away, sad at the disconnection but feeling like she should say something. He sighed and pressed his forehead to hers, still holding her tight. She realized that he was trembling as much as she was. That he was confused and excited by it too—Brock Fitzgerald, the ladies' man, super-hot, flirt machine was shaking in her arms right now. And his lips...dear Lord help her, she wondered what he'd think about her if she admitted how perfect he made her feel with something as simple as a kiss.

"Damn, woman," he said with a small smile.

She closed her eyes, relishing the moment even as the absolute understanding that it would never be more than this rushed in to smother her happiness. She'd never have a normal sex life. All she knew was pain, ugliness and filth. Her brain seemed to open up, to overflow with the horror of her childhood years.

She wrenched herself out of his arms and backed away, hand to her lips, tears burning her eyes. It was as if a faucet had opened up wide, busting past a kink in her mental garden hose, flooding her senses with sights and sounds and smells. All the sex she'd been forced to have well before a little girl should be worrying about anything other than which of her friends she wanted to invite to her next sleepover.

"Kayla, don't." Brock's voice tried to break through the wall of noise in her head. But she kept backing away from him, loath to put the space there, but knowing it was best for them both. "I didn't mean to..."

She held up a hand. "It's not you, Brock," she said as tears spilled down her face. "I'm sorry." She turned and ran up the stairs, willing the old memories gone, wishing the newest ones—the ones involving Brock's arms, his lips, his strong, safe body pressed against hers—to the front. But it was useless. She was full to bursting again. Her skin was tight and painful. She needed something to release the pain, to distract her from all of it.

She ran into her bedroom, blind with remembered agony. The pills she'd started taking had blunted things for a while but had sent her spiraling down a different path, one she now wished she'd had the guts to finish. Death from overdose would be easier than this — this shit show of complicated emotions that had sent her rushing away from Brock.

She dropped to all fours and crawled the last few feet, reaching under the sink where she'd put her supply — the things she never allowed herself to be without, even if she didn't use them. Her fingers closed around the small plastic bag, which sent a jolt of sick relief down her spine. The memories faded as she sat with her back to the giant soaking tub, one of the many amenities bought and paid for by her successful baby brother and now part of her life.

Just holding the bag of razor blades, antiseptic ointment and gauze bandages calmed her for a few minutes. Her breathing slowed. Her pulse rate dropped to a semi-normal rhythm. Her hand was curled so tightly around the bag she felt the edge of the razors, which touched off the part of her that had sent her up here in the first place.

Fingers shaking, she opened the bag and pulled out the blade, letting the other stuff spill onto her lap. It was a familiar tableau, and one she understood, unlike the terrifying moment downstairs when she'd believed that she wanted more from Brock. That she'd allow him to touch her, to make love to her like a regular person. A low groan escaped her chapped lips. She fumbled with the razor, holding it in the usual way. The light from her bedroom caught the metal, sending a reflective shard into her eyes.

"Don't," she heard herself say. "Don't do this. Go back to Brock. He's your anchor now, not this." But before she knew it, she had the lethal end pressed into the tangle of scars on the inside of her upper right arm. The release…she craved it, required it, it would make her better. Cutting the ugly out of herself, giving herself the pain that had been part of her life for so many years.

"No," she said, even as she saw the blood speckle the business end of the blade. "No…oh…God," she sighed and leaned her head back as the endorphin rush her body had been trained to experience at the sight and sensation of her own blood running down her arm made her groan. Her body pulsed with that weird energy she didn't understand but welcomed because it shut out the yammering ghosts of memory — including the one of Brock's face when she'd bolted from him earlier.

"No," a voice said as she relaxed into it. She wondered if she were still talking but didn't care. The release — the relief — was so great, she didn't want it to end. "No," she heard again. Her eyes were so heavy, she couldn't keep them open. The blood was warm as it oozed into her open palm.

"No, God damn it, Kayla, I won't let you do this."

Shocked, she found herself nose to nose with Trent. He was on his knees, prying the razor from her fingers. His eyes — so much like hers it was like staring into the mirror — were dark with worry.

"I'm sorry," she whispered, reaching for him but finding herself too depleted from the hormonal, adrenaline rush of her encounter with Brock followed by the blood-letting she'd engineered for herself. "Oh, T... I am so sorry. I'm ruining your weekend."

"Shut up and let me get this bleeding stopped already."

She flopped back. Her head felt like a giant bowling ball, too heavy for her neck to support. She watched as if from miles away as he used a warm cloth to clean up her arm and hand, his touch gentle, his expression intent and non-judgmental. "Hold this," he said, pressing a dry cloth to the fresh cut. She did as he told her, while he wiped the floor clean.

She sensed herself fading, falling, entering the blessed empty blank space where she didn't have to constantly be fighting all the demons. She saw him then, sensed his presence, tasted his lips, felt his arms around her. "Brock, I'm sorry," she said, reaching out for him.

"What did you say?" Trent's harsh voice near her ear jolted her back to consciousness. "Kayla, answer me. Did he...do something to you? Make you want to hurt yourself?" She touched her brother's clenched jaw. He jerked out of her reach. "Don't make me ask him, K. Tell me what happened."

She watched as he smeared the new wound with ointment and bandaged it, before he dropped down next to her with a low moan. "God damn it, if that Fitzgerald punk put a hand on you..."

"No, Trent. It's not... He didn't, I mean... We, um...shit."

Her brother jumped up, his eyes blazing, his hands balled into fists. "I knew it. I knew he couldn't be trusted. I don't care how great you and Melody tell me he is."

"Wait, don't." She tried to get up but stumbled. Trent caught her, picked her all the way up and carried her to the bed. "Brock isn't..." But she was so fucking tired. All she wanted was to close her hot eyes and drop into oblivion for a few hours. "He's..."

"Sh, K. It's all right. I'll take care of it."

A soft blanket covered her. Trent touched her cheek. Kayla tried like hell to struggle past the looming fog, to tell him what happened so he didn't misunderstand. But it pulled at her, whispering sweet nothings, and the last thing she remembered for a while was Trent, promising her he'd "take care of everything."

Chapter Seventeen

"Nice move, Fitzgerald," Brock muttered at himself as he watched Kayla scurry up the steps like a scared little kid. "Jesus." He felt boneless, cored out and empty in a way that confused him. Finding the leather chair right before his knees gave out and left him on the floor, he blew out a breath as he sat.

He felt as if he were moving in super slow-mo. His arms weighed a thousand pounds each as he raised one hand to touch his lips, reliving their incredible kiss only a few minutes ago. He'd been blown away by it. Even as he'd let her take the lead on purpose, knowing that if he came on too strong she'd bolt.

And heaven help him, she'd done it. She'd pressed those soft, perfect lips to his and his entire universe had exploded behind his eyes. The simple act of kissing a woman had never affected him that way, except maybe the first few times he'd experienced it. The kissing bit had always been a pleasant enough pre-tune to the foreplay for him. Something he'd prided himself on, knowing that women used phrases like 'toe curling' and 'panty melting' about that stage with him.

But damn Sam she'd taken him by such surprise he couldn't tell which end was up for a few seconds. She'd tasted of chamomile and vanilla, with a back bite of cinnamon. Her small tongue had probed, uncertain, while she'd been unsure where to put her hands at first, keeping them pressed between them until he'd gotten a hold of himself and pulled her into his arms, where she belonged.

From that moment, when he'd held her so close he could feel her heart pounding against his chest, he'd been done for, a goner, ass over teakettle. Her lips were so sweet, her slim body perfect, he'd almost lost his mind. But again, it was in what he considered to be a normal way.

Sure, he'd popped a woody. What normal man wouldn't have? But it didn't come with the painful urgency that he'd always associated with his typical sexually aroused state. He didn't want to shove a hand up her skirt, or to cup her breasts or clutch her ass. He'd wanted, simply, to kiss her. To put her at her ease in a slow, easy-going way that was so at odds with his usual M.O. it made him dizzy even now.

He swallowed hard and glared at the ceiling, ignoring that fact that his erection was still straining his zipper. He pondered this new-found control as his body worked its way down off the horny edge in a way that didn't piss him off, or make him reach down and jack off so he could breathe. He found that he could breathe just fine. His heart was steady, not racing. His face devoid of the cold sweat that always accompanied arousal.

As he smiled, figuring that it had been a decent start anyway, even if she'd freaked out at the end, he let himself drift. It had been a damn long day – chock full of drama and, in his case, deflection and redirection. The meal had been delicious, although the company had still been strained, thanks to the teenager's chokehold on everyone's emotions.

But they'd made it through two solid days of stress and tomorrow the wedding part would be accomplished, despite Taylor Hettinger's ongoing attempts at sabotage. And he had just kissed the woman he was starting to believe might be the elusive soulmate, despite all their combined thousand-pounds worth of baggage. He chuckled under his breath at the concept, and wandered out onto the deck that spanned the entire width of the house. The tiki torch flames were flickering in the breeze that had picked up in the last hour, so he went around and extinguished them all, his body still languid with anticipated satisfaction, his mind a smooth blank slate.

As he was about to take a seat on one of the cushy lounge chairs, thinking outdoors here might be as good a place as any to sleep, he heard a bizarre, almost animal growl behind him. He turned and caught the full force of a left hook to his nose from nowhere. It sent him spinning backward, where he collided with the deck railing with a loud grunt of pain. At first, he believed that someone had broken into Trent's mansion and was assaulting him first since he was the only one downstairs.

He whirled back around, fists raised and got in a vicious uppercut to someone's ribs and a roundhouse swing to the temple before a cloud slid aside overhead, and the moonlight hit the face of his attacker. Trent was backing away, blinking fast, one hand to his no-doubt broken rib, his other raised and ready to lash out again.

"What the actual fuck, man?" Brock stutter-stepped back and dropped his arms. Maybe Trent had thought he was an intruder, out here lurking in the dark when he had his own place to stay. "It's me, Brock." He held up his hands to let Trent know he'd disarmed himself. "Sorry about the rib—oof." His breath rushed out of him when the man tackled him in the midsection, driving them both to the deck. Still confused, he struggled but the bigger man had him pinned. His nose broke with an audible crack before he could leverage his wits and strength and shove the guy off him. "What the hell is wrong with you? Christ!" He touched his poor nose with a wince, noting that the man was up and coming at him yet again. "Stop!"

Trent hesitated, one fist raised, his eyes shining in the moonlight. "The hell I will," he growled before making another tackling move. Brock was ready for him this time and dodged under his arm. "You fucking shitty excuse for a man, don't you run from me."

"Listen, dude, I'm a lot of things but a shitty excuse ain't one of 'em." His voice was nasally and echoed in his head. "I don't know what happened between our friendly card game and now but if you don't mind telling me before you beat the shit out of me I'd appreciate it."

"Fuck you, douchebag." Trent spit a wad of blood onto the deck then raised his massive fists again. "You're gonna wish you'd never laid a finger on her."

"Wait, hold up." Brock's mind wrapped around that revelation. But Trent was rushing him like a Brahmin bull so he ducked and whirled around, his own fists at the ready. "I don't know what the hell you're talking about. Laid a finger on who?"

"Don't lie to me, you useless junkie dickhead."

"Christ, man, talk to me, will ya? I really don't want to make your face any uglier than it is for your wedding day."

Trent growled and ran at him, managing to shove him back against the railing. The pain in his kidneys was visceral. He let out a loud groan and twisted to one side, not managing to block the blows raining down on his face. They stopped abruptly, as if the beating-Brock-to-a-pulp switch had been flipped to the off position. He slumped forward, his body a mass of agony from his bruised back to his thrashed face.

"What the fuck! Get the hell off me!" Trent was bellowing a few feet away from him. He couldn't see who it was that had saved him, but he had an inkling. "I mean it, Fitzgerald. I'm gonna kill…"

"No, you're not," Austin said from the gloom, his voice as still as the surface of the lake. "Sit. Calm the hell down and tell me what happened."

"I'm not telling you…shit! That's my fucking shoulder, asshole."

"Yeah? Well that's my brother and best I can tell he's been a big help to you these last two days so why don't you get a grip on yourself and tell me what's going on?"

"Fuck off," the bigger man grumbled.

But as Brock wrapped his mind around the pain and got on top of it long enough to take a full breath of air, he realized the steam had gone out of his fight. He lunged for an empty chair, groaning as he sat, still trying to inhale enough oxygen to contribute to the conversation.

"Nope," Austin said as he shoved Trent into a chair, two removed from where Brock sat, gasping like a fish on the sidewalk, marveling how he'd gone from kissing Kayla and relishing how normal he felt about her to this mass of quivering agony, thanks to her brother. Wondering if he needed to get his kidneys checked, he figured if he started pissing blood he'd worry about it. Wouldn't be the first time, after all.

"Fuck me," he grunted as he tried to move his nose back into its proper position.

"You'd better shut up, you goddamned prick," Trent called from across the deck.

"All right, I'll bite," Brock said, his anger rising in the face of whatever shit the other man was slinging at him. "What in the hell did I do? Whose honor did I besmirch?"

"Shut up, or I'm gonna…"

"Sit, God damn you," Austin barked from the doorway. He held two beers and a water bottle. The sight of it made Brock's head ache worse. He could already taste the glorious malt and hops-infused liquid sliding down his throat. But he took the water bottle and downed half of it in a few gulps.

Trent took the beer. Brock studied him as his eyes adjusted further to the moonlit darkness. He took a long slug of it, wiped his lips with a wince, then set it on the table next to him. "You," he said, his long finger pointed straight at Brock. "You…did something to her. You made her want to hurt herself. I found her…tonight…"

Brock rose, his mind clear and focused on one thing. He had to check on Kayla. Now.

He marched past the two men watching him with their mouths agape. Someone grabbed his arm but he jerked himself free without a thought as to who it was. "Touch me again, Hettinger and I'll make sure your future wife doesn't recognize you tomorrow, do you get me?"

"Brock," Austin warned.

"Shut up. I mean, thanks for getting this crazy shithead off me but shut up. I need to check on her."

"She's asleep," Trent said. "And if you think I'm letting you within a country mile of her you'd better have another fucking think, if your addled junkie mind can manage it."

"Guys," Austin pleaded, standing up between them. "Listen, I get it that he's not exactly Prince Charming but you need to back the fuck off a minute," he said to Trent before turning to address Brock. "And you. You need to come clean. What happened? Did you guys…uh…"

"No, not that it's any of your fucking business." His shoulders slumped. His pulse raced with anxiety and worry over Kayla. "Where did you find her? What had she…done?" But he knew already. She'd cut herself. And it had been his fault. "Shit," he said, dropping into the chair next to Trent. "I didn't do anything to her. I swear to God."

"Fuck you, loser," Trent grumbled. But he was holding his beer and looking out across the vast expanse of grass that would tomorrow serve as the scene of his second wedding. "I want to help her but I don't know how." He tossed back the rest of his beer and threw the empty bottle over the deck railing to the grass below. "I can't fucking do this thing. My existing daughter hates my future wife. My future wife is dog-sick twenty-four-seven with my future kid. Ugh." He leaned forward, his elbows on his knees, spitting blood onto the deck surface.

Brock and Austin exchanged a look. Brock took a deep breath. "I didn't do anything to her, Trent. We...we kissed. That was it. And she initiated it. She got upset though, and ran upstairs. End of story."

Trent heaved a huge sigh and lay back, arm over his face. "Do you even know what she's been through?"

Brock frowned. "Yeah. She's an ex-junkie. Booze, painkillers, heroin. The gamut. Same as me. We would've thrown a mean party together, once upon a time."

"No, Brock. That's not all." Trent's words sent a jolt of panic through him. When the man sat up and met his gaze, his eyes were no longer rage ignited. They were flat, exhausted, resigned. "I thought you knew."

"Well," he said, stalling for time as he ran his hand through his hair. "I mean, we've gotten to know each other these last few months. Meetings...and shit." He stopped, realizing how lame that sounded. He didn't know what else the man was talking about but he had a clear and sickening feeling that he didn't want to know. "Maybe she should tell me herself," he said, getting to his feet so he could see for himself that she was all right.

Austin pulled him back down. "I think her brother wants to tell you."

"I'm not sure that's..."

"I am. Sit."

He sat. But all his nerve endings were humming on high alert. When Trent spoke, he kept his face turned away, looking out over his domain. The words poured out of him, slamming into Brock like hurricane-force winds, sending him reeling until he stood and stumbled inside, hands over his ears. He made it to the downstairs bath in time to throw up his dinner. He flushed the toilet but couldn't get up from the floor. He sat, hunched over the bowl, staring into its watery depths. Trent's revelations were bouncing around in his skull, careening off each other and back again. "Oh, God," he moaned, dry heaving until his ribs ached as bad as his lower back.

After rinsing out his mouth, he stood staring at himself, wondering how in the hell the universe had conspired to throw the two of them together. A colossal joke — a big fat cosmic chuckle — that was what it was.

Even as his mind tried to remind him of how she affected him, about how great he felt around her — no longer fighting the sick compulsion to fuck and fuck and fuck some more — he realized it would never, ever work. Not in a million lifetimes. They were doomed to the sort of co-dependent friendship that would end with them ignoring each other out of self-defense.

He closed his eyes against the horror show of his busted nose and swollen face. She filled his consciousness then — her sweet, soft lips, her fragile frame, her smile, her laugh, everything about her that had compelled him for so long until he found himself here, smack dab in the middle of her lifelong nightmare.

The ultimate predator — he'd managed to locate the perfect prey.

That brought on a fresh wave of nausea but he muscled past it, rinsed his mouth again and splashed ice-cold water onto his face. He had to set things straight with Trent. He had to let him and his own brother know that he, Brock, had no intention of doing anything more with her. Of course she had no concept of a healthy sex life and he was the wrongest of wrong guys to teach her how to have one. Him and his disgusting urges, all the faceless, nameless women he'd screwed. The nights he'd spent trolling bars in whatever city he'd flopped in, high as a kite, slugging back water and searching out the ones who'd leave with him and take off his razor-sharp edge for a few hours. The drug-fueled orgies he'd gotten himself into, where he'd wake up the next morning with his head pounding, his mouth coated with slime, and his naked limbs coated in dried sweat.

He stopped halfway through the kitchen, groaning at his stupid old life, furious at the tease of a new life. And wanting a drink so bad it made his eyes water. Austin was at his side then, guiding him past the fridge, past the liquor cabinet, sitting him down on the couch and handing him another water bottle.

"Sorry, man," Trent mumbled. "I didn't mean... I mean, I did, because I thought...oh shit." He tossed back his own water and glared down at the empty bottle. "This is such a fucked-up mess."

"Yeah," Austin said, patting the guy on the shoulder. "But it's almost two in the morning on the night before your wedding. You ought to get some shuteye."

Lightning flashed, followed by a clap of thunder so loud it made the windows rattle. "Oh, good Christ," Trent moaned into his hands. "Now what?"

"Kayla has the tent on standby," he said. "We'll get them on the phone first thing. No worries."

Trent sighed and met his gaze. "I really am sorry, Brock. I don't know what got into me."

"I'll be fine." He hesitated. "She's... She cut herself? Tonight?"

"Yeah. Not too bad, but you know, bad enough."

Brock sighed and sipped his water, already missing her but knowing what he had to do now. A woman who'd lived through the hell Kayla had deserved a much better man. One who could control himself, who didn't have to take drugs to numb his inappropriate urges. "Yes, I do know." He rose. "I should head back to the Inn."

"You can stay here," Trent said.

"No, I can't," he said, his voice firm. "And rest assured, I won't be doing...anything more with your sister. I get it. I'm the polar opposite of the guy she needs."

"I don't know... I don't know anything anymore." Trent's voice was flat.

"Well, I do. And I can tell you without hesitation that you don't have to worry about me laying a hand...or anything else, on your sister."

"She's gonna kill me for telling you."

Brock snorted, wincing at the pain in his nose. Exhaustion washed over him, making him unsteady on his feet. "Guess you should've thought of that before telling me anything. Much less the shit you laid on me tonight." He stood.

His brother and Trent stared up at him. Shaking his head, fury warring with frustration and a looming despair, he took his leave, flinging himself behind the wheel of his truck and squealing out into the dark Petoskey street.

Chapter Eighteen

"I am so, so sorry about this. Shit, God damn it..." Melody's tirade segued into Spanish as she sat in front of the mirror, her face blotchy from crying.

"Well, as big and important as you and Trent might think yourselves, I hate to break it to you that you do not control weather." Kayla kept her tone light as she brushed Melody's long black hair. A bright flare of lightning filled the room. Kayla's neck prickled right before the clap of thunder that followed made her flinch.

"This is not a good start, is it?" Melody sniffled and patted her hair, which hung loose and silky down her back. "As if it were good anyway. All the sunshine and blue skies in the world wouldn't change how much Taylor hates me."

"Oh, it's not as bad as all that," Evelyn assured her.

"Oh, actually it is." Melody's red-rimmed eyes stared at her reflection. "This is a huge mistake. All of it." She let her hand rest on her stomach.

Kayla noted that in her loose, silk dressing gown, you could make out the slightest hint of a baby bump.

"She'll get over herself. Don't let it ruin your day." Kayla fussed around, tidying up for lack of anything better to do. Rain lashed the windows. Lightning and thunder continued their back-and-forth dance.

"Huh, okay. Guess I'll focus on the lovely weather for my midsummer outdoor wedding then." Kayla glanced at Evelyn, but the other woman had her gaze fixed on Melody. Her lips twitched, then she giggled, which made Melody do the same. The two women ended up draped over each other, trying to catch their breath between laughing. Kayla smiled in relief.

"Hey, I think it's letting up a little." She peered through the sliding glass door and took in the fact that it was, in fact, raining even harder. This sent the ladies behind her into more paroxysms of giggles. "Anyway, I'll go check on…things." She ducked into the upper hallway, eager to escape the unhappiness, mixed with borderline hysteria. It made her nervous, twitchy, in need of a drink or a hit.

Brock. She needed to find Brock.

She was unable to suppress the smile as she headed down the steps to the barely controlled chaos in the main room and kitchen. She'd slept so hard the night before, after Trent had tucked her into bed. She woke at six-thirty feeling fresher than she had in years. She'd found Elle and the hired staff bustling around the kitchen, setting out the morning meal while others worked away on the evening's feast.

She and Elle shared a quiet mutual respect, each of them sensing the other's strength after past personal trauma without having to enunciate it. The other woman was more at home in a kitchen than anyone she'd ever seen. Kayla could watch her for hours, moving around the space, managing prep for multiple meals. This morning, Elle had put her in charge of the coffee and tea for breakfast, as well as making sure everyone was up and at it early enough.

Trent had to be dragged from his bed, which surprised everyone as he was always one of the first one of them awake. But she figured it for nerves. Evelyn had intimated that the men had stayed up way late, well past the time she and Brock had been left alone together. He'd managed to avoid her, which worked, as she was embarrassed at the scene she'd made in his nice bathroom that he'd had to jump in and handle.

She pressed her fingertips to her lips, reliving the amazing kiss, as every inch of her skin tingled from the memory.

"Where's Brock?" she asked the crowd in the kitchen and great room.

"Haven't seen him yet," Ross said as he distracted fussy toddler Rose around on the floor. Only a little irritated by this, she refilled water glasses and took a quick look out onto the top of the massive white tent she'd ordered at seven-thirty that morning. The installers were wrestling with the wind while attaching the sides with their fake windows. She'd also had them bring in more gas heaters and extra strings of lights. She still couldn't quite get over how easy things became when there was plenty of money to spend.

Elle had set up her staging area for food in the walkout basement, using the almost-as-big-as-upstairs kitchen down there for ease of service later so the whole house was already teeming with people, which rubbed her the wrong way, for no good reason.

Brock. She needed to lay eyes on him. To be eased by his wink and smile as he went about his caretaking duties for the day. She pulled out her phone and sent a quick text.

Hey. You're slacking. Get your ass over here. Pretty please?

She waited a few beats then followed that with:

I'm sorry I wigged out last night. It was a nice moment and I ruined it. But I won't the next time. I'm sort of not good at the kissing thing. I'll explain why someday.

She frowned when the little 'delivered' message didn't show up right away. But when Taylor appeared in the kitchen doorway, she allowed it to distract her.

"Hi. Want something to eat real quick? I've got to run these up to Melody. I'll be right back."

The girl didn't speak, just moved aside so Kayla could get past her.

"You should get a shower, Tay. I know we've got some hours to go still but…"

"Whatever."

With a sigh, she headed upstairs, deciding to give Mr. Invisible a call. She needed his help today. After handing off the water glasses to the now-recovered Melody and Evelyn, she ducked into her room and touched 'call' next to Brock's name on her text screen. The sound of his voice requesting that she "leave a message" that hit her ears after only one ring made her anxiety ramp up fast.

Recalling what a mess he'd been upon arrival two days ago, she stuck her head into Melody's room and motioned for Evelyn to join her in the hall. She glanced around, nervous and fidgety. "Hey, what's wrong?" Evelyn put cool hands on her upper arms, which made Kayla instantly recoil for fear the woman would see the mess she'd made of her own skin there. "Sorry."

"No, I'm… It's okay, but, um, do you know if Austin's heard from Brock this morning?"

Evelyn frowned and crossed her arms. "I don't know. I haven't talked to him since last night. He was dead asleep when I got up with Rose. Ross was up so I handed her over to him once Melody needed me."

Before Kayla could explain her concern, Trent's bedroom door opened, revealing him in his full, fight-club-faced glory. "Oh, my God and sonny Jesus in Heaven, Hettinger, what have you done?" Evelyn whisper-shouted.

He blinked fast, as if confused, then sighed. "Oh, right." He touched his swollen nose. "Got into a bit of a…"

"Whatever it is, it's nothing compared to what Melody's gonna do when she sees you."

"Yeah, I know. So can you help me out and make sure she doesn't see me until she has to marry me later today?" He shot Kayla a weak smile. Her Brock radar pinged like mad. She took a step toward her brother. He took a corresponding step back.

"What did you do, T?" She glared at him. He averted his gaze like the little kid he'd once been, confronted by her for some trivial, childhood reason. "Look at me."

He dragged his gaze up and met hers. His eyes were bloodshot. One of them would be a brilliant purple and gray by tonight, she knew. The hand he kept pressed to his side gave away that he had bruised ribs or worse.

All of a sudden, she knew what had happened. Anger filled her skull, followed by embarrassed horror.

"You fought with him," she said, her words matter-of-fact.

"Fought with who?" Evelyn demanded. But Kayla kept her focus on Trent. He nodded and looked at the floor again. The incongruity of this—of her tall, strong, rich-as-God brother unable to meet her angry gaze—was lost on her as she felt her knees wobble. "What's going on?"

"Hey," Melody called from her doorway. "What's all the whispering about?"

Evelyn glanced over her shoulder then moved so she and Kayla were blocking the possible view of Trent's mangled pre-wedding face. "Nothing," she called out while glaring at Trent, whose face flushed even darker under her scrutiny. "Get back in there and take that bath I told you to take already."

"Is that *mi esposo*? I want to see him."

"No!" Kayla and Evelyn both yelped as they turned to face her and Trent slunk back into his room. "Don't be silly," Evelyn segued, smooth as silk. "It's bad luck. Now get your ass in there and soak it. Pronto!"

Melody's dark eyes narrowed at the two of them. Kayla slapped a reassuring smile on her face but when the woman gave up and shut the bedroom door behind her, she almost slid to the floor. "Jesus," she muttered into her hands.

"Okay, first things first," Evelyn insisted. "I'm going to get Austin up and over to the Inn to check on Brock. You"—she pointed to the closed door—"you're on keep-Trent-out-of-her-sight duty."

"Okay, but..." Kayla stopped, unwilling to share anything with this tall, imposing and obviously pissed-off female. "Fine. I've got her. But tell Brock to call me or something?"

Evelyn sighed. "I will. Where's Taylor?"

"Sulking around but I hear a shower so maybe she's at least doing that."

At that moment, a toddler-issued howl rose from downstairs. "Shit," Evelyn muttered, glancing at her watch. "I'm gonna leave that for Ross. Go on." She pointed to Melody's door again. "Keep her calm and away from your brother until the last possible moment."

Kayla nodded and headed for Melody's door, her heart pounding with worry over Brock and what had happened between him and Trent while she'd been passed out the night before. Distracting Melody distracted her for an hour or so, but when the time came to help her into her dress—a gorgeous, custom-made cream silk sheath that highlighted her deep bronze skin and raven's-wing black hair—she still hadn't heard a word about Brock's whereabouts or wellbeing.

She snuck out of her assignment room, leaving Melody lying quietly on her bed in her dressing gown a few more minutes, and headed downstairs, wishing she could hear his voice sorting through the chaos as only he could. But all she found when she got to the great room were Ross, still with Rose, who was fussing louder than ever, and Austin who was staring out onto the rain-lashed deck, his phone clutched in one hand. When she touched his shoulder, he flinched.

"Any word?"

He shook his head and glared down at his device. Deciding that adding her panic to his wasn't a good use of either of their time right now, she smiled at him and turned away, keeping her worries to herself.

Guests began arriving about an hour later, guided from vans by the staff equipped with giant umbrellas around to the tent that now encompassed the entire back yard. Over a hundred people were expected, including the Governor and First Lady, so parking arrangements had been made with a couple of hotels, and shuttles scheduled, even before the weather had turned to absolute shit.

Thankful she and Brock had decided to get the extra lighting, heaters and seating, Kayla watched from an upstairs window, willing him to materialize from one of the vans, smile up at her and head indoors, forgoing the umbrellas for the sake of haste. But as hard as she tried, she couldn't conjure him.

"Hey, Earth to Kayla, time to dress the bride." Evelyn's voice was high and bright which gave her stress away.

"You bitches are being weird, now," Melody insisted as she sat pulling a brush through her long, silky hair. "Come clean. What's wrong? I mean, other than the obvious." She held up a hand as the wind howled around the corners of the house.

They exchanged a look which Kayla realized was a mistake, given the guilty nature of it. Melody rose, smoothed her hands over her dressing gown and marched past them to the door. Evelyn moved fast, blocking her way. "Oh no you don't. We have to put your dress on you and get you downstairs. Your guests and future hubby await." Her smile was huge and fake.

"Move out of my way," Melody insisted, her voice a low, almost-growl. "There's something wrong with Trent and I want to see him. Now."

Kayla put a hand on Melody's arm, but she threw her off, still glaring at Evelyn who hadn't budged from her spot blocking the door. "I mean it. Move."

The women managed a few more seconds of stare-down, then Evelyn slumped and shifted to one side. Melody yanked the door open and bolted out into the hall. Kayla remained where she was, between the bed which was draped with the dress and veil, and the window which revealed the tent flapping in the wind that had only gotten stronger in the last hour. She was frozen in place, horrified by this whole mess and convinced it was all her fault. She'd ruined Melody's weekend with her silly behavior that had forced Trent to do something he shouldn't have.

A loud shriek of surprise from somewhere in the long hallway unfroze her. She rushed out behind Evelyn, heart in her throat, skidding to a stop on the hardwood floor when she nearly ran smack into Melody's back. The woman was babbling in Spanish, hands on her hips, glaring at someone Kayla couldn't see at first. But of course, it was her brother, with his cage-fighter face.

"Come on, honey. It's nothing. He's fine," Evelyn was saying, trying to tug Melody away. "You need to watch your blood pressure."

"Get off me," Melody cried, holding out her arms. "What did you do? You..." More Spanish that she assumed Trent understood. He'd gone out of his way to learn it, she knew, once he'd figured out he was head over heels for Melody Rodriguez. "That's it," she finished in English. "This marriage is doomed." She whirled to face Evelyn and Kayla, her eyes wild, her face sweaty. "Call it off. Call it all off!"

Kayla glanced around the woman at her brother, who stood looking amazing in his dark suit with a single deep red rose in his lapel. Well, perfect but for his face, which was now swollen up so much he was almost unrecognizable. "Jesus, T," she muttered, turning to try to help Evelyn calm the bride.

"I mean it," Melody screeched at Trent. "This is just another God damned sign."

"But…" He walked toward her but she backed away, both hands held up in front of her.

"Stay away from me. You go down there and tell all those people to fucking leave!"

"Hey, what's with all the noise?" Taylor joined their little party, stepping out of her bedroom dressed in the light-blue sundress she'd chosen for her maid-of-honor duties. She was beautiful, Kayla couldn't help but note, with upswept hair and tan skin. "Dad?" She moved to her father, who was standing with his hands jammed into his trouser pockets. When he met her gaze, she gave a little gasp but, to her credit, didn't add to the general freak-out. "Wow, so…" She turned to Melody who was spitting out Spanish a mile a minute as she backed toward her bedroom door. "Mel, hang on a minute."

Everyone, Melody included, stared at her. She'd never once called her future stepmother anything but "step monster" as a half-joke that they'd all let slide to avoid acknowledging it. Melody's mouth gaped open as she stopped the invectives mid-stream. The wind howled. Rose kept up her ongoing whining. Kitchen staff clattered around downstairs.

Melody closed her mouth and straightened, crossing her arms and glaring down the hall at Trent. "Your father…"

"Is so madly in love with you it's sickening," Taylor finished for her.

"But look at him!" She pointed at Trent's face, which had gotten even more gross in the last few minutes. "He's...ruined this, as if it weren't ruined already."

Taylor moved toward her but Melody backed away. "Don't even pretend you like me. I know you don't. *Dios Mio*...this just isn't meant to be." She hit the wall next to her door and slid down.

Evelyn started for her, but Kayla held out a hand, keeping her gaze on the teenager, who moved fast and was crouched in front of Melody in a flash.

"T, go out there and tell everyone we've had a slight delay of game," she said, while Taylor spoke quietly to Melody. He walked up to her and was headed for his daughter and fiancée but Kayla stopped him, too. "No. Go do what I told you. Christ, you're like a monster. But I still love you. And so does she. Now go." She shoved at his shoulder. He glanced at the women muttering to each other on the floor, then back at Kayla. "It's all right. We've got this. We'll be down in..." She checked her watch. "Forty-five minutes. Open up the bar. Since it's all under one tent now, everyone can have a drink while they wait."

Rose let out another loud howl. Evelyn winced. "I really need to spell Ross. Austin's out in the tent already, schmoozing."

"Okay, Taylor and I will handle Melody. You go on." Kayla felt calm and in control, even happy for the distracting chaos. Evelyn nodded. "Make sure he gets out to the tent," she said, indicating Trent who was still lurking around looking helpless. As Evelyn marched him to the stairway, Rose let out another cry, this one of pure delight.

"Boooooock! Bock! Bock!"

Kayla's face blazed hot. Evelyn dragged Trent with her as Taylor pulled a crying Melody to her feet. She was torn, wanting so desperately to see Brock while at the same time knowing she had to stay here, to keep this positive momentum going.

When his voice rose up the stairs and hit her ears, relief coated her nerves, calming her enough so she could help Taylor guide the bride back into her room.

"*There's* the most beautiful little girl ever," were the words filling her brain as she closed the bedroom door and helped Taylor put Melody back together.

Chapter Nineteen

The wedding, once underway, was beautiful, despite the howling winds and off-and-on blinking of the lights inside the tent. It had been helped along by alcohol lubrication during the near hour and a half it took to coax Melody back into bride mode and get her own dress — a pale yellow version of the blue one worn by Taylor and the light green one worn by Evelyn — on and her face made up for the occasion.

Even Trent looked a little better, aided no doubt by the dim lighting in the tent. And when he saw her — the gorgeous Melody in her perfect dress, her hair flowing like an inky waterfall down her back — he lit up in a way that almost made everyone forget the condition of his face.

Brock had elected to keep the restless toddler up at the house for the ceremony, which disappointed her since she hadn't laid eyes on him once and her need to do that was becoming visceral, like a taste in the back of her throat she wanted to experience. But for now, she was beyond thrilled that this damn wedding was almost over. As her brother and Melody spoke their brief vows, she saw Taylor's eyes fill with tears, which set her off — something she'd sworn not to do. But the girl had been incredible earlier, convincing Melody that if she didn't marry her dad, the man would jump off the Mackinac Bridge or something just as dire.

When it came time for the kiss, even Kayla got embarrassed by the enthusiasm of it but joined the crowd cheering for the couple, whose lip-lock was something out of a fairy tale as far as she could tell. Finally, they parted and only had eyes for each other for a few seconds, before turning to the crowd, their faces alight, both sets of eyes bright with emotion. The jolt of jealousy Kayla experienced was eclipsed when Taylor, who'd been standing between her and Melody, gave first her father, then her new stepmother a huge hug and kiss.

The event flipped into a different mode, while half a dozen staff dismantled the chairs and altar, and transformed the now double-sized tent into a spectacular party space. Kayla hugged her brother and Melody then left them to their guests. She'd agreed to help Elle supervise the food table setup, while Ross managed the bar, which kept herself distracted for the next hour and half that she barely noticed Brock's continued absence.

But once the buffet tables had been cleared of their tapas-style offerings and it was time for the cake-cutting and other silly rituals, Kayla decided she needed a break and headed inside. Half hoping she'd run into Brock and half wanting to lie down and sleep for a few days straight, she trudged up the steps and into the mudroom where they'd had their first moment a few days ago. Now, the room served as a staging area for all the empty wine and beer bottles, and the aroma hit her like a wall of alcohol.

She staggered backward, thinking she might be better off back down in the basement. There were also a couple of bedrooms she could hide in while the party got serious. She heard laughter and music over the still-howling wind and pounding rain. The basement was deserted but for a few of the hired help, cleaning off dishes and stacking them in their cases for return to the rental company. The laughter ramped up, took on a raucous edge, before she heard feminine squeals and various other sounds.

It all made her exhausted. She'd had her fill of family togetherness this last week. She couldn't wait to get home to her quiet, small space and back to her calm life. As she wandered around the massive space that opened out onto the lawn under the deck and leading to the back of the tent, she even felt a kernel of anticipation over what might happen next with Brock.

As uneasy — as downright terrified — as she was at the thought of taking their incredible kiss to the next level or stage or whatever you called it, she also had to admit that she looked forward to it. Even if it meant awkwardness at first. She was ready to tell him everything. There would be no secrets between them. She would reveal her past as abuse victim, as survivor, and maybe, just maybe, they could craft some kind of an adult relationship out of the ashes of their pasts.

The thought made her grin widen. She touched her fingertips to her lips, reliving last night's encounter.

A flicker of movement at the tent flap caught her eye. The rain had let up in the last few minutes she'd spent in some weird la-la-land of romantic fantasy so she ducked out from under the deck and walked across the sodden grass, eager to catch up with him. The DJ was getting cranked up. The bouquet had been thrown. The cake had been smashed into faces and now lay cut into dozens of pieces on a side table.

Kayla craned her neck around trying to catch sight of him in the crowd. Finally, she saw little Rose up high, sitting on Brock's shoulders. She had hold of his hair with one hand and the other thumb jammed into her mouth. She didn't look like she wanted to party.

"Hey! Brock!" she called out, waving at him. But he must not have heard her because he turned away and headed to a soft seating area in one corner, where Melody perched on Trent's lap, holding court with friends and family and other guests. Cursing under her breath, she shouldered her way over there, determined to speak to him, to ask if he'd like to get away from this scene for a bit, take a walk or something now that the rain had stopped.

He kept his back to her, talking to Austin and a few other brewery types, while Rose kept a death grip on his hair. Kayla glanced up at her in time to see that her eyes were drooping closed. She reached out and caught the child as she was sliding off Brock's shoulders.

"Hey," he said, spinning around.

Kayla held Rose close and smiled at him, until she saw that his face looked even worse than Trent's. He smiled. Then, as if flipping a switch, he frowned and faced away from her again, as if she weren't even standing there. Reality rushed back in, filling in all the silly, empty spaces she'd been inhabiting, thinking she'd be allowed to have anything like a normal life, or a normal, healthy adult relationship.

Unable to speak, she backed away, holding the toddler, shaking her head until she headed inside, tears blurring her vision. She heard him calling her as she headed into the basement, but she ignored him, intent on escape, on her own room, her bed, her own solitary life.

Chapter Twenty

Brock's entire body felt encased in concrete. His mind was sluggish. Even his heartbeat seemed slow as he watched Kayla run into the house with Rose. The sight of her had lifted his spirits, as it always did. But then, before he could say or do anything, he remembered Trent's words. The brutal description of her God-awful life, abused by countless men, which had no doubt led to her various addictions.

Nausea rose in his gut but as he hadn't managed to eat anything since puking the night before, nothing happened, other than saliva filling his mouth for a few seconds. After a quick check to make sure Trent wasn't watching, he ran after her, calling her name, unsure what he'd do or say if she stopped and faced him but unable not to do it.

He'd lain awake the entire night once he'd made it back to the Inn. The place smelled mildewy and gross, convincing him that he'd either talk his mother into selling it or commit some of her vast funds to improve it. The old sounds he and Austin had labeled as ghosts during some of their summer nights spent there followed him as he'd paced through the cavernous living and dining rooms, the empty kitchen, the old parlor.

By six a.m. he'd been in his car and determined to head back to Grand Rapids. As he'd pondered his various, viable excuses, all of them hinging on Austin backing him up about a "problem at the brewery," he'd played the memory loop of their kiss through his mind over and over again.

It had been, in a word, perfection. It had been beyond that, were there a word for such a thing. He'd never in his entire almost forty years of life felt so at ease kissing a woman. In one or more of his many sex addict anonymous meetings, he'd heard about this. Stories of men and women cured by the love of a soulmate. As a dyed-in-the-wool cynic when it came to love and all its attendant bullshit, he'd always scoffed, convinced that while it may be a stopgap, once he was addicted to sex the way he'd been, he'd always be that way, soulmate or no.

But last night, he thought he comprehended the concept. Kayla brought out something in him he'd never believed he possessed—a kind, gentle, loving, normal demeanor. He could be the guy who, while he wouldn't argue with the opportunity to hop in the sack and enjoy a tumble with Kayla, was not a raving lunatic of testosterone-driven ugliness. He was no rapist, of course. He'd never, ever had sex with a woman without her consent. The problem was, consent had sometimes gotten a little slippery when all the drugs he'd used to get high and stay that way for hours had taken hold of his brain.

No. He was hands-down a monster. No better than Kayla's stepfather or the men after him. He had to let her go. He'd only hurt her, and she didn't deserve any more hurt.

He leaned against the open sliding glass door, listening to the happy sounds of the wedding turning into a dance party. With a sigh, he closed his eyes and felt Kayla in his arms again.

"Fuck." He headed out onto the wet grass, not even hearing the distant warning rumbles of thunder or feeling the initial pinpricks of more rain on his face. Space. He needed it like he needed oxygen. His skin burned. His heart was pounding so fast it almost deafened him. Shame filled every corner of his being. Mortification at everything he'd done or said in the pursuit of pussy for almost twenty-three years of his useless life made his chest ache as he stumbled on the sand on his way to the dock. Seeking distance, space, breathing room.

The ants were joined by an army of mosquitoes, treating him to repeated tiny stings on his exposed skin as he remained on his hands and knees, trying to catch his breath. He'd taken his meds on time, as usual. Done his check-in with Austin at four-thirty to confirm it.

But the fact remained that he did not want to be here at all. Had not planned to be, but for a phone call he'd made as he'd sat, shivering in the heat of his car, attempting to man up and get his ass where it belonged, no matter his horror at seeing Kayla again. He'd called the number on autopilot, not sure why and not even aware he'd done it until he'd heard her familiar voice in his ear.

"Hello? Brock? You there?"

He'd sat, breathing heavily like the perv he was, trying to formulate coherence.

"Brock? Are you okay?" Caroline's voice sounded concerned.

"No," he'd managed as he'd wiped a hand down his sweaty face. "No. I'm not."

"Where are you?"

"In Petoskey. I'm supposed to be going to Trent and Melody's wedding, but I'm thinking about ditching it."

"Why?"

"I… It's complicated."

"Are you taking your meds? Going to meetings still?"

"Yeah, I am." He'd run his hands along the expensive leather steering wheel, feeling himself rev up at the sound of her voice. It had been sickening in its familiarity but at least he'd understood it. His dick had been so hard he'd had to unzip to relieve the pressure as he'd leaned his head back against the headrest.

"Brock, honey, why are you calling me?"

"I need…to hear your voice. You're the only one who fucking understands me, Caro."

"Bullshit," she'd said, but her voice had been soft and sexy. He'd groaned as his back teeth had begun buzzing, like he'd been biting down on tin foil.

"What about Kayla? Isn't she there?"

The sound of Caroline speaking Kayla's name had been like a pinprick to his inflated libido. His brain had fuzzed over and he'd been able to take full, deep breaths for the first time in hours. "Yes," he'd said, his voice breaking a little. "She is. How do you…? Never mind. I'm sure…"

"Austin told me, just in case you did call or show up or pull one of your usual, um…stunts."

"Ah, I see." A spark of fury had ignited behind his eyes. "So you know about her."

"A little," she'd admitted. "I'm… I'm happy for you, Brock. You know that, right?"

"There's nothing to be happy about, I assure you. She's… She's an abuse victim, Caroline. She was raped by not only by her stepfather but by a bunch of his buddies before she ran away and hit the streets. Which is when she added junkie to her résumé. I can't…" He'd pressed his palms against the wheel, trying to drive out the urge to kill the men who'd done that to her.

"Oh, God. That's awful. But she's all right now? You guys go to meetings together and stuff, right?"

"Yeah." He'd swiped his nose, wishing he had something normal in his damn life.

"Well then, I suggest you get your ass to that wedding. I'll bet you've been helpful. You always were great under pressure."

He'd snorted but had felt an easing of his stress at her words. "I can't," he'd whispered, needing her to say more to convince him, to remind him that he wasn't a useless douchebag of an addict posing as a man, as Trent had so poetically described him the night before.

"Yes. You can. Now go on, scoot. Enjoy the rest of the weekend, and be a friend to Kayla, if nothing else, okay? For me?"

He'd ground his teeth. "I…loved you. A lot."

"I know you did. But we all know how that turned out."

"Are you happy…there, in D.C.?" He'd wanted to hear that she was miserable, broke, hating life and as single as fuck.

"Yes. I love it. My job is amazing. And…"

"Great. Cool. Say no more, please." He'd straightened up, not even sure why he had any right to be jealous of her life. She deserved the best. She always had. They all did. They all deserved not to be hampered by him.

"Go on, Brock. Stop being a pussy."

"Nice mouth, Miss Thing."

"I mean it. You really are an amazing man when you put your damn mind to it. Go prove that…to her." Her voice had dipped at the end, as if she hadn't wanted to say it.

He'd ended the call, turned the car around and driven straight here. But had gone well out of his way to avoid seeing Kayla as long as he could. Now, having seen her, he believed that his heart might break. Such sappy bullshit—but nothing was more true.

He got to his feet as lightning split the evening sky and thunder filled the world. With a primal roar of his own, Brock tilted his head up and accepted the rain to his hot face. He was soaked through to his skin in seconds but it felt great. The lightning made him laugh. The thunder answered with more growling as he stood there, willing himself into some other life.

"You are a nut job," a voice broke through all the noise. "What is the matter with you?"

He wiped the rain out of his eyes and stared down at her, at Kayla, the woman he believed he loved— the way adult people are supposed to love. And the woman he had to reject, outright, to save them both.

"That is a proven fact," he said, not smiling at her. "And the answer to your question would fill a fucking book so I'll spare you." He shook his head, spraying water in all directions like a dog. The rain had let up some but not stopped. She stood in her bridesmaid's dress and a dark denim jacket, almost as soaked as he was even though she was gripping a tiny umbrella.

"So you duked it out with my baby brother last night, eh?"

He blinked then touched his sore nose. "Yeah. He had some points he needed to make."

"About me," she said, her eyes darkening.

He looked straight up, opening his mouth and drinking the rain for a few seconds by way of evasion.

"Tell me what happened, Brock. All of it." Her hand gripped his biceps, which put her close, way too close, for his comfort.

"It's between me and him." He pulled away from her.

"Why won't you look at me, then?" she demanded, yanking him around again, surprising him with her strength. "What did I do to deserve this cold shoulder bullshit?"

"Nothing. I'm not... I didn't mean to... Shit." His shoulders slumped. Rain ran down his face but he couldn't feel it.

A loud shout of laughter and other noises waxed and waned from the tent behind them as people came and went, slogging through the rain, some of them stopping to kiss or otherwise make out in the near-dark. "Missing a good party." He motioned behind her.

"Yeah, what else is new? Brock, you'd better tell me what's going on in your head. I just... I mean last night I... I did something I never thought I'd do, much less enjoy. And I enjoyed it a lot."

"I did too. But Kayla..."

"Don't you 'but Kayla' me. What the fuck is going on? Why didn't you come back this morning? Where *are* you right now?"

Frustration filled his head. "I'm here God damn it. Right in front of you."

"No, you're not. You're some other damn place. And if you don't tell me what is going on I'm going inside and you can forget anything else with me."

He reached out for her then let his hand drop. "Maybe that's for the best," he said in a whisper.

"What did you say?"

"I said…"

But he couldn't finish because she had launched herself at him and had her arms around his neck and her lips on his before he could say anything else. The sensation of sinking into her, into this moment, suffused him as it had done the previous night. The taste of her mouth, the way her body fit to his, made his mind go blank as he kissed her back, desperate to communicate something, anything, before he had to give her the news that they would never, could never, be more than friends.

But dear God help him he loved this, loved her so much right then, the urge to somehow overcome it all together, to give it even more of a college try than he'd been doing for the past few years overcame him. He dropped to his knees, pulling her with him. The sand bit into his kneecaps. The rain pelted them, soaking their faces and hair again as they clicked teeth and bumped noses in an unpracticed way.

The urge to protect her, to have her trust him was stronger than anything — even stronger than the desire to make love to her and prove how a real man treated a woman, although that compulsion was gaining a firm foothold. Could he do it? Would she trust him? He cradled her face with his hands as he broke from her, giving her lips one last swipe with the tip of his tongue.

As she stared up at him with those huge, green-brown eyes, he realized that the answer to the question was a profound "no". He let go of her and dropped onto his heels, breathing heavy, his eyes burning with tears he didn't know how to shed. "I'm sorry," he said when she tilted his chin up so he was forced to look at her. "I'm so, so, so sorry, Kayla."

"Sorry about what?" But she seemed wary all of a sudden, on guard in a way she hadn't been with him in months. It ripped at his guts, but he knew it for what it was. She was afraid of him. As she damn well should be. He reached for her, wanting to kiss her, to reassure her, but she jumped to her feet, clutching her arms close to her sides. "Sorry. About. What?" Each word was a knife blade to his chest.

He rose, keeping his distance, watching her expression morph from wary to furious in an eye blink.

"Hey! What's going on over there?" Trent's voice broke through the silent standoff. "K, are you all right?"

She kept her angry gaze on Brock but spoke to Trent, who'd approached them, beer in one hand, suit coat off and tie askew. "You," she said. "You told him."

"Honey, I don't know what you're…"

"You betrayed me, Trent," she said, her voice raising with every word. "You…you nosy jerk!" She was screaming by the end, backing away from them both. "You had no God damned right to tell anybody."

Trent glanced at Brock, but Brock had nothing left. He'd gone and done it again. Hurt her without meaning to. Making this whole mess even worse.

"Kayla," Trent said, trying to lunge for her. But he was halfway to drunktown. Brock could smell the booze on him. He stumbled and dropped onto the sand, leaving Kayla standing over him. Brock helped him up just as the heavens broke open and spilled what felt like a gallon of water on them all at once.

"I hate you," she screamed over the noise. "I fucking hate you both!"

As he watched, his body once again encased in concrete, Kayla ran across the lawn and up the deck stairs, leaving the two of them staring after her with their swollen eyes and busted noses.

"Gosh, that went well," Brock said.

Trent glared at him through the bruises. "You're an asshole," he muttered. "But if you don't go up there and talk to her, calm her down and tell her you don't care about her past, I'm gonna throw you off the fucking boat back there."

Brock lifted his chin. "I thought you didn't want me within a country mile of her."

"I don't. But my wife reminded me that I am not in charge of her, or of you. If you're the one to make her happy, you'd best get on that, pronto."

Brock sighed. "I can't do it, man. I'm...a shit. I don't deserve—"

"Fucking-A, Fitzgerald, get over yourself already. Be a man. Be the man my sister deserves." He lifted a fist. Brock waited for the blow but it never came. And when he opened his eyes into the rain again, Trent was gone.

Chapter Twenty-One

Three weeks later

"My God, this place..." Melody walked in after her long honeymoon in southern France, looking healthy, happy and very pregnant. "What sort of miracles have you worked in here, Kayla?"

Kayla blushed but kept tidying the glassware. She had no real concept of how to take an honest compliment, so she deflected them or ignored them altogether. "I changed a few things. I hope you don't mind too much."

"Hell no I don't. This layout is a million times better." As she eased herself onto a bar stool in the quiet before a busy fall Friday night, Melody exhaled with relief. "My feet... Your brother made me walk all over France, I swear it." She leaned forward, peering at the sketch book Kayla had left open near the service area of the bar. "You're chock full of surprises," she said, turning the thing around. "This is beautiful."

Kayla reached for it and slapped it shut, her face flushing hotter. "It's nothing. Therapy shit. You know." She'd been obsessed with drawing kids lately. Little kids playing, eating, sleeping, all in normal homes. But her drawings contained something darker. Every child she drew seemed miserable and terrified — at total odds with their apparent happy surroundings. They haunted her. But she couldn't stop drawing them.

As she tucked the book under the bar, she changed the subject, taking the opportunity to fill Melody in on everything she'd missed. While they were catching up, Kayla sensed herself relaxing, re-inhabiting her happy place — the one she pretty much only found here, at work in the FitzPub, pouring booze she could never drink.

"All right, *chica*, I'm gonna check the back of the house and spend a few hours on my computer. Trent wouldn't even let me bring the thing, you know. Such a bossy pants, that man."

Kayla smiled at the sight of her new sister-in-law, thrilled beyond measure at the fact of her, that the woman had gone out of her way to find her and pull her into Trent's universe. Something she doubted she would ever have done on her own. Which meant she never would have met Brock, of course.

The thought of him sent dark clouds scudding across her blue-sky attitude. He'd avoided her like the very plague since the wedding weekend. Hell, he'd managed to avoid her the rest of the wedding night. Not that she'd made herself accessible. She'd run inside, taken a long hot shower and fought the urge to cut herself for a few hours before falling into bed while the rest of the guests danced and drank the night away not far below her. The next morning, he'd been long gone by the time she'd made it down to the kitchen for a quiet breakfast while everyone else had slept off their hangovers.

She'd resumed her life, slipping back into it with ease while Trent and Melody honeymooned overseas and Taylor spent the month with her mother. It had been a relief. But she missed him more than she'd ever thought possible. And every day it got worse.

Her phone buzzed its way across the bar where she'd left it. She picked it up, her pulse racing at the sight of the number.

"Hello, is this Kayla Hettinger?"

"Yes, hi." She walked around to the other side of the bar and sat before she fell over.

"Hi. This is Andrew Walker with Child Protective Services."

"Yes, I know." She winced. "Sorry. I'm just…eager to know the answer."

"Yes, well, ah… I'm afraid I don't have great news for you."

"Oh." She picked up a coaster and bent it in half, trying to keep from cursing the guy out. "So…the answer is no."

"I'm afraid so. Your history, you see. You've been committed for drug addiction and you have a police record. I realize that you've turned things around but…"

"But I'm still a useless junkie and can't foster that little girl."

"That's about the sum of it, yes."

"Can you tell me one thing?"

"I can try."

"Is she safe? Is she with a real family? Not one who fosters for the extra dough?"

"I can't... Hang on a second." She heard some shuffling around and the click of a door. "Ms. Hettinger, I'm not allowed to tell you anything about the child."

"About June, you mean."

"Yes, June. But..." He hesitated. "We have a family that's trying to adopt her, not just foster her."

"Oh." Kayla knew she should feel happy for little June Dessen—the baby who'd clung to her for dear life that God-awful afternoon in the hospital. But she didn't. She'd wanted to believe that her face-to-face plea to the Child Services people would have convinced them. But once a junkie, always a junkie. "Good," she said, trying like hell to distance herself from it, from the girl, from the whole thing. "Thank you." As she was about to end the call before she embarrassed herself by bursting into tears, the guy stopped her with his next words.

"I did check to see if they'd let you volunteer somewhere. You know, so you can help other kids. Not every agency's amenable to people with records like yours but..."

"But?"

"I'm going to email you a list of places that said they'd consider your application. I suggest you try one of them, if you want to help."

"Okay. I will. Gotta go." She ended the call and gripped the phone for a few seconds, forcing herself down and away from the irrational anger. *June Dessen is going to be adopted, not fostered. She's going to be fine. Move on with your life, now, Kayla.*

She straightened her shoulders and got to work for the night, shoving baby June and grownup Brock out of her head as best she could. When Trent landed in one of the bar chairs, there to pick Melody up a while early so he could have a beer and talk to her, the sight of him made her ears buzz. She hadn't wanted to ruin Melody's wedding weekend any more than it had already been tainted by the weather and various trauma-dramas so she'd acted as normal as possible around her brother.

But she would never, ever forgive him for spilling the truth about her disgusting past to Brock, no matter his motivation. As he settled in, trying to get her to look at him so he could gauge the level of her anger, she ducked into the kitchen to avoid him. When Melody wandered out of her office, packed to go home, she smiled at Kayla and tried to pull her out into the bar. "Let's get dinner, just the three of us. You're off in twenty and it's not busy anymore."

"No, no, thanks. You guys go on. I have...some things to do."

Melody peered at her, her dark eyes concerned. "What did he do?"

"Who? What? Nothing," she insisted as she bent to putting silverware and napkin packets together.

"I'm sorry, but that's not how this family is going to operate." She put her hands over Kayla's, forcing her to drop the napkin. "It's taken us too long to get our collective act together, Kayla. And I'm not going to waste any more time lying to each other. Tell me what's wrong."

Kayla sighed. "Can we not do this here?" She jerked her chin toward the kitchen staff.

"Fine. Come with me." She leaned out into the bar. "Trent, *mi amore*, join us in my office, please?"

"No... Melody, please."

"Excuse me, but did you not hear me a few seconds ago?" The woman's eyes flashed. Kayla bit her lip, realizing that she had nothing in the face of her sister-in-law's strong personality. "I thought so. Now, come on."

She and Trent sat in the chairs across from Melody, who sat behind her desk, her hands folded on the surface in front of her. "So, who's going to tell me what's going on?"

Trent glanced at Kayla then at his wife. "I told Brock about her...about the abuse. The night before the wedding. We fought, as you know, because I thought he'd hurt her. That he'd put some bullshit move on her which had made her cut herself." He lifted his chin. "I stand by it, though. He needed to know."

Melody's eyes widened. She glanced at Kayla for confirmation. Kayla nodded, her guts roiling. Everyone knew about her—about how disgusting and filthy she was. She shivered, picturing herself in one of many hotel rooms, waiting for whatever man was paying her stepfather. "I need to go." She stood. "Now that we're all clear here."

Melody motioned for her to sit then turned to face her new husband. "Trent, that is a serious betrayal of Kayla's trust. I don't blame her for being mad at you." Her nostrils were flaring. Kayla could tell she was keeping a tight rein on her anger and admired her for it.

Trent sighed and slumped into his chair. Kayla almost forgave him then. Last thing he deserved was both his wife and his sister ganging up on him. But then she recalled how Brock had looked at her after she'd thrown herself at him for that last kiss in the rain. He'd been sickened by her. And she knew why now.

"Don't worry about it, Melody. Trent and I will work ourselves out." She sensed Trent's gaze on her. But she refused to meet it. "You guys should go on home. You probably need to get off your feet." She elbowed Trent, knowing he'd leap to attention if he thought Melody was overtired or otherwise taxed. As she figured he would, he flew into bossy mode, demanding that Melody stop playing at psychotherapy and get home to rest, pronto.

"I haven't seen or talked to him since that night," she blurted out as the two of them were headed out of the door. "If that's any comfort to you, *brother*." She emphasized the last word, still furious with him, but figuring it for the best — as Brock had said that night.

"It's not, K. I don't want you to be unhappy. And I told him that night to go up to the house and find you, talk to you, work through it. I take it that he didn't do that."

She twisted her fingers together. At night, before she drifted into restless sleep, she could hear his voice, calling her name. His fist, pounding on her bedroom door that night until he'd given up and had gone away, leaving her in peace. "He tried," she admitted.

Melody touched her cheek. "I hate to see you so upset, *chica*."

"I'm a grownup, Melody. I'll sort out my own shit. Now go on and rest, enjoy your married life back in Michigan." Things were out of balance again, now that they were back. It was making her antsy. It was making her want Brock even worse — just to see him, hear his voice, know he was around. But he'd steered clear of her and she didn't have the nerve to ask Evelyn about him, not after that God-awful wedding. No matter how badly she wanted to, or how worried she might be about his mental state. She'd gone back to her old meeting place, the crappy community center near her just as crappy halfway house, thinking—hoping—he might join her. But of course, he hadn't.

He knew her worst secrets. She had no doubt, based on his disgusted reaction to her after their last kiss, that he found her as filthy as she was. So at least she knew that much about him. That if she'd gotten around to telling him everything, he would have bolted in horror. So maybe she should be thanking Trent for saving her some heartache, not shunning him, unable to even look him in the eye without wanting to scream.

Chapter Twenty-Two

Two weeks later

"Fuckin-A I can't do this anymore!" Brock dropped the weights, letting them take an illicit bounce on the rubber mat. "You're a God damned torturer. You're fired."

His trainer, a sixty-year-old dude who had no right looking as good as he did, smiled and pointed to the treadmill. Every muscle and sinew in his body screaming for mercy, Brock limped to the device, climbed aboard and started running. Twenty minutes later, he lay on the massage table, while some burly chick dug into his calves and hammies with what felt like knife-shaped knuckles.

"Ow," he said, over and over again. But it fell on deaf ears. By the time she'd finished with him, he was a limp noodle, well past exhausted, which is exactly how he liked to spend his evenings—so tired he couldn't even lift a soup spoon or a sandwich before he fell face-first into bed.

Tonight, he took a long shower in the gym's fancy spa-like locker room after a thirty-minute soak in the hot tub, then headed for the juice bar, figuring he might as well drink his dinner. The cute girl behind the counter tried her usual hair-flip, eyelash fluttering mating dance on him but one other advantage of working out six days a week until he could barely walk was an inverse reaction to this sort of behavior. He flirted, of course. That much was ingrained in him. He'd consider it an insult to a beautiful woman if he didn't. But his body remained unaffected. His brain blank.

As he watched her throw his dinner replacement smoothie together, he flipped his car keys around in his hand, antsy for some reason. He kept hearing sirens from emergency vehicles as they screamed past his gym. The first one when he'd been almost finished with the treadmill, and the rest while attempting to relax under massage torture. And now, there were more. It was as if the entire city of Grand Rapids were on its way to some kind of a crisis.

"Oh, wow, check it out," the girl said as she handed over his drink. She was looking up at one of the many flat screens in the facility, angled so that you were never in any position not to see one. "Where is that?"

Unnerved, Brock ignored the outstretched smoothie and turned to take in the news, hoping it wouldn't hamper his commute home from this suburban oasis of hell. What he saw on the screen took him a few seconds to comprehend, but once he had, he ran flat-out for the glass doors, the images etched onto his brain.

"Large warehouse fire on city's south side consumes uncertified and illegal living spaces. Many already feared dead as firemen battle the blaze."

He leaped in behind the wheel and screeched out onto the quiet street, realizing he was a solid twenty minutes on a good day away from that warehouse. The place Kayla refused to move from, no matter how hard Trent had tried to convince her otherwise.

After their violent confrontation and now-shared knowledge about Kayla, he and Trent had stayed in close touch since he'd returned from his honeymoon. Although Brock had gone out of his way to assure the man that he had no intention of 'dating' Kayla, or of anything else. Their situations were too fraught, too complex, carried way too much proverbial baggage.

The truth was, Brock missed her so much it kept him awake most nights, pondering what he might have done differently in his life, to deserve to be the man she needed. It had been a brutal set of weeks as he did all he could to avoid her, in direct opposition to how their relationship had been progressing before the wedding. He'd lurked a bit, making sure she worked her shifts, observing without being observed, out of loyalty to Trent, he self-justified. Which had not helped his psyche one bit.

He'd skipped meetings for a couple of weeks, burying himself in work. The water clean-up program did not require his direct oversight or presence, but he gave it anyway, as he researched the foundation's next beneficiary — Boys and Girls Clubs of Greater Grand Rapids. While he had not gone off meds — something he'd been guilty of before during times of high life-stress — he realized after missing the routine, he needed it, so he resumed his spot in the church basement, listening, sipping coffee, offering support where he could.

When his therapist suggested that he drop one of his twice-weekly sessions with her and attend a sex addicts anonymous meeting instead, he'd agreed. So now he got the church basement scene twice a week—once with the drug junkies and once with the perverts.

He skidded to a stop at a light and touched the 'voice call' icon on his car's fancy media screen. "Call Trent," he demanded. As he waited for the guy to pick up, he pressed his fist against the steering wheel, still hearing the sirens echoing in his brain pan.

"Hettinger," the voice came through the car's fancy speakers.

"Fire," Brock blurted out. "Where are you right now? Can't you hear the sirens?"

"What? Why? I mean…what fire?"

"Fuck, man. It's Kayla's building… It's burning the hell down. I'm trying to get there but I'm stuck in fucking…suburban…traffic…hell!" He hit the horn with each of his last four words, urging the soccer moms and stay-at-home dads through the damn traffic signals.

"Her…building?"

"Yes. I don't know if she's working, but I don't think so. It's Thursday, usually her day off."

"I'm on my way. Coming from downtown."

"You'll make it before me then. Ask Melody if she's there."

"Yeah. Got it." The call ended before he could say anything else. He cursed and honked his way through the suburbs and hit the expressway at ninety miles an hour, willing some cop to try to stop him.

As he was exiting, he could see black smoke rising into the evening sky. His entire body seized up in panic but he kept the pedal mashed to the floor and ran three stoplights to get through the long stretch of auto dealerships between downtown and the south side, where Kayla's building was going up in flames.

The scene was out of some nightmare movie version of a five-alarm fire. A half-dozen ladder trucks were assembled, all directing as much water as possible onto the blaze. Another dozen or so support vehicles ringed the building, with an outer phalanx of cop cars forming a barricade. Ten ambulances were lined up, their staff in varying degrees of helping survivors or staring, helpless in the face of the inferno.

Even stopped as far back as he was forced to, the heat was unreal, like standing inside a furnace. He could make out Trent's Jeep a few cars ahead of him but couldn't see him anywhere. As he shoved his way forward, determined to get closer and see if Kayla was one of the people being treated outside, praying that she was, and realizing that he may have hesitated and lost his one shot at happiness, he could hear Trent's voice. Loud shouts of anger interspersed with increasing threats of physical restraint filled his ears as he snuck around one car and saw what was going on.

"My sister is in there, you fucking asshole. Let go of me!" Trent gave a final wrench of his arms, stumbled forward past the line of ambulances, and right at the burning building.

"Fuck," Brock muttered as he snuck closer, getting glimpses of the soot-stained victims being given oxygen, some being loaded into the rigs, as more waited to take their place. He prayed that Trent had enough sense not to run into the damn building.

It would appear, however, that he did not.

As Brock watched in horror, Trent sidestepped a line of firemen, barreled right over another line and headed for an opening where the door used to be. "What a...hey!" A hand clamped around his upper arm. He turned to find himself face to face with a sooty fireman. "Sorry. I... I know that guy and..."

"I'm sending someone in after him, but I don't want to do it. We've gotten everybody out we can. That building has about fifteen seconds before it collapses. Now, get the hell out of the way. Back there." He gave Brock a none-too-gentle shove. He moved but stayed as close as he could, keeping tabs and praying harder than he ever had in his life.

Three firemen scrambled forward, following Trent into the building while the rest kept dousing the place with streams of water. He counted to twenty, then thirty, and the building stayed upright. When he got to seventy-five, he saw the upper floor flattening in slow motion, pancaking down and collapsing the lower floor under its weight. The flames shot up higher, singeing his eyebrows.

But there, out of the rolling smoke, he saw three figures emerge. The firemen, with a body draped over one of their shoulders. Without another thought, he ran toward them, terrified to see if it was Trent, or Kayla. The medics rushed forward, slapped the body onto a gurney and raced to an ambulance.

"No time! No time!" one of them was yelling. "Full saturation. We've got to get him to the hospital."

"Move! I've got to cut a trach. He's crashing!"

"Wait, watch out for the swelling. You'll cause a PE."

Brock stood, helpless, while the medics tried to save Trent's life, wondering if the world had lost two

Hettingers even as he understood that it was now up to him to find Melody and tell her.

The ambulance doors slammed shut in his face. His knees gave out and he dropped to the hot pavement, gasping for breath. Hands helped him up and guided him to another ambulance but he broke away from them, coughing even as he insisted he didn't need anything. He had to leave. He had to find Melody.

"Wait! Sir! You should let us…"

But he ran from the hellscape toward his car, ignoring everyone and everything in his panic. As he drove like a bat out of hell toward the brewery, not knowing what else to do, he said, "Call Austin" to his onboard computer. But his voice was hoarse and he broke down coughing so long and loud the computer lady voice said, "I'm sorry but I didn't get that. Who am I calling?"

"Forget it," he muttered, swiping his lips and noting that the back of his hand came away black with soot.

Chapter Twenty-Three

"God but you are a lifesaver, yet again."

Kayla smiled at Melody, shrugging off the compliment as usual. "It's not like I have anything better to do," she said as she grabbed a clean FitzPub shirt from the rack and headed for the employee bathroom. She'd come in to cover a shift mid-afternoon, thankful for the distraction. And when Melody had rushed up to her, panicked because two of her best servers had called in sick, which made them short for a private party in the FitzHall—the large rental space that backed up to the other side of the kitchen—Kayla had been doubly relieved.

Covering parties in the Hall was pretty easy money, most times. And she was eager to grow her tiny savings to hit a milestone that would allow her the wherewithal to move. Of course, Trent had been after her like a dog with a bone to get her into someplace safe. But she was still in polite mode with him, unwilling or unable to admit that she had to do this first step herself. If she could save the three grand she needed for a deposit and first month's rent on a tiny studio she'd found, it hit a major goal in her independent life. Her life as a normal, non-using adult.

It had taken Melody's firm — and loud — insistence to get Trent to back off, which he had done. Although he'd kept trying to work his way back into her good graces, something she'd continued to resist.

Tonight's tips, unexpected and welcomed, would put her almost to the point at which she'd feel comfortable pulling the trigger on a new lease. She changed out of her beer-splattered shirt and into a clean one, pulled her hair back and splashed water on her face. Operating most days on three or four hours of sleep did not make her the sharpest of tacks by the evening, but she'd tough this one out. She needed the money. She craved the distraction. Time alone was not her friend. Time alone meant memories of Brock, which always led to a wave of disgust at herself.

The event was a big one — a going away party as best she could tell. By the time she joined the fray, the food had been consumed and ninety percent of the attendees were past the point of no return. Unsure how to deal with some of them, as she'd been trained not to serve anyone who was so obviously over-served, she sent a quick text to Melody, asking for her to step in and make the call.

Together, they poured pitchers of water and fought tiny battles with drunk assholes until they decided that it was time to confiscate everyone's keys. Kayla climbed up on the bar to the sound of catcalls and let out a shrill whistle. "Okay, people. The only way we are going to serve another beer to any of you is if you put your car keys in the bowl that my boss is bringing around."

Loud complaints and curses followed.

She waited. "Anyone in here want another beer?"

The crowd roared. "I thought so. Give up your keys. We'll pour one more round for each of you then I'm calling cabs for everybody."

"Party pooper!

"Bitch!"

She smiled. "Yes. All of the above. Keys, boys. Or no nightcap."

Melody took the bowl of keys to her office and locked them up, then returned to help the overwhelmed staff. "Jesus, remind me never to let this guy book a party again," she muttered as she began the daunting task of cleaning up while four male bartenders encouraged, poked, prodded and in some cases dragged people to the side door to wait for their taxis.

It was almost ten p.m. by the time they had it all cleaned up, and Kayla had been on her feet for almost twelve hours straight. Her back and knees were screaming for mercy and her stomach rumbled, reminding her she hadn't eaten for almost that long. She half sat, half fell into a chair, propping her feet on another and taking a proffered glass of water with a grateful smile.

"I'm ordering us some food, *chica*. You sit tight and let me handle it."

"I should get home," Kayla said, but she didn't move. She didn't think she could right then.

"After we feast. Bean burger, right?"

"Right. Thanks." She finished the water and lifted her arms over her head, trying to stretch out the many kinks and knots in her back and shoulders. She'd been stuck in this windowless room for so long she felt a strange surge of panic.

Brock. She needed to see Brock. The need was so strong it forced her to her feet and across the empty floor to the bar where she'd left her phone. But a quick touch to the screen revealed that the damn thing was dead. Her ears rang. Her pulse raced. Her mouth was so dry she lunged for the pitcher of water and drank the rest of it down in greedy gulps. As she swiped her lips, Melody appeared, bearing plates of food that smelled so good, Kayla's mouth watered.

But she was shaking as she took hers and the first bite tasted weird in her mouth, almost like smoke or ashes. Melody groaned and put her feet up as she picked at her food. "I thought I was hungry," she said, echoing Kayla's reaction. She put the burger down and wiped her lips as the ongoing sense of panic made every inch of her skin crawl.

"Melody!" a voice called from the kitchen. "*Telefono!*"

"*Una momento,*" she said, getting to her feet. "*Mi Dios,* my body hurts."

Kayla nodded, staring down at her dead phone's screen and wondering why she was so wigged out. As she had decided to chalk it up to sheer exhaustion, the voice called out again.

"*Prisa! Es una emergencia!*"

Both Kayla and Melody froze. Melody blinked fast then ran toward the kitchen while Kayla stood, gripping her phone, her mind dancing over the many disasters that might have occurred in the last few hours that she'd been cloistered in this damn room.

She listened but couldn't hear Melody over the clanging and banging in the kitchen. Taking this as a good sign, she walked to the bar, thinking she'd drink more water to get the ashy taste out of her mouth. The sound of a door slamming against the wall behind her made her drop the full pitcher of water, dousing her lower legs and sending the plastic container bouncing merrily along the concrete floor.

A figure stood in the doorway. She couldn't make out the face but could tell it was a male, tall, well-built, short hair. But his face seemed to be coated in a layer of mud. Confused, she glanced toward the interior door that led to the kitchen, wondering if she should call for help. The muddy guy let out a loud, throat-rasping cough, then looked right at her and said, "Kayla, is that you?"

Her heart seized up, leaving her gasping for breath as she processed that the man in the doorway was Brock. He was coughing again, hanging on to the doorway and staring at her from eyes that were white-rimmed, hollow in his dirty face. She walked out from behind the bar and toward him, even as she heard Melody's shriek and a loud bang of something dropping in the kitchen.

Brock reached for her, stumbling forward to get at her, saying her name over and over again in that shredded-sounding voice. As he yanked her to him, the smell of smoke and chemicals filled her senses. She let him hold her as she gripped his waist, ignoring the stench and burn in her throat.

"Oh God, oh God, I thought…you were in there." She peeled him off her and stared at him. The soot was mingled with other wetness on his face. "Kayla, honey. We have to go. We have to get Melody and get to the hospital, now." He was tugging her, pulling her toward the open door.

"Wait…why? What burned? Who is…?"

Melody ran up to them, her eyes wild. "Can you take us, Brock? I have to be with him."

"Be with...who?" Her mind refused to calculate this. She felt herself shutting down, backing away, wanting to escape. But Brock had a firm grip on her hand.

"Let's go. My car's right out there." Melody marched out ahead of them, a determined set to her shoulders. Kayla's feet would not cooperate and obey her mental orders to move.

Brock hesitated, turning back to her. "Kayla, honey, it's Trent. He went into the...the...building."

"What building?" She realized she was being irrational and causing unnecessary delay but she had to hear it for herself.

"Your God damned building, Kayla. It burned to the fucking ground about half an hour ago but Trent tried to go in and find you and he—" His sentence ended with more violent coughing. "We have to get to the hospital before—"

But she was already out of the door and climbing into the back seat of his still-running car before he could finish. Melody was in the front seat, staring straight ahead, hand resting on the shelf of her belly. Her eyes were dry, her jaw clenched as Brock got in and screeched out into the night traffic without a word to either of them.

Chapter Twenty-Four

"I'm sorry but you all can't go in at once. Mr. Hettinger is in critical condition. Only one visitor at a time, only immediate family members...hey!"

Brock shrugged at the hapless nurse when both Melody and Kayla ignored her and walked into Trent's room together. He got a glimpse of a wall of machines and heard a cacophony of noises before the door shut behind them, leaving him alone, shaking and adrenaline depleted. Not to mention starving.

Instead of seeking out food or water, he sat, staring at the closed door, unsure what to do now that he'd fulfilled his part of things. He guessed he should go home. Leave the family to their wounded and their healing.

An alarm began to clang and a red light flashed over Trent's door. Several medical types ran in as Kayla stumbled out, hand over her mouth, tears streaming down her face. Brock rose and went to her, holding her while she sobbed into his shirt. He pressed his lips to her hair, unable to resist the need for more connection. She sniffled and looked up at him. Her face was soot-streaked, he realized from earlier, when he'd grabbed onto her out of sheer disbelief that she was there, at the damn bar, alive and well.

"He's… I don't… How did this happen?"

"He thought you were in there. He wanted to save you."

"You were there too?" She wandered to a set of chairs and fell into one.

He joined her, taking her hand and pressing her knuckles to his lips. "Yeah, but I've got this aversion to running into collapsing, burning buildings, I guess."

She smiled then put her hands over her face and shook so hard he glanced around in search of a nurse in case she needed one. "Well, I guess I know who my real hero is, then," she said, accepting the tissue he held out from a box he'd found nearby.

"Without a doubt," he admitted. She sighed and leaned into his shoulder.

He held on to her as they waited, together, while Trent's door stayed closed in front of them. At some point, Austin appeared, with a terrified Taylor. Kayla got up and hugged her then pulled her toward the door. He followed them, his need to protect her stronger than ever. It opened, revealing a bunch of scrub-wearing types, and Melody, curled up next to Trent in the tiny hospital bed.

Before the door could swing shut, Kayla held it and pushed Taylor inside then turned back to him and wrapped her arms around his waist. They stood like that for a while, until a doctor approached them.

"Are you family?" he asked, poking at his tablet screen.

"Yes. I'm his sister." Brock stood with his arm around her shoulders. "That's his wife and daughter in there. Should I get them?"

"Yes, please. I'd like to talk to all of you at once."

"I'll get them," Brock said, ducking into the room where he talked the Hettinger women away from the bed with promises of medical updates waiting outside.

"Okay, so I think we've established that Mr. Hettinger was not fully saturated as was first feared."

"Saturated?" Melody asked, her voice calm.

"Yes, we were afraid that the smoke had suffused his lungs to the point where it was poisoning his bloodstream, but that isn't the case. He only had a few cuts that seem minor and his skin wasn't terribly affected. We've kept him on steroids a while and want to keep the intubation in place overnight. But all in all, he is a very lucky man. He should make a full recovery."

"Oh, dear Jesus," Melody moaned and slumped against the wall.

The doctor took in her obvious condition and motioned for a nurse. "Let's get you into a bed, shall we? I don't like the way your skin is flushed. Just a quick blood pressure check and…"

Melody yanked herself away from them and stood straight. "I will stay with my husband. Anything you want to do to me will have to be done in his room." She marched herself back in there, leaving the earnest-looking doctor and nurse at a loss.

"So he's…he's going to live. And he won't be damaged or anything, right?" Kayla heard the weak sound of her voice at the same time her stomach let out a loud growl. She glared at the doctor. "How long before he can go home?"

The doctor nodded toward the room then glanced at his tablet again. "Three days, tops. As long as nothing unexpected arises."

"Okay." She slumped into Brock who tightened his hold on her shoulders. "Okay, then. Good."

The doctor gave them a quick smile then headed down the hall to his next crisis. Brock guided her back to the seats, where Austin waited, holding bags of delicious-smelling food.

"I don't know about you, but my stomach is going to rebel if I don't put something in it," he said, helping her into a chair then grabbing the bag with a quick thanks to his brother. He pulled out sandwiches and fries, handing some to her before devouring one so fast he barely tasted it.

His own throat felt ragged, as if he'd swallowed glass, but he powered past it, needing the food more than worry over something that would go away on its own. Kayla ate a few bites then put the food on the table in front of them and leaned back, her eyes closed. "I can't believe he did that."

"Me neither," Brock said around a mouthful of fries. "But thank God he's all right."

She opened one eye and peered at him. "I've missed you," she said, surprising him. "I mean, I don't have anyone to make snarky comments to during meetings anymore."

He grinned then sipped from a water bottle, feeling nearer to human than he had in hours. "Yeah, that would have been worth near death from smoke inhalation. What was I thinking?" He smacked his forehead. She frowned and threw some fries at him. He picked them off his shirt and lap and ate them with gusto. Without thinking, he grabbed her hand again and pressed it to his heart. "I thought I lost you today, Kayla. I didn't care for that very much." Understatement of the century but he knew he had to go slow, not to scare her.

She blinked fast and bit her lip.

"No need to say anything. I just wanted you to know." He let go of her and leaned back in the seat, settling in for a long wait. They sipped water in silence. When she took his hand and threaded her fingers through his, he felt as if his whole universe had righted itself. Keeping it low-key, he shot her a quick smile then kept drinking, relishing the sweet warmth of her hand in his.

After about an hour, Melody and Taylor emerged from Trent's room. Kayla ran up and hugged them then turned to Brock. "You don't have to stay, you know. But I'm going to stick it out here tonight."

He rose, stretched and gathered up the remains of their dinner before tossing it into a bin. "I'll stick it out too, if that's okay?"

Kayla ducked her head but he saw her blush. Melody nodded and gave him a quick hug. "Can you find me something to eat, maybe? Tay? You need anything?"

"On it, ladies." He snapped a quick salute once Taylor admitted that she was starving, too. Before he headed out to seek and find the comfort food they required, he turned to Kayla, took her hand and blurted out something he'd been thinking for the last hour. "I want to take you out on a date. A real date, like with clothes that don't reek of bar or fiery inferno. To a place where the food is so expensive they don't even put the prices on the menus. Can I interest you in such an outing, Miz Hettinger?"

He saw Melody and Taylor smile behind her but was discouraged by the frown on Kayla's face at his question. "You're got a nerve, Fitzgerald."

"So I've been told," he quipped, hoping to calm her with an attempt at humor.

"You think you can distract me from the fact that you didn't rush into the burning building to save me with a date? Seriously?" The left side of her lips lifted, reminding him of the first time he'd seen her and marveled at her slow, subtle smile.

"God, Aunt Kay, lighten up. Go out with him. He's cute." Taylor gave her shoulder a fake punch.

"Okay, fine. But I'd better not get the menu with the prices on it."

Brock kissed her knuckles, much to the delight of the watching women and to the further deepening of Kayla's blush. "Never. The places I'm talking about always make sure the man gets the prices. I'm a pig that way."

She chuckled and pretended to push him away, but the way she looked at him — with hope, and relief, and happiness — stayed with him for hours.

Chapter Twenty-Five

Trent ended up hospitalized almost two weeks, fighting an infection that had settled in one of the supposed minor cuts on his arm. Kayla stayed in his loft with Melody and Taylor during that time, fighting the urge to panic every time her phone rang, assuming it was more bad news from his doctors. He was released on a Thursday afternoon, and both he and Melody had insisted that she stay with them through the weekend.

Friday morning, she got up early and made a big pancake breakfast, complete with fresh fruit and maple syrup. As they all sat, basking in the fall morning sunshine streaming through the wall of windows and sipping the dregs of their coffee, Kayla began to feel like she was a part of something — part of a family — that might be the real deal.

"What're you smiling about?" Melody asked her as she walked around collecting the mugs.

"Oh, nothing."

"Nothing, huh? Does his name start with a B and rhyme with rock?"

"What? No...I mean. I wasn't thinking about him right then, anyway."

"When's the big date?" Taylor asked over the top of her tablet.

"What date?" Trent asked, his voice still raspy from smoke damage.

"None of your business. Actually. I should go." She got up, nervous in the face of Trent's glare, her wellbeing of a few moments prior dispersed into the ether.

"Wait. Sit down a minute. We need to talk."

"I have to get to work," she insisted as she helped load the dishwasher. "Tell your wife to sit down. She looks tired."

"Stop trying to distract me, damn it."

Melody nudged her. "Go on. Let him get it off his chest. Then you can go. You're not opening today."

She sighed, wiped her hands on a dishtowel and made her slow way back out to the main loft room, where her brother sat in one corner of a huge leather couch, his feet up on the ottoman. He was thin and wasted after his two weeks on hospital food and IV drugs. The sight of him lacerated her heart with guilt. She sat on the ottoman next to his feet and folded her hands in her lap, willing to listen to him. She owed him that much at least.

"That's more like it. Jesus, you women are going to be the death of me."

"Ha, yeah, literally," Taylor quipped.

He glared at her then focused on Kayla. "I found a place for you to live." He turned his computer tablet around so she could see the screen. "Go on, scroll through the pictures."

She did, already formulating arguments in her head. After a few seconds, she glanced up at him, confused. "Did you hit your head while you were playing hero-rescuer or something, baby brother? These are pictures of this place."

He put his hands behind his head, looking satisfied with himself. She frowned down at the tablet again. "I don't get it. Sorry."

Melody appeared in the doorway, hand on her baby bump, which had grown in the past few weeks. "We're moving. I wanted a house and a yard and all that comes with it. I found one. We made an offer and we'll be moving in about a month."

"You're...moving?"

Taylor grinned at her. "Yeah! I get a whole princess suite and shit for my last year home before college. Can you stand it?"

"I'm going full McMansion again, I'm afraid," Trent said, holding out his hand to his wife who slid into his lap. "Anything for *mi esposa*, here." They kissed. Kayla rolled her eyes at Taylor then cleared her throat. He pulled away from her with an even wider grin. "But this time, it's a renovated older home, so it comes with character as opposed to crappy construction."

Melody moved to sit beside him and took the tablet from Kayla's hands. "We want you to have this place. It's perfect, no?"

"I'm... I can't..."

"Yes. You are and you can. And by dint of me almost dying to save your non-existent ass in that fucking flop house, you will not argue with me. Got it?" His eyes glittered at her.

"I'll think about it. I mean, it's such a kind offer. Too kind. You don't have to… I mean, couldn't you make a ton of dough if you sell it? I hear the market is smoking hot for this kind of hipster paradise."

"I don't need the dough, sister dear. What I need is to know you're living somewhere safe, within a ten or fifteen-minute drive of me and my growing *familia*." He ran his hand across Melody's tummy.

"I…don't know what to say."

"It's easy. Say — Thank you hero brother of mine. I will take you up on this offer and, in the meantime, will continue to camp out in the extra bedroom."

"You're trying to bribe me out of being mad at you for…" She glanced over at Taylor, who was ignoring the annoying adults around her. "You know."

"Perhaps. But as I said, I am now beyond the reach of that potential error of judgment, remember?" He pointed to the bandage covering the hole the EMTs had to cut into his throat so he could breathe.

"Look at it this way," Melody said, leaning into Trent and draping one of her long legs over his. "This place has tons of room for…more people."

She blushed fast and hot. "There won't be any more people, Melody," she insisted. "And like I said, I'll think about it. But I'm not staying here for another month, underfoot. This may be a palatial lofty mansion but it's not big enough for four and a half of us." She winked at Melody. "I've found a temporary place and I can afford it so allow me the dignity of doing that, at least, while I decide what to do about your too-generous offer."

Trent waved her off. "Fine. Fine. Think all you want but in a month, this will be your new address, mark my words, Kayla."

She pecked the top of his head, patted Melody's shoulder and gave Taylor a quick hug in passing. "I'm moving into my extended-stay hotel tonight. I'll see you tomorrow, Melody. Brother, you rest up. Doctor's orders. No master of the universe bullshit for a few days."

"I'm just sitting here, master of my own universe right now, K." His eyes were bright.

She nodded, her chest tight with emotion at the sight of him, happy at last with a woman who could handle him and a daughter who handled them both.

An hour after she started her shift, Brock wandered in, laptop at the ready. He'd been hanging out at the bar a lot while she was there, not talking to her that much but soothing her with his presence. They had talked about one thing—their commitment to the Boys and Girls Clubs. She'd already been through the volunteer approval process and went two evenings a week to mentor a couple of teen girls who thought they were the hardest asses around. It was a buzz, getting to know them and letting them know that they didn't have to be so tough all the time. She'd gotten them interested in drawing. Since she'd lost her old sketch books in the fire—her only truly valuable possessions—she'd been filling new ones like crazy, inspired by the renewal of her friendship with Brock.

She smiled and waved at him from her spot at the line of beer taps, watching as he got himself settled in, chatting with everyone around him. When she had a few minutes to spare, she leaned on the bar, taking in the spreadsheets on his computer screen. "Looks super boring," she said.

"It is," he admitted. "Boring data. But necessary. I want to allocate the foundation's funds fairly and I am inundated with requests, now that my passel of magical interns has gotten us so much damn publicity." He shut the laptop and gazed at her. "So, about our date."

Kayla flinched. It wasn't as if she hadn't been fantasizing about that very thing for a couple of weeks. But hearing him say it shot a bolt of anxiety all the way through her. "What about it?"

"How about tomorrow?"

"I can't, Brock. I'm moving into that place I told you about. The extended-stay motel thing."

"Those are expensive. I wish you'd let me pay…"

She held up a hand. "I won't. Please don't waste energy saying any more."

He fiddled with his coaster. "Well, then, how about this? I'll make us dinner at my place."

"No. I'm not quite ready for that yet." But her skin prickled in pleasant anticipation of it in spite of her base knowledge that it would never happen.

"Fine. I'll pick up sandwiches and bring them to your new digs."

"You *are* desperate," she said, enjoying the light flirtation. "But I thought I was getting the super-expensive dinner thing. Why can't we just postpone that a little while longer?"

She had her hand on the bar next to his computer. When he picked it up and pressed her knuckles to his lips, she shuddered, but not out of any fear or anxiety. Out of something else. Something she had zero frame of reference for. Something anticipatory, scary, but pleasant.

"Because I'm done waiting. I'm ready to pick things up where we left them the night before the wedding."

Kayla's mouth dried out at the sudden, crystal-clear memory of their kiss. She blew out a breath and tried to reclaim her hand but he held on tight. His eyes were shining in a way that made her warm from the inside out. "You're terrible," she said, for lack of anything more coherent.

"Guilty. But also persistent. So…what are we doing for our date tomorrow eve, fair lady?" He let her go and leaned back in the bar chair.

She crossed her arms but figured he could tell how flustered she was. "Fine. Tomorrow. Bring dinner to my place. I'll text you the address."

Brock's boyish, handsome grin widened as he propped his elbows on the bar and motioned for her to move closer. After glancing around as a stalling mechanism, she leaned into him, getting a whiff of his soapy-clean scent. "I want you to make the first move again, okay?" His whispering breath blew against her ear. He grazed the edge of her jaw with a fingertip then withdrew, opening his laptop and focusing on the screen again.

Chapter Twenty-Six

As he perused the options at the local over-priced, prepared food store, Brock was shocked when he realized that he had no real objectives for the night ahead. That he honestly wanted to spend some time with Kayla, eating said over-priced prepared food and maybe some decent coffee and just...talk.

He'd missed her. She'd been such a great sounding board while he'd gotten his feet under him as the foundation's president. Their casual, unemotional discussions about the reality of making a damn bit of difference in the mess that was the Flint water crisis went a long way toward convincing him to toss the foundation's first million-dollar grant in that direction. She was so straightforward, so honest about her opinions – it was a breath of fresh air.

Air he'd been missing for too damn long, he mused, waiting for the guy behind the counter to weigh the couscous salad, the sweet potato fries, and the rest of the vegetarian crap they'd recommended when he'd stated his desire for a "full veggie meal to go". That was one thing about her he'd have to work on. As a full-on carnivore himself, he couldn't quite fathom life without the odd steak, pork chop, or bacon slice.

He smiled to himself, realizing he'd done it again. He'd thought about Kayla and himself in terms of having 'a life' as in 'together'.

"Here you go, sir," the oldster behind the counter said as he handed over a bag stuffed full of biodegradable boxes filled with various forms of non-meat dishes. "If you need a wine recommendation to go with—"

Brock held up a hand. "No need, but thanks."

He whistled under his breath and placed the food, a couple of bottles of expensive fizzy Italian water and some flowers on the checkout counter. At the last minute, he indulged in an impulse buy, tossing a bar of chocolate up on the belt that declared itself 'decadently dark and sweatshop-free'.

"Can't pass up sweatshop-free dessert, now, can I?" he asked the bored-looking checkout girl with no fewer than eight piercings along one ear cartilage. She pretended to smile at his lame joke. "Never heard that one before, right?"

"Something like that. Paper bags okay?"

"But of course." He tapped his black AmEx, not registering the amount. "Have a great evening," he called over his shoulder before heading for the door. He felt exuberant, ebullient, even, dare he think it, ecstatic at the thought of being around Kayla, just the two of them, for a few hours.

He pulled up the text containing her address and transposed it into the truck's navigation system. The evening was picture perfect. Cool, after a warm day he'd spent half in the office and half under the care of his gym buddy, pushing himself ever harder in the pursuit of pure exhaustion. Then the quick, deep-tissue massage, dip in the hot tub and short nap at home.

All so normal, so regular-guy. As if on cue, he got a familiar twinge — the one he always got when the devil side of his brain was taking over.

"Normal is boooooring, Brock. Regular is stupid. Only losers accept the sort of day you had as something good. Only soccer dads and similar assholes think a half day at the office and a half day at the gym constitutes a decent Saturday. Jesus, man. You're fine now. Don't bother with those stupid pills. Let's go out! Have some real fun!"

He gripped the steering wheel, stiffening his arms until the noise in his head faded to something he could ignore. Normal was all he'd ever wanted. All he'd ever craved. And Kayla could give that to him. In some fucked-up, bass-ackward way they seemed to be able to give that to each other.

He pulled out into the light weekend traffic and cranked the satellite radio to something Primus-like. Screaming filled the car, helping drown the devil in his ear, tickling him with his reminders that the only way he, Brock Fitzgerald, would ever feel good is if he were out fucking first one, then another, then another willing hottie. Not babysitting some fellow junkie, sex abuse survivor and eating — God help him — tempeh burgers.

He touched the volume button on the steering wheel, determined to overcome this momentary lapse in his happiness. He'd not missed a dose of his pills. He'd been attending both addict meetings and therapy sessions — which had become more cheerful once he'd been able to admit how he felt about Kayla.

When he sat at a stoplight, drumming his fingers on the wheel, the music cut out for a split second, right before the sound of an incoming call almost burst his eardrums.

"Shit, God damn it." He ramped the volume down before answering. "Hello?"

"Brock?"

His heart did a tiny stutter-step in his chest. The polite Midwesterner behind him beeped his car horn, reminding him that he'd been sitting at a green light for a few seconds too long. The car lurched forward. He swiped the sweat off his upper lip. "Hey, Caroline. How're things?"

"Oh, pretty good." She sounded out of breath, or maybe excited. "How's your bod?"

"Fitter than ever. You really gave up on me too soon. I'm fucking Captain America these days."

"I'll bet," she said. "And the rest of you?"

"Oh..." He was out of breath for no reason. The Devil was poking his temple with something pointy, reminding him that if he went over to Kayla's tonight with his vegetarian feast, he'd be going home blue balled.

And did he want that?

Really?

He slapped his cheek, trying to drive out the persistent, needling inner voice.

"Brock?"

"Hey, yeah. Sorry. Mosquito in the car."

"Oh. Well, anyway, I have some news."

"Oh?" Something in him wanted to hang up. To go to Kayla's and regain his normal-guy equilibrium. To not hear Caroline's news. "What's up?"

"I'm engaged!" He heard bar noises behind her then, as if she'd just walked into one, or back inside one after dropping her bombshell. Brock put on his blinker, then his hazard lights, and pulled to the side of the road, lest he risk harming himself or others due to a sudden lack of oxygen to his brain. "Aren't you going to congratulate me?"

He sat, hands on the wheel, staring into the now sinister-seeming darkening sky. Why wouldn't he congratulate her? Why did he have the sudden urge to find her fiancé and kill him with his bare hands? Caroline was his. They were the only ones who understood each other.

He took a deep breath, dragging something his therapist had once said about Caroline to the forefront of his brain—'*You and Caroline were the dictionary definition of co-dependency. And a co-dependent bond is one of the hardest in the world to break. You can't be friends with her so don't try. A clean break is for the best.*'

"Congratulations," he said, *sotto voce*.

"What?"

"I said, fucking congratulations, Caroline. Jesus." He let go of the wheel, flexing his hands which were sore from gripping it so tightly.

"Well, hell, Brock, you don't have to be an asshole. I thought you'd be happy for me." He heard the teary edge in her voice and hated himself for it. Not a new sensation when it came to her. "Have you taken your medica—?"

"You know what, fuck you, all right?"

"Fine. I can see that I've called at a bad time. Sorry."

"No...wait, it's not... Shit. Caro, I'm sorry."

She remained silent. It was the sharpest blade in her arsenal and she knew how to wield it. The realization of that made him bone-deep tired. He glanced at the clock on the media screen. "Is he a nice guy? I mean, would I approve?"

She sniffled.

"Caroline, spare me the cold shoulder. You called me, remember? Tell me about the lucky bastard."

"He's a junior senator from Illinois. His name is Brandon Giles. We met the first weekend I was here, when I was so homesick…"

"A rebound fuck, eh, darlin'?"

"You're such a colossal prick, Brock." The bar noises faded. He heard a door shut and her sniffles got louder. "I don't even know why I called you."

"Me neither. But I will say this, you'll make a fine first lady someday, Caro."

"I love him. I really do."

"I don't recall asking you if you did, but okay. I'm sure Senator Giles will be thrilled to know that." He was being a dickhead but fucking-A she brought it out in him every time. "How is he in the sack, babe? I know that's important to you."

"God, I hate you. You're a selfish asshole and you always were."

"Yeah? Well, then don't call me anymore. Go on and have your fancy new D.C. life. Just remember, politicians lie worse than I ever did."

"He may be a politician, Brock, but he is more man than you ever thought about being—by a long shot." Her voice had slid into ugly and he realized she was drunk. Very drunk. He'd know a drunk Caroline voice from however many miles he was away from her. He wondered if her fab new senator man knew his hot, redheaded fiancée had drunk-dialed her old junkie boyfriend.

"Oh, honey, that's a damn low bar to set for him. Don't be so easy on the guy." He wanted to sleep, to hang up, crank back the seat and pass out. He felt along the space between it and the console, knowing he'd once kept a stash of weed there, for just such emergencies. But of course, his meddling-ass brother must have found it and tossed it on his behalf because the damn stuff was nowhere to be found.

Caroline was sobbing now, calling him every name in the book and then some. He sighed and slumped over the wheel as her familiar voice filled the car's interior, swirling around, provoking the devil who was still hard at it inside his head.

When he closed his eyes, he saw her. Not Caroline, she of the killer bod, the deep green eyes, the legit red hair—curtains and rug he knew for a fact—but Kayla. Kayla's thin, exotic-looking face with her olive-tinted skin and huge hazel gaze. Her slim fingers, cool palm, sweet, comforting lips.

"Okay, okay, enough," he bellowed, cutting off the blubbering and insults. "Stop it, Caro. Cut it out. Listen to me, you need to get out of the bathroom of whatever bar you're in, go find your friends, drink a gallon of water and get a ride home. Do you hear me?"

She kept sniffling but hadn't hung up yet.

"I am sorry for being a dickhead earlier. I'm maybe just a tad bit jealous. I can admit that. If you can admit wanting to make me that way by calling me, all tuned up on a Saturday evening, just to break your glorious news."

He waited, forcing himself to take long breaths to calm his racing pulse. "Well? Didn't you want me to react this way? Isn't that why you got lit up and called me?"

"Maybe," she said, her voice soft.

"Right so, here's the thing. I'm about to go out on my first real date in what feels like centuries. With Kayla, remember? The ex-junkie, sex abuse survivor? Yeah. That. So what I need for you to do is tell me you'll drink some water, get your ass home in a cab or ride share or call Senator Giles to come get you, I don't care. I need you to do that. To truly move on with your life and leave me to mine." He was panting like a dog now, sweaty and shaking in the cool interior of the truck. "I'm happy as hell for you, Caro. I hope that he treats you well, the way you deserve. Because God knows I never did."

"Brock…honey."

"No!" He squeezed his eyes shut, realizing this for what it was. Caroline, dragging him into her shit, so that she could say no to the good future senator. Making him want her in that inexplicable, sick way she always managed to do. Using him as an excuse to say no to a marriage proposal to a nice, normal man. "No, God damn you. I am *not* doing this anymore. I know I started it, so this is me by God ending it. I want you to be happy. Go, be that way. And don't call me anymore."

As he was reaching out for the media screen to end the call, she got in her last dig.

"Fine, Brock. I'll do what you say. And yeah, I wanted to make you jealous. Because you've trained me that way, you sick fucker. I hate you."

He closed his eyes as the resonant *beep-boop* of being hung up on echoed around the inside of his head.

"No less than I deserved," he said, digging the heels of his hands into his eye sockets. The phone buzzed. A text message appeared on the screen.

Kayla: *Where are you? I cleaned and everything. Only kidding. Just making sure you're all right. See you when you get here.*

Panting and sweaty all over again, he picked up the phone and tapped out a response.

I got stuck at the whole paycheck store. All those free samples. I'm stuffed. Might need to reschedule tonight.

He dropped the phone on the seat with a groan. His head was pounding. His throat dry. His dick, which had surged to attention at the sound of Caroline's voice like some kind of pervy Pavlov's dog, retreated, allowing blood to flow to his outer extremities once more.

Her text appeared on the media screen in seconds.

That's fine. But something has me worried about you. Like my user-junkie radar is pinging, you know? Don't come over if you don't want to but know that if you don't, I'm calling Austin to check in on you later.

After about five minutes, he had his breathing under control. He fired up the navigation system, pulled the car into traffic and made a beeline for Kayla's extended-stay hotel, desperation roiling around in his brain, making him sick to his stomach at the thought of not seeing her tonight.

Chapter Twenty-Seven

Kayla looked up from her sketch pad at the sound of a sharp rap at the door. Surprised, and more than a little relieved, she opened it up and found Brock, fit as a fiddle, holding two big bags from the most expensive grocery store in town.

"Dinner is served." He strode past her. "Does this place have a microwave?"

"There." She pointed it out in the mini kitchen. Her radar kept pinging as she watched him dashing around, getting the meal together in near-manic fashion. Deciding to stay silent and let him calm down on his own, she opened the fizzy water and poured them each a serving over ice. She sat, sipped, and observed him, getting more worried by the minute.

At one point, she got up and put her hands on his shoulders. He stiffened then turned to her with a wide smile, holding up two full plates.

"Here we go," he said, plunking them down on the small table and putting out silverware and a couple of paper napkins.

She took a seat, picked up her fork and tried to eat. But she could sense Brock's leg bouncing up and down and believed that she could hear his heart beating through his chest wall.

"What happened?" She put down the utensil and leaned forward. He moved away from her, chuckling and wiping his lips. "Brock. Look at me."

He did. She frowned and gripped his chin. "Are you using?"

He wrenched out of her grasp and stood. "Fuck no. Jesus. I'm just...I don't know...nervous." He raked his fingers through his hair.

"Excuse me, but I call bullshit on that." She kept her seat, fighting the urge to go to him, to hold him close like she'd done in the mudroom of the lake house. But this was way worse. This was borderline hysteria. She stayed seated and waited for him to explain himself.

He paced the small confines of the room, rubbing his stubbled jaw or running his hands over his hair. He stopped and leaned against the small stove. "Aren't you hungry?" He gestured to the untouched plates of food.

"No. Not really."

"I'm sorry. I'm ruining our date."

"Maybe a little," she admitted, sipping her water, and waiting for more from him. The nurturer in her was clamoring to get at him, to hold him and soothe and promise all would be well. But the nature of their personalities meant that he had to come to that conclusion on his own. Anything she did to assure him would only allow him to shove whatever was eating him aside and under, undealt with, unexposed to the sunlight.

He sighed. His jaw unclenched enough for him to speak. "You're not making this easy on me."

"That's not my place, Brock, and you know it."

"I hate it that you know all the buzz phrases better than I do."

She chuckled into her fizzy water, snorting when some of it went up her nose.

"Sexy," he declared, handing her a tissue to blow into.

"Well, that's one thing I assure you that I don't worry about. Being sexy." She kept her movements slow and non-threatening. The guy was twanging and sparking like a downed electrical wire. She knew she had to tread carefully. "You know you can trust me, right? That you can talk to me?"

He glared at her then seemed to collapse in on himself. Shoulders slumped, hands shoved into his trouser pockets, he was the epitome of misery.

"What happened, Brock?" She touched his arm and stood there, close enough for them to be considered a hair more than just friends.

"Caroline," he began, but then spat out a curse and tried to shove past her. She blocked his way.

"Your old girlfriend. The one you talk about at meetings sometimes."

"She's… Dear Jesus, this is so lame. I can't even stand to hear myself say it."

"Nothing that has you this worked up is lame."

He stood, staring down at the hand she had on his chest, stopping him from escaping the small kitchen area. Without another word, he pushed her hand off him and moved back to the stove. "I realize that you know everything about me. I can't help but think…" She bit the inside of her cheek. "That you think I'm…"

"No, Kayla, honey. No." He reached for her, dragged her close and held her tight. So tight she had trouble breathing. But she didn't mind. Closing her eyes, she sucked in deep breaths of him. The soapy, clean manliness of him, devoid of sour beer or old cigarettes or week-old sweat. "It's just me. And her. She's… She's getting married and she called to tell me, and it fucked me all up and if that isn't the stupidest shit any man could say when he's standing holding another woman in his arms, well I don't know what is." His voice was muffled as he had his lips pressed to her hair, but she heard every word. "God, this feels so good." She shifted, molding herself into him, feeling the firm press of his muscles against her chest, stomach and legs.

"Yes." She shifted her arms so they were up and around his neck. "It does feel good."

"I'm no good, Kayla. I was no good for Caroline, and I won't be any better for you."

"I think you're jumping to conclusions," she whispered, unable to resist the impulse to touch her lips to his neck. She tasted saltiness there. "And I think you should let me decide who's good for me and who isn't. I'm hardly a teenager, you know."

He chuckled into her hair but didn't let go of her. "Okay," she said as her need to taste his lips became too much to bear. "Brock?"

"Hmm?"

"I'm gonna make the move, now. You ready?"

He stiffened, but she held on tight, pressing soft kisses to his neck. "I don't know why but I can't not do it. So, here I go."

She pulled back so she could look into his eyes. His face was a mask of anxiety and pain. But she decided to ignore that and go with her gut. Which was in slow meltdown mode again, leaving her languid and a little woozy. "I don't think we should…"

But she shut him up, slanting her lips over his, making room for their noses. This time, she pressed her tongue to his lips and he opened himself to her, gripping her face and meeting her halfway in a tangle of tongues and teeth. A strange sort of shock hit her brain and traveled down her spine, settling low in her back and belly.

She gasped when he turned them, then picked her up and set her on the tiny kitchen counter, all the while keeping their lips locked. The urgency to feel him, to hold him close to her, skin to skin almost blinded her. Fear tried to trickle in around her edges but she shoved it away, ready for this, for him, for the whole nine yards, right fucking now.

He slid his hands up her arms, threaded his fingers in her hair and went deeper with the kiss, exploring every corner of her mouth before easing off, nibbling her lips, making her want to explode. When he held her closer, which forced her legs apart, she moaned into his mouth, not understanding any of this but wanting to so badly it was like a bright pain nestled in the center of her chest.

"I…I can't…" he said, pulling away, panting for breath, his hands on her upper thighs. "Kayla, I'm sorry. But this… This isn't right."

"What the hell are you talking about?" Anger pierced the fog of desire that had enveloped her. Her face felt white hot. Her belly felt heavy. Her legs and arms pebbling as if the room was charged, like it had been at the lake house for their first kiss. But he was moving in the wrong direction. The one away from her, leaving her sitting on the damn counter, legs spread, mouth hanging open. "Brock!"

His head snapped up. Eyes dazed and cloudy, he held up a hand and stumbled into the small living area adjacent to the bedroom. She jumped down and followed him, trying like hell to square what he'd done to her with what he'd said about it not 'being right'.

"Oh, I see," she said, arms over her chest. Her skin was getting that tight sensation again. The one she could only alleviate with razors and blood. "I get it. I'm the dirty girl. The one everybody's fucked. The disgusting hole they've all shoved their dicks into. I don't blame you for running away from me." Her eyes burned with tears that she refused to let fall.

"No…Kayla…it's not that."

She looked down at his crotch, made a point to do it so he'd know she was staring at his erection. "You know what? Fuck you and your flirting and bullshit. I don't know what's gotten into you, and since you can't seem to share it with me I think you need to leave."

He was shaking as he hit the wall and sank down to his heels, hands over his eyes. "No, you don't understand. I'm not right for you. I'm no good for…this."

"For God's sake, Fitzgerald. Just go. And don't come back to the bar or anywhere else near me pretending you want another date."

He kept backing away, as if her words had triggered something in him. In a few steps, he was up in her face, hands on her cheeks, his intent, beautiful eyes gleaming with the sort of want she had swirling around inside her. "I love you, Kayla. But I ruin the things I love."

She was speechless at his proximity, or perhaps it was his words, but without a doubt the way their bodies seemed drawn to each other. A rogue tear slipped from one eye. "See? I've made you cry already."

"Oh, dear Jesus, shut up and kiss me, then."

His smile was sad, but when their lips touched, she grabbed on to him and opened her mouth, her heart and her soul, willing him to feel and understand it. To comprehend the magnitude of her feelings for him — of her trust in him.

He dropped onto the stiff hotel couch, pulling her down with him. But before she could slide underneath him, he held her in place. "No. You sit here. You set the pace." He nipped her lower lip then dove in again as she allowed herself to feel a man's erect dick under his pants against her panties and not be horrified, or terrified, or disgusted by it.

The kiss had a life of its own and she fell into it, full immersion, enjoying all the new and thoroughly pleasant sensations coursing through her. She realized at one point that she was pressing down and forward with her hips, seeking some sort of contact that she didn't understand.

"May I?" he asked before lifting up her shirt and unhooking her bra. For a few seconds, she wanted to cover herself, to cower in the corner and escape his stare. "I want to kiss you here. Is that all right" He cupped one of her small breasts, dragging the pad of his thumb across her nipple. That made her groan so loud she slapped her hand over her mouth in embarrassment. "May I, please?"

When he kissed her on her exposed nipple, a bolt of electricity shot down her spine. He glanced up at her. She nodded, breathless and scared and elated all at once when he sucked her nipple into his mouth. "Oh…oh…oh my God!" Her hips were moving again. She got warmer and wetter in a way that should have made her blush but instead made her spread her legs wider, hold him closer to her, and moan with unfamiliar pleasure.

He gave her other nipple the same attention, driving her mad, making her feel plumped up and full. "Brock," she gasped as he sucked and teased the tender tips of her breasts. "I'm… I don't know… I want…"

He released her nipple and pulled her off his lap, wincing when he adjusted the crotch of his trousers, but not unzipping, which she appreciated. "I know, baby. I know. I'm going to give you an orgasm and one you'll never forget. But first, let's move over there." He pointed to the bed then yanked her up and tossed her there, making her giggle. "Can we lose these too?" He unzipped her jeans, kissing her exposed belly skin. "Hmmm?"

"Yes," she gasped. "Take them off. Hurry."

He grinned and slid them down her hips, then hooked his finger in her panties and gave them a quick tug. She lay, naked and exposed and yet, unafraid. He stood and stared down at her, his eyes full of wonderment, as if she were the first nude woman he'd ever seen.

"Perfect," he whispered. He dropped to his knees and tugged her hips toward him. "So very perfect."

He began kissing the inside of one thigh, stopping when he got to her sex—that mysterious part of her she'd hated for so long—and starting over with her other thigh. But God help her, she was lifting her hips, angling them toward his face in a way that shocked and horrified her but that she was unable to stop.

"I want to kiss you here, now, Kayla. Is that all right?"

She propped on her elbows. His face was flushed. His lips swollen from their marathon kissing session. "I won't, if you don't want me to."

"I don't know," she admitted.

"How about this?" He dropped down beside her and began teasing her nipples again. "I think you need more kissing here." He teased her lips, shoved his tongue into her mouth then retreated, all the while pulling on her nipples and making her moan and writhe, while her hips kept thrusting up of their own accord. "I want to touch you, Kayla. May I?"

She nodded, keeping her hands tangled in his hair, drowning in him and happy to do it. She felt fingertips move down her stomach, stopping where her pubic hair began. "You sure?" His voice was hoarse. His breathing as ragged as hers. "I can stop. Any time. You say the word."

"Don't you dare stop," she said, staring into his eyes. "Just…keep kissing me. Don't stop kissing me while you touch me…down there."

"Of course." He traced the edges of her sex with his fingertip, making her shiver with a combination of lust and a shred of fear. "It's all right," he whispered.

She nodded, sliding her hand up his shirt, wanting to feel his skin under her palm. His fingertips were light, non-threatening. Some kind of a strange sound escaped her as he focused on one spot, somewhere near the top. It almost hurt. But yet, it didn't. He stroked her there, in that tiny spot, until she was gripping his biceps and arching her back. She kept expecting him to shove his fingers into her and was tensed all over, waiting for that painful penetration.

"Relax, my love," he whispered, breaking their kiss and smiling down at her. She kept her grip on his arm and stared into his eyes, still anticipating the inevitable pain even as his small movements focused on a part of her she'd never known about, never understood and now felt as if it held her entire universe. "Let go, Kayla. I'll catch you. I swear it."

He lowered his lips to her nipple. The speed and firmness of his touch on her changed. Kayla's vision dimmed but she kept hold of him, fear now shadowing the exquisite pleasure he was providing. "I'm...I'm...I don't know...oh..."

"Relax, sweetheart," he repeated before pulling her nipple into his mouth hard, then he released it and stared at her again. "God help me, but I only want you to be safe and happy. Please, let me do this for you. Just once. Please." He pressed his lips to her neck, at some mystery spot where it connected with her shoulder. She felt his teeth there, nibbling, while his finger did something amazing at the same time.

She heard herself moaning and crying out his name but it was coming from far away. Light exploded behind her tightly clenched eyelids as a tidal wave of pleasure rolled up her body, leaving her gasping, shivering, and clinging to Brock like a drowning person. She pressed her legs together, relishing the odd sensations centered there, wanting to capture them.

Her face was wet but she couldn't recall crying. Brock held her close, making soothing noises in her ear. Her body calmed and her brain cleared. "Oh, shit," she said, letting go of her death grip on his arm. "Sorry."

He chuckled and nuzzled his nose into her neck, bringing on a fresh round of full-body shivers. "That was beautiful," he said before pressing his lips to hers.

Letting her mind wrap around what had just happened, she took a deep breath. "But you didn't...I mean you only touched me, um, on the outside."

"Yes, that's where you needed to be touched. What? You didn't like it?"

She wrapped her arms around his neck, tasting the sweat on his neck. "You didn't even take off your clothes. I mean... Don't you want to, uh...?" She hid her hot face, confusion and happiness swirling around in a crazy stew in her brain.

"Oh, honey, I'm just fine." He pressed her back on the bed. "I wanted to give that to you. So you could feel an orgasm and understand how...how..."

"How damn incredible they are? Sheesh." She flopped back on the bed, still embarrassed by her nudity and the strange, mildly spicy odor that was wafting up from between her legs. "A girl could get hooked on that." She glanced over at him. "Hey, I found something to be addicted to that isn't going to kill me! Score." She held up a hand as if to high-five him.

Brock's face seemed to shut down on her before he rolled away and sat on the far side of the bed, head hanging low. Fear hit her hard. She scrambled off the bed and positioned herself in front of him on her knees, hands on his thighs. "It wasn't fair to you, though. I can... I mean, I know how to..." She reached for his belt, but as he put his hand on hers to stop her, she saw the damp splotch darkening the crotch of his khaki trousers. "Oh." She leaned away from him.

"Yeah. I'm no better than a teenager around you." His voice was flat. "Let's sleep, okay? I just...I want to hold you."

She nodded and rose, but the whole thing was off now, the energy in the room shifted away from pleasure and into unhappiness. But she was tired all of a sudden and nothing in the world sounded better than falling asleep in his arms after the life-shattering experience they'd shared. He pulled down the cover and sheet and helped her under, then climbed in behind her, curving his body against hers, one arm under her head, the other draped across her hip. It was like something out of her wildest dreams. She smiled and burrowed in deep, filling her nose with his scent and her brain with all the other longed-for but never imagined sensations. Even as something tickled at the back of her brain, like a half-forgotten conversation, something they'd said and she'd filed away to pick up later, after...

"Brock," she whispered as she touched the knuckles of the hand he had stretched out in front of her.

"Hmm?"

"I feel like there's something more."

He shifted, and she sensed his anxiety as if she were experiencing it herself. She tensed then heard the word he'd kept muttering in her ear as he'd stroked her to her first ever orgasm. "*Relax*," he'd said. She relaxed and kept her voice light. "I mean, more that we should talk about."

He sighed and tightened his hold on her. "Tomorrow, okay? I need to sleep."

"Okay." She waited a few beats. "Brock?"

"Huh?"

"Thank you."

"The pleasure was all mine." He kissed her bare shoulder. She smiled. Right before she drifted off he spoke again, his voice low and muffled as if he were talking to himself. "I love you, Kayla."

She stiffened, but her body's demand for sleep overrode her anxiety. She threaded her fingers in his, half of her wondering how he could rest if his arm went numb under her head, the other half not caring, relishing this unimaginable, yet 'actually happening to her' moment.

Chapter Twenty-Eight

Kayla lunged up from sleep to sitting as if she'd been shot from a canon. Breathing heavily, holding the now-cool sheet to her breasts, she gave herself a few seconds to let the nightmare release its grip on her psyche.

Brock. She needed Brock.

Something in her was not at all surprised to find his side of the bed empty. But that didn't make it hurt any less. She dragged the blanket with her when she crawled out of bed and headed for the kitchenette. After gulping down three glasses of water, she noted that their un-eaten dinners had been cleared away.

As her eyes adjusted to the gloom, she spotted a folded sheet of her sketch book paper on the counter. She picked it up and held it for a few minutes, unwilling to accept what was no doubt inside it. A big kiss-off — a that-was-fun-but-you're-spoiled-goods-so-see-ya-round Dear Kayla note. That was what had been missing, left dangling and unspoken. His actual goal, to get her off and bolt.

Anger shoved its way into her muddled brain, making her rip the note in two before even reading it, leaving it on the kitchen floor while she ran for the bathroom, seeking the only release she could ever count on. Her skin was tight again, but in a new way. A way she hated, now that she'd experienced what true sexual pleasure meant.

She yanked the small bag from under the sink where she'd stowed it a few hours before. Still tingling between her legs, cursing and crying and sniveling like the loser she was, she flopped onto the pristine bathroom floor and pulled out a blade.

"*Relax,*" she heard his voice remind her. "*I love you,*" he'd claimed, the lying bastard.

Shaking with anticipation, she put the business end of the blade to her skin, needing the release so much it was scary close to the sensation she'd experienced on the brink of orgasm. She waited, counting to ten, giving herself a moment to reconsider before letting the blood flow.

"*Relax, Kayla,*" she could hear him say.

"Shut up!" She hurled the razor across the room then scrambled for another one. Jaw clenched, she put the metal to her skin. She could already smell the rustiness, feel the release of pressure she required.

"*I just want to make you happy,*" his voice insisted.

"Oh, God," she groaned. The blade dropped to the floor, unsullied. She stared down at her body, exposed under the harsh bathroom light, laid bare by the blanket that she'd let fall to the floor beneath her. The soft triangle of hair where he'd touched her. The nipples, hardened in the cold, that he'd kissed and sucked and worshiped, drawing her ever deeper into true, adult pleasure. She passed her palms over her breasts, down her stomach, and rested them on her pubic hair. Eyes closed, she touched herself, finding that tiny spot that he'd shown so much attention to, using her other hand to tug one of her nipples, wondering if she could recreate the feeling herself before giving up, sprawled out on the bathroom floor.

The first streaks of pink and orange light were filling the horizon as she rose, collected all the blades, the ointment, the bandages. Jaw set, still naked as a jaybird, she strode into the kitchen and found one of the bags he'd brought. She shoved everything into the bag then into the garbage bin, slamming the lid down with satisfaction.

After a long, hot shower, she put on jeans and a loose sweater, forgoing a bra, wanting to experience the fabric brushing against her now sensitive nipples. Coffee, a banana and some yogurt helped the hunger pangs as she waited for a decent hour to arrive so she could make a few calls before she had to leave to open the bar. Sunday — a slow day, thank God. She needed time to process and think and plan.

At eight-fifty-seven a.m. she grabbed her phone and hit Trent's speed dial button. As she waited for him to answer, the ripped white sketch book paper on the floor of the kitchen caught her eye. She picked up the pieces and spread it all out on the table in front of her as the call went to his voice mail. With a curse, she ended the call and sent a quick text.

I'll take you up on your offer of the loft. Thanks. I love you. Tell Melody I'll see her later.

She felt as light as air, as if she'd been tied down with a heavy chain that had been busted open sometime in the night. The concept that she'd been set free by an orgasm made her roll her eyes but she'd be damned if she had any other explanation for it.

Of course it wasn't the act, but the man who'd bestowed it. Brock. Fellow ex-junkie, class clown, baby whisperer and, dare she even admit it to herself, man she loved. She touched her face, which burned as those words passed across her consciousness. Feeling restless, she paced from one side of the small room to the other, avoiding reading his note, until she couldn't stand it another minute.

As she pieced the thing together, the words formed into sentences, and her heart pounded at the realization that she'd been right.

Dear Kayla,

I want you to know that tonight was hands-down the most amazing one of my life. Weird, in a way, since I had no big-boy self-control on the one hand, but incredible in so many others. Ways I wish I could explain to you but have decided that it's best if I don't.

It's not that I don't want to. I do. But I have no idea how to even admit to you the awful things I've done in my life. The horrible feelings and urges I've been unable to manage. The meds I take help. But now that I've fallen for you, I'm afraid. I'm afraid of how I'll act with you, that I'll lose it and revert to my old, worst self.

You deserve so much more, Kayla. I hope you find him someday. I'm going up to the Inn for a while, to think about where I'm going to go next. But I can't be here, around you, wishing I were a different, much better man.

Yours,

B

She crumpled the note in her fist, tears leaking down her face. Her phone buzzed with a text. Trent, ecstatic that she'd come to her senses.

I want your life to be a million times better, K. And I think you're well on your way to that.

She sighed and swiped her eyes, holding the crumpled note to her chest as she sat on the stiff couch, looking at the bed where her life had changed, at least for a few hours.

* * * *

She muddled through her shift, woozy and tired but somehow jumpy and on edge at the same time. Everything irritated her, from the beer taps shooting foam all over her shirt to the high-maintenance table of twenty-somethings who kept asking her for something "like a Budweiser."

When she'd get a moment, and would close her eyes, she saw two things — the sharp, comforting edge of the razor blade, and Brock's face over hers as he'd pleasured her for the first, and, she hoped, not the last time.

"Relax, my ass," she muttered as she jumped up to serve a fresh set of newcomers settling in at the bar. By the time her shift was supposed to end at five, the place was almost full, and the sounds of their chattering was driving her up the wall.

Melody caught her leaning slumped against the wall next to the restrooms, hands over her eyes. "Kayla? What's wrong?"

"What? Oh, sorry, I...have a headache."

Melody's dark eyes narrowed. "Do not bother lying to me, sister. I can read you like a book."

Kayla sighed and slumped. "Fine. Whatever. But my shift is over so I'm out of here."

"Wait, don't go. Let's eat something. You still need to put on some weight and I'm making that my mission in life."

"I'm not hungry. I need to go home and lie down." She smiled at the woman who was now her sister. "Don't worry about me."

"Right. Like I'm going to do that." She clucked her teeth but left Kayla alone, as if sensing that she'd pushed it as far as she could for today.

Kayla dragged herself back to the bar, her feet as sluggish as her mind. As she was packing up her sketch book and pencils, shoving them into the thrift-store denim backpack she'd scored a few weeks ago, the bar door flew open. Squinting into the back light, she had a thrill of hope. Maybe he'd come back, ready to declare his love for her in front of all these people, and would carry her out, *An Officer and a Gentleman*-style.

Right. Get a grip, Kayla. Your ending will never be of the happily ever after sort.

"Have you seen him?"

Confused, she found Austin standing at the bar, his eyes wild with worry.

"No," she said, knowing who he meant without asking. "Excuse me. I have to go."

"Kayla, wait." Austin reached across the bar and grabbed her arm. She pulled away from him but waited, out of respect for the fact that he owned the brewery and the bar where she worked. "Can we talk?"

"What about?" She shouldered the backpack, shoving down a growing anxiety about Brock's wellbeing.

"Please. I'm worried about him right now and I think… I think there's something about him you should know."

She rolled her eyes. "You and Trent are super great at this secret-revealing thing, aren't you?"

His expression hardened. "Yes, I guess we are because the two of you can't seem to communicate fully and we all think…well, we believe that you're good for him. That you guys are good for each other. So, I'm going to tell you what he won't. And then maybe you'll understand why he acts the way he does sometimes."

"Fine." She crossed her arms and waited.

"Not here. Come on." He motioned to the door behind her.

Her legs shook as she followed Brock's twin, the man who'd built the Fitzgerald Brewing business from small to hugely successful. So successful he had excess money to set aside in a foundation, and had given his ex-addict brother a job running the thing. She sighed at the convoluted nature of all of this, while Austin led her up to Evelyn's big office overlooking the old brewery floor. He shut the door behind them and took a long breath, jumping right in before she could even catch her breath.

"Once my parents got over themselves and got him to professionals his first year of college, Brock was diagnosed with…" He hesitated, blinking fast. "He's a sex addict, Kayla. He… He started having sex with older women when he was fifteen or something, and it… Well, he's been getting in and out of trouble with women ever since. I mean, I don't know most of the gory details but I do know it's something he takes a specific medication for, every day at four-thirty, along with his anti-anxiety pill." He glanced at his watch and blew out a breath.

Kayla stared at him, her ears burning and the words 'sex addict' roaming around in her mind like grinning, evil ghosts.

"He always checks in with me every afternoon at four-thirty. It's part of our deal. And he's done it for months, over a year now. Until today."

She stared at him, her mouth hanging open. He wiped his lips. She saw how much his hand was shaking. She started to ask if he'd called or texted Brock but realized how stupid that question would sound. Of course he had. "I think he might be up north. At the Inn."

"He's not," Austin said. "He's gone there before, when he's in a bad place. I had the rental company go and check, but it's locked up tight."

"Oh." She backed up and sat down hard, coming to terms with all of this, with how what Austin said squared with all the strange things Brock had intimated to her, both last night and in the note he'd left.

Austin sat and took her hand. "I'm sorry to drop this on you, but we have got to find him. I can't even fathom what would happen, what he'll do, if he falls off the wagon again. Have you seen him? I mean, I thought you guys had a date?"

Her face flushed. Was nothing a secret in this family? She guessed not. She took a breath. "Yes, we did. He brought food to my extended-stay place. We… He… Oh, God." Tears rolled down her face.

"I know it seems weird that people with your respective histories might find each other, but trust me when I say that my brother is madly in love with you.

I've never seen him so happy as when he's talking about you or about to see you."

"What about Caroline?" She let the words escape, hating them even as they hung in the air between her and Brock's frantic twin brother.

"Brock and Caroline are over. He knows that. He loves you. And I think...well, I hope you guys are... Oh shit, this is embarrassing."

"You think?" She winced at how hysterical she sounded.

Austin groaned and leaned back. "I told Evelyn she should do this. But she insisted that I tell you." He dropped his elbows on his knees. "Kayla, he's gone off the grid. And Brock never does that unless he's going way off, jumping off all his wagons with gusto, do you understand what I'm saying? I don't know what happened, but something triggered him and I need your help."

She took a breath. "Do you have Caroline's number?"

Austin blinked and pulled his phone from his pocket. "Yeah, I do."

"Okay. Dial it and give me the phone." She'd never felt more resolved and sick with worry at the same time. She took the phone from him and walked to the large glass wall overlooking the brewery. Leaning her hot forehead against it, she waited for Brock's longest-running girlfriend to answer.

"Hello?" Her voice sounded sleepy. "Austin? What's wrong?"

"Hi, uh, Caroline. This is Kayla."

The beat of time it took for Caroline to respond was filled with more awkward emotion than Kayla ever thought existed in the universe. She broke the silence.

"I'm Brock's friend. And I'm worried about him. Have you heard from him since you guys talked yesterday?"

"Um…no."

Kayla waited a few seconds to gather her courage. "Would you have any idea where he might be, or go, if he's…in a bad place in his head? We've tried the Inn up North already."

"I don't think so. I mean, he used to go to some places…a few bars, you know?"

"Yes, I do. Where are they, if you don't mind telling me."

"No, I don't mind."

Kayla motioned for a piece of paper, which Austin slid over to her with a fancy pen from his shirt pocket. She scribbled down names and addresses.

"Okay, thank you. Sorry to have bothered you."

"It's no bother."

Kayla waited through another brutally awkward silence.

"Kayla," the other woman said. "I'm… I hope you guys can work it out. Brock is… Well, he's…"

"He's a complicated hot mess with a shit ton of baggage. And I'm in love with him."

She heard a sharp inhale through the phone line. "Oh my God, you have no idea how happy that makes me."

"Well, good." Unsure what else to say, she was about to end the call when Caroline broke in.

"Wait, wait, I think I know where he is."

* * * *

As Kayla rode with Austin through the early fall evening, she had no eyes for the sunset, or the colorful leaves raining down in the wind like something out of a movie. She had her hands clenched tight in her lap and one thing on her mind — find Brock. Tell him it was okay, that she understood, that she loved him. Before he did something so stupid that they'd never get him back.

"Here it is," Austin said, screeching to a stop outside a bar that might win the award for the diviest shit hole in Grand Rapids. There was one window featuring a blinking macro beer sign. The door was scarred. The sidewalk littered with broken glass, cigarette butts, and, sickening and yet familiar to her, several empty ziplock bags. "Let's go."

Kayla put a hand on his arm before he could get out. "No, Austin. I need to do this."

He frowned but slid back behind the wheel, gripping it and staring straight ahead. "Go on. Hurry. Please."

She got out without a word and made her way to the door. Loud, pulsing beats of unidentifiable music seemed to leap out at her. Sour old beer and liquor odors filled her nose. Her shoes crunched over unnamable detritus. When she got to the door, she hesitated, wondering how this might work for them. They were, by definition, co-dependents. They could end up feeding on each other's weaknesses, pushing each other back into vice without even knowing they were doing it. They were sick, so sick.

She said a quick prayer and tugged open the door. Enveloped in the smoke, booze and noise, she let it pull her toward the bar. The place was packed with pool players, drinkers, couples making out in corners. And of course, tweakers. She could see them everywhere.

As she moved through the crowd, ignoring the come-ons, the invites, the outright ugly suggestions, she focused on finding him. He wasn't at the bar, which sent her pulse racing with panic. She'd somehow counted on him being there, sucking back beer or booze and trying to score — or already having scored, would be shooting up in the bathroom.

She headed toward a dark, smelly hallway where she assumed she'd find the men's room, she saw him. Sitting alone at a table, a bottle of whiskey and an empty glass in front of him. He was doing something with his hand and arm she couldn't quite make out. When she got closer, she realized he was flipping a coin.

When she slid into the booth across from him, he didn't acknowledge her presence, continued with his coin, flipping and looking at it over and over again. She waited for almost five minutes in silence, observing, noting that the glass had not been used. That the whiskey bottle's seal remained unbroken.

The quarter made yet another downward trajectory. She reached across the table and snagged it out of the air in front of his face. He frowned, blinking fast as if noticing her for the first time.

"Go away." He took another coin out of his pocket. "I'm busy."

"I see that," she said, letting him get into his rhythm before grabbing that coin, too. "Brock, look at me."

After a solid twenty count where she thought he might have already gotten his hit and was now deciding between drinking or finding a female, he met her gaze. But when she stared into his eyes, she knew he was clean.

"I love you," she declared as she plunked his coins on the table.

"Doesn't matter." He fiddled with the unopened seal on the bottle. "We'll just end up hating each other. Co-dependents can be…whatever it is we might be. I'll fuck you up just like I did Caroline."

"So, what's with the coin flip thing?"

He sighed. "Heads, I drink. Tails, I drink."

"Don't lie to me, Brock Fitzgerald. I can read you like a book." She parroted this saying of Melody's even as she acknowledged it as the gospel. She *could* tell he was lying, and at that precise moment she knew they were meant for each other. They had to be. Who else would tolerate them if they couldn't?

He propped his chin on his hands. She could see him through the bottle, his face distorted by the amber liquid between them. "Fine. I was flipping to see what kind of a man I was. Heads, I'd go to you, try to make it work. Tails, I'd run away."

She grinned, picked up both of the quarters, and tossed them high, watching the dim bar lights glint off each one. Catching them both in mid-drop, she slapped them onto the table. "There. Now are you happy? Let's get out of here. This place gives me the creepy crawlies."

He stared at the dual George Washington profiles glinting up at him from the scarred wood table, then up at her. "I…don't know…"

"I do. I understand everything now. About you, about me, about us."

He raised an eyebrow but she kept going, figuring that if she stopped, she'd chicken out. She held out her hands, palms up. He put his in them. She felt him trembling and believed that she could sense his zinging nerves deep in her soul. She held on to him, tight, like he had done for her the night before. "We aren't co-dependent, Brock. That word is no longer allowed in our vocabulary. We're co-survivors, okay? We've been through hell and back and now…we're gonna survive together."

He smiled. "Co-survivors, eh? Nice."

"Yeah, I thought of it all on my own." She put her palm alongside his stubbled jaw. "Can we please get out of here? We have some unfinished business, I think."

"Do we?" His dark eyebrow raised. The sparkle in his eyes made every inch of her skin tingle. "What sort of business might this be, madam?"

"Personal business, mister."

"Ah, yes, my favorite kind." He got up and pulled her to her feet, and they walked out of the stinky, smoky old life into the crisp Michigan October night.

Chapter Twenty-Nine

One year later

Once Brock woke, he realized something was wrong. After noting the empty space next to him, the sheets hardly mussed, he climbed out of bed. He padded barefoot down the long hall toward the main room, a small box from his bedside table tucked in his PJs pocket. He blinked into the dark space, lit only from streetlights below the wall of windows, and heard the soft strains of the Bob Dylan song that they both agreed defined the moment that their relationship changed.

He spotted her sitting at the massive dining room table that was covered by sheets of architectural renderings he'd been studying before going to bed. Her hands were wrapped around a mug of tea, her eyes focused out onto the Grand Rapids streetscape below. She'd gained weight since they'd moved in together, thanks to his cooking, which had the side bonus of making her hair and skin glow with good health. They were both glowing, and he liked to claim that having a healthy sex life for the first time was the reason.

Deciding that standing across the loft great room and watching her was what he wanted to do right then, Brock leaned against the wall, arms crossed over his bare chest, humming along with the chorus of *Tangled Up in Blue*. Kayla remained still, the cup in one hand, her gaze fixed outward.

The moment shimmered with portent on one hand, but felt so ordinary, so normal, Brock smiled in the dark, his skin not crawling, his body not urging him forward to do something to her, with her. He could stand here and look at her and feel happy. The sensation still gave him a bit of pause. He'd been conditioned to mistrust happiness in most any form that didn't come with an external, chemical high. But as their new therapist reminded them, they had to adjust to happiness, learn to accept it on its own terms. To understand that it was okay to feel it. It was fine to trust it. That there was no reason to upset it for the sake of upset, as had been their mutual *modus operandi* for years.

Kayla met his gaze in the gloom then crooked her finger. He straightened and glanced over his shoulder before pointing to his chest and mouthing "me?" She tilted her head, accommodating his bad joke. He stuck his hand in his pocket and curled his fingers around the ring he'd bought six months ago.

When he reached her, he saw she had a computer tablet in her lap, open to email. Leaving the ring hidden for now, he plucked the tablet up and read the message she'd had opened last. She remained as still as a stone while he read it again, then once more, to ensure he was seeing the words correctly. A surge of pride filled his chest. "Kayla," he whispered, pointing to the message glowing in the dark. "Honey. Is this…what I think it is?"

She nodded but kept her gaze averted. Tears stood in her eyes. Her hands shook as she put the tea mug to her lips. Brock put the tablet down and took the mug from her, pulling her up and into his arms. She remained wooden, stiff, her arms hanging at her sides. He held on to her, giving her his body warmth, his wordless support, until she softened and wrapped her arms around his waist.

"I can't do it," she said into his chest. "I never meant for people to…to…"

He pulled back and stared into her eyes. "For people to want to give you money—serious money—in exchange for your art?"

She sighed and buried her face into his chest again. He stroked her hair, relishing the normalcy of his mind and body for the millionth—zillionth?—time since she'd pulled him out of that dive bar. Holding her close, filling all his senses with everything about her, was all he needed most days. Well, that and regular attendance at meetings, therapy sessions, a full medicine cabinet of drugs, a fridge full of ginger ale, exercise…the usual.

Once a junkie and all that.

As they stood there, the Dylan tune swirling in the air around them, the blueprints on the table caught his eye. A whoosh of anxiety filled him, making him look away. It was too much. She was right. Too many things were going so great right now for them. It was a matter of time before the other shoe dropped—before one of them slipped, fell, used, or worse.

He pressed his nose into her hair, eyes squeezed shut. As if sensing his lapse, she tightened her arms and lifted her face to his. "Did you see that number?"

He nodded, willing his brain to settle. Which it did, thanks to the kiss she laid on him. He broke away and touched her face. "I'm so proud of you. I told you those pictures were incredible. So did the gallery owner."

She shook her head but remained in his arms, their bodies mashed together the way they both preferred it. "It was only supposed to be a charity thing. You know, pictures by losers and shit."

"It was for some people, but for you..." He pressed his lips to her forehead. "You are the real deal, it would seem."

Her collection of self-portraits had been included in a large gallery show as part of the Fitzgerald Foundation's latest fundraiser. The weekend-long event included a walking tour of all the galleries in town, with the art provided by recovering addicts and others with mental health issues. She'd been reluctant to show him the charcoal drawings, so he'd seen them for the first time at the Friday opening reception. He'd stared at them while the party swirled around him, amazed and horrified at how completely she'd captured herself. He'd stood there, frozen by the raw emotion she'd poured into the simple portraits, until his intern crew had pulled him away for interviews and face-time with local muckety-mucks.

Two weeks after she'd saved him, he'd decided to sell the Inn to a local non-profit that provided therapies for children and teenagers who were survivors of any number of life's horrors—abuse, abandonment, drugs, alcohol—the gamut. He'd signed the deed over with his mother's blessing for a single dollar, then launched himself into the effort to raise money to renovate the main building to house offices, classrooms, therapy room and the adjoining cabins into short-term residential options for kids who had no other place to go. He'd talked the architects into donating their time, as well as lawyers, and a few contractors. But he wanted people to get paid something for their work, so he'd pledged a matching donation up to a million dollars and the non-profit, well-named Survivor's Club, had been in hardcore, no-holds-barred fundraising mode for almost a year.

He tucked a lock of Kayla's hair behind her ear, kissed her neck, then pulled the ring from his pocket. She smiled as he slid it onto her finger. They'd agreed to get married the following spring, had worked out the details between them, but had decided not to make a big announcement or fuss.

"You promised," she whispered, holding her left hand up so the light from outside caught the facets of the brilliant round amethyst surrounded by small, sparkling diamonds all set in heavy platinum. "Oh, shit, Brock."

"I heard that bitches love big rings," he said, threading his fingers in hers. "That true?"

"But we said nothing showy."

"I changed my mind," he said, pulling her close again, swaying to the music which had changed to Etta James.

"Did you set this up? I mean, you're not the 'anonymous buyer' who wants to pay me half a million bucks for my whole collection of scratchings, are you?" She leaned away from him, her eyes narrowed. "I wouldn't put that past you."

"Now *that* would have been super romantic and cool, but no. I don't think I could have those things here."

She nodded and molded her body to his again as every single line of the song seemed to describe exactly how he felt, right here, right now. He was dead serious about the pictures. They were harsh and brutal in a way that had left him breathless. The work had been featured on a few national morning chat shows, once his passel of promo geniuses had worked their magic, and now the art world was yammering about her non-stop.

But he hated them. Despised the damn things with a burning, consuming passion that had kept him up all night after he'd seen them the first time.

They were six self-portraits, all of them the same dimensions—a standard, student-sketch-book size. Three of them were etched onto his brain as if by laser. The one she'd titled simply *K* was in a mirror image-style, her face thin and drawn, her eyes haunted, her hand to her neck. *Pain* was a frank rendering of the state of her upper arms, cross-hatched with thick scar tissue, shown lifted over her head as if in surrender.

The worst—or the best, depending on your perspective—was one called *High*. It depicted a grinning, made-up, beautiful Kayla, decked out and ready to party, holding a cigarette in one hand, a bottle in another. It gutted him on so many levels—not the least of which that he recognized what she meant by it. That being high made her feel beautiful, for a while. It gave her control, for a time. And no matter how far she—and he—got away from that life, no matter how much they understood that it wasn't the case, they would never, ever forgot that sensation—in some cases, addicts never stopped chasing it. They both understood that the danger was never far from the surface. Life's myriad temptations were always lurking, whispering their poisonous entreaties, urging them both back into the dark.

"So," he said, when the touch of her lips to his neck and her hands moving downward toward his ass made his body harden and his skin tingle. "I say we make the big announcement." He kissed her ring finger. "Tell all the pertinent family members and friends. Invite them to the ceremony next year. That sort of thing."

"Maybe," she said, gripping his butt with one hand and his erection with the other. "Mmmm…this for me?"

"I can't imagine who else it would be for, future Mrs. Fitzgerald."

She gazed up at him, her eyes haunted, before letting him go and dropping back into her chair. He fell to his knees and put his head in her lap, his arms around her calves. "It's all right." She ran her fingers through his hair. "I'm all right, Brock."

"Hmpf," he said into her thighs. "Maybe I'm not. Maybe I'm wigging out." He looked up at her, happier and more content at this precise moment than he'd been in his entire, shitty life. "Or, maybe I just like this position." He pulled her knees apart and yanked her forward, making her squeal. "Yes. This is my happy place, without a doubt. Hang on, my dear." She hooked her legs around his waist with a grin. Using the strength of his legs and back, he rose, bringing her with him, heading for the massive leather couch.

"Kiss me," she demanded in a whisper. He did, and when he sat with her straddling his lap, he kept doing it, even as she shoved his PJs down and lowered herself onto him. They moved with languorous ease, lips locked, hips rolling in unison, skin dampening with sweat. As he approached his release, Brock broke the kiss and stared up into her eyes.

This woman.

This woman is my very oxygen. No. She's my gravity.

Her head dropped back as she ground down, gaining the outer friction she required, along with the deep angle of penetration he provided, moving fast, and faster. He watched her skin flush, felt her body tighten around his, heard her cry out his name right before his vision dimmed. And he was at peace, at long, long last.

About the Author

Amazon best-selling author, mom of three, Realtor, beer blogger, brewery marketing expert, and soccer fan, Liz Crowe is a Kentucky native and graduate of the University of Louisville currently living in Ann Arbor. She has decades of experience in sales and fund raising, plus an eight-year stint as a three-continent, ex-pat trailing spouse.

With stories set in the not-so-common worlds of breweries, on the soccer pitch, in successful real estate offices and at times in exotic locales like Istanbul, Turkey, her books are unique and told with a fresh voice. The Liz Crowe backlist has something for any reader seeking complex storylines with humor and complete casts of characters that will delight, frustrate and linger in the imagination long after the book is finished.

Don't ever ask her for anything "like a Budweiser" or risk bodily injury.

Liz loves to hear from readers. You can find her contact information, website details and author profile page at http://www.totallybound.com.

Home of Erotic Romance